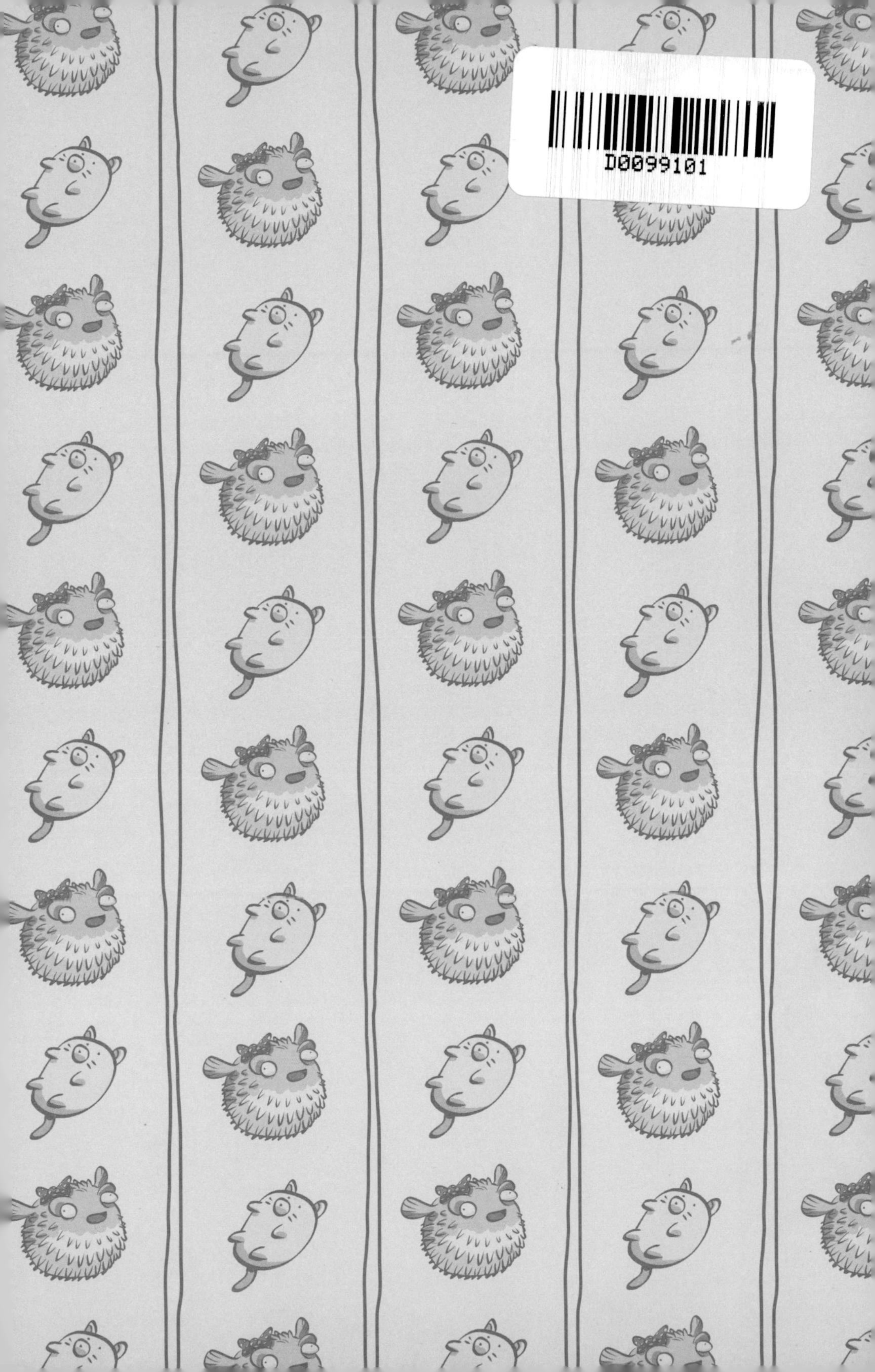

PLANTS VS. ZOMBIES™

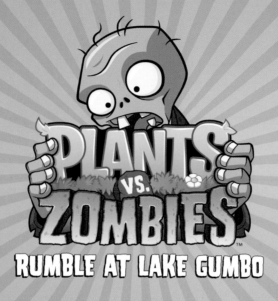

RUMBLE AT LAKE GUMBO

Written by PAUL TOBIN
Art by RON CHAN
Colors by MATT J. RAINWATER
Letters by STEVE DUTRO
Cover by RON CHAN
"Zomboss' Fashionable Beach Wear!"
Bonus Paper Doll Kit by
CHRISTIANNE GILLENARDO-GOUDREAU
"Tales of Stirring Romance"
Bonus Story by
KEVIN BURKHALTER

DARK HORSE BOOKS

PLANTS VS. ZOMBIES

RUMBLE AT LAKE GUMBO

Publisher **MIKE RICHARDSON**
Editor **PHILIP R. SIMON**
Associate Editor **MEGAN WALKER**
Designer **BRENNAN THOME**
Digital Art Technician **CHRISTINA McKENZIE**

Special thanks to Alexandria Land, A.J. Rathbun, Kristen Star, and everyone at PopCap Games.

First Edition: June 2018
ISBN 978-1-50670-497-5

10 9 8 7 6 5 4 3 2 1
Printed in China

DarkHorse.com
PopCap.com

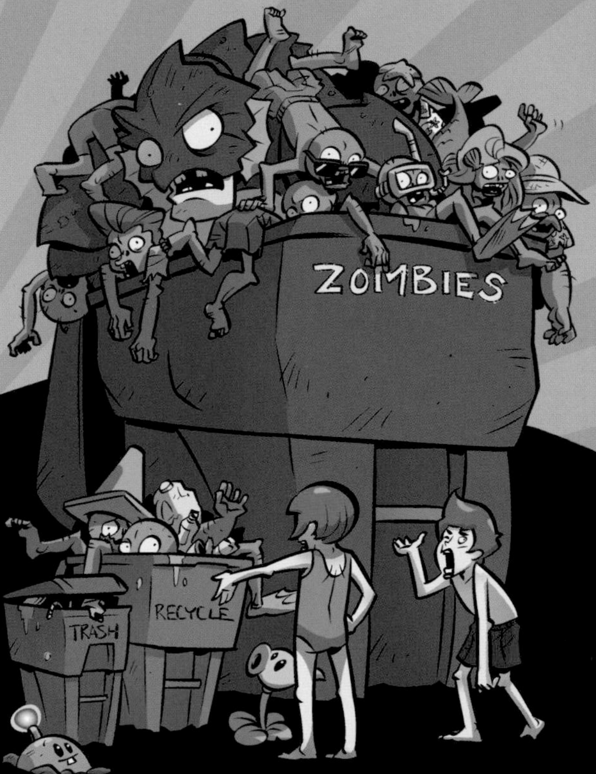
ZOMBIES
RECYCLE
TRASH

No plants were harmed in the making of this graphic novel. However, the Party Crabs did cause quite a neighborly disturbance, with several noise complaints, and the Kelptomaniac unintentionally swiped twenty-seven dollars, a coffee shop punch card, and a Mr. Stubbins fan club membership card from the editors' wallets.

PLANTS vs. ZOMBIES: RUMBLE AT LAKE GUMBO | Published by Dark Horse Books, a division of Dark Horse Comics, Inc., 10956 SE Main Street, Milwaukie, OR 97222 | To find a comics shop in your area, visit comicshoplocator.com |

Library of Congress Cataloging-in-Publication Data

Names: Tobin, Paul, 1965- author. | Chan, Ron, artist. | Rainwater, Matthew J., colourist. | Dutro, Steve, letterer.
Title: Plants vs. zombies. Rumble at Lake Gumbo / written by Paul Tobin ; art by Ron Chan ; colors by Matt J. Rainwater ; letters by Steve Dutro.
Other titles: Plants versus zombies. Rumble at Lake Gumbo | Rumble at Lake

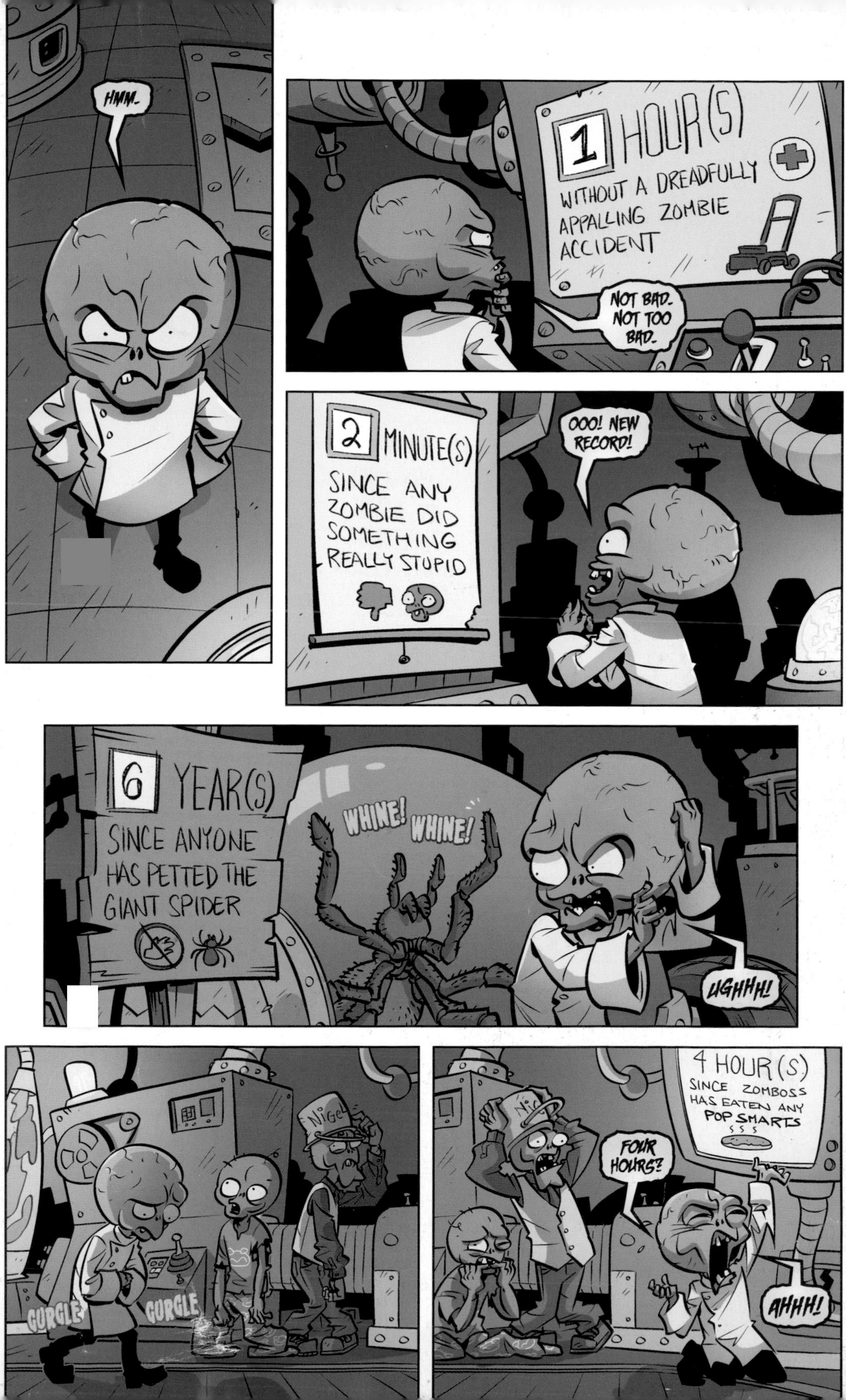
HMM.
1 HOUR(S)
WITHOUT A DREADFULLY APPALLING ZOMBIE ACCIDENT
NOT BAD. NOT TOO BAD.
2 MINUTE(S)
SINCE ANY ZOMBIE DID SOMETHING REALLY STUPID
OOO! NEW RECORD!
6 YEAR(S)
SINCE ANYONE HAS PETTED THE GIANT SPIDER
WHINE! WHINE!
UGHHH!
GURGLE
GURGLE
NIGEL
4 HOUR(S)
SINCE ZOMBOSS HAS EATEN ANY POP SMARTS
FOUR HOURS?
AHHH!

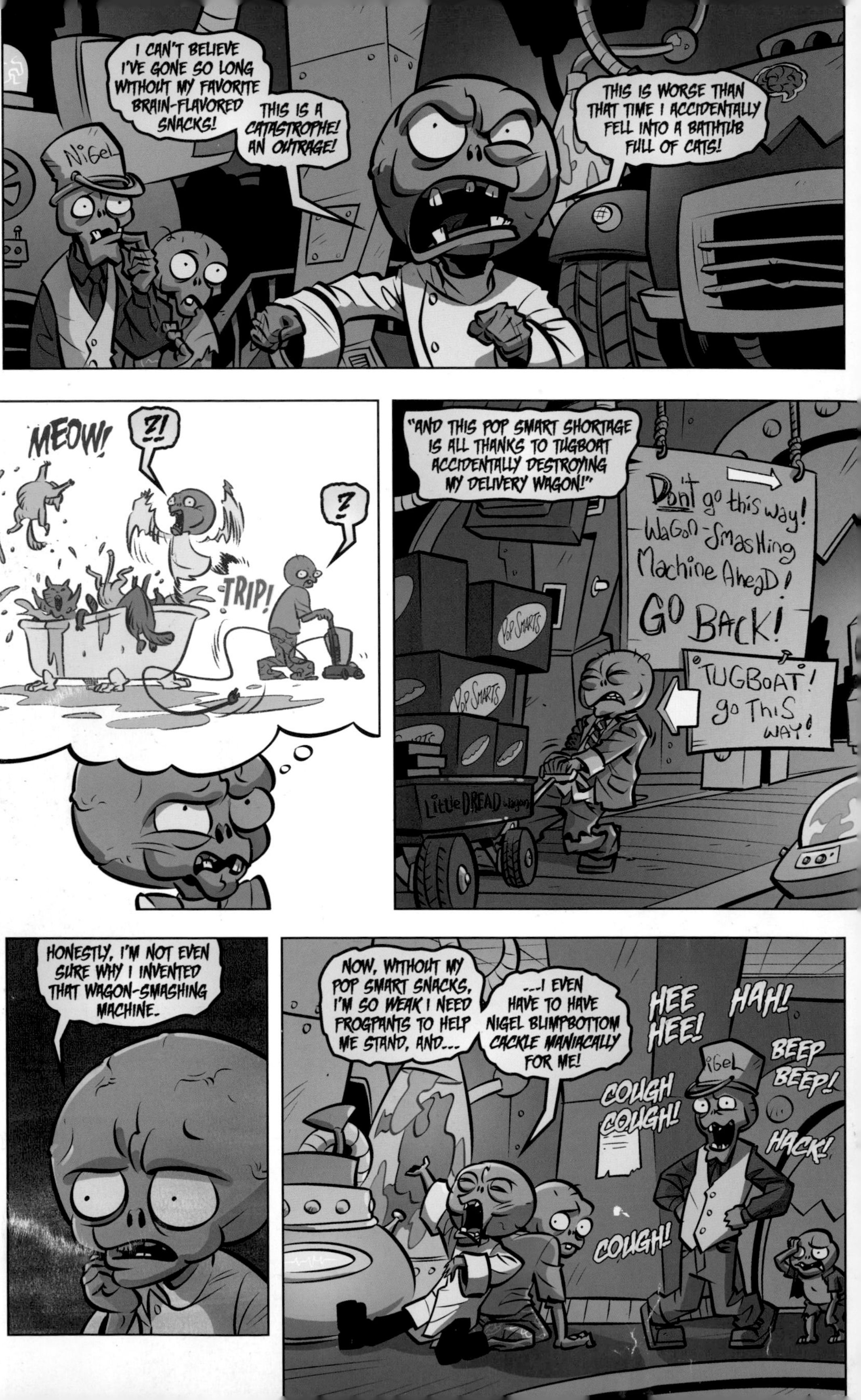
I CAN'T BELIEVE I'VE GONE SO LONG WITHOUT MY FAVORITE BRAIN-FLAVORED SNACKS!
NiGeL
THIS IS A CATASTROPHE! AN OUTRAGE!
THIS IS WORSE THAN THAT TIME I ACCIDENTALLY FELL INTO A BATHTUB FULL OF CATS!
MEOW!
?!
?
TRIP!
"AND THIS POP SMART SHORTAGE IS ALL THANKS TO TUGBOAT ACCIDENTALLY DESTROYING MY DELIVERY WAGON!"
Don't go this way! WaGon-Smashing Machine AheaD! GO BACK!
TUGBoAT! go ThiS WAY!
PoP SMARTS
PoP SMARTS
Little DREAD wagon
HONESTLY, I'M NOT EVEN SURE WHY I INVENTED THAT WAGON-SMASHING MACHINE.
NOW, WITHOUT MY POP SMART SNACKS, I'M SO WEAK I NEED FROGPANTS TO HELP ME STAND, AND...
...I EVEN HAVE TO HAVE NIGEL BLIMPBOTTOM CACKLE MANIACALLY FOR ME!
HEE HEE!
HAH!
BEEP BEEP!
COUGH COUGH!
HACK!
COUGH!
NiGeL

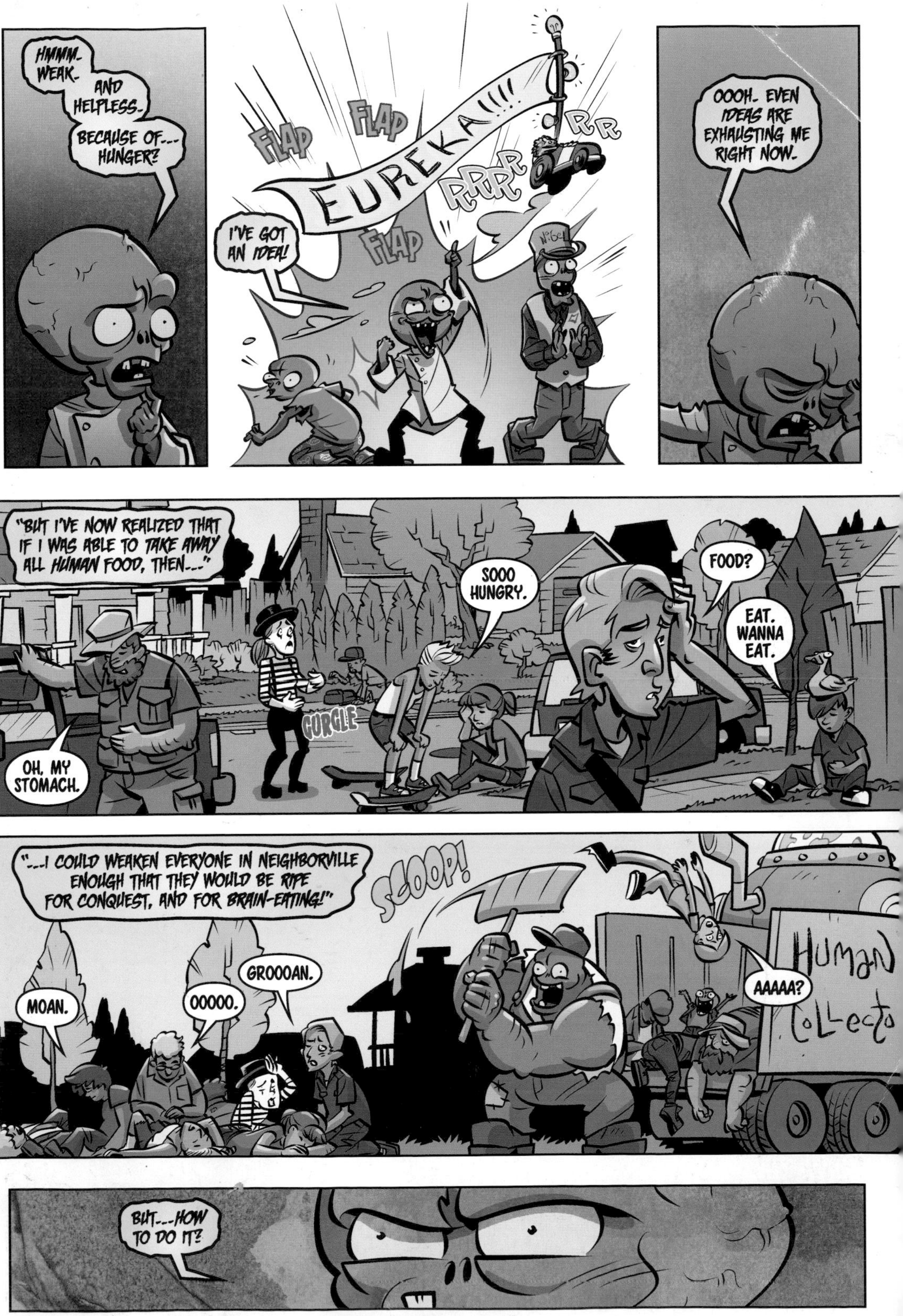
HMMM... WEAK...
AND HELPLESS...
BECAUSE OF... HUNGER?
I'VE GOT AN IDEA!
EUREKA!!!!
FLAP
FLAP
FLAP
RRRRR
RRR
OOOH... EVEN IDEAS ARE EXHAUSTING ME RIGHT NOW...
"BUT I'VE NOW REALIZED THAT IF I WAS ABLE TO TAKE AWAY ALL HUMAN FOOD, THEN..."
SOOO HUNGRY.
FOOD?
EAT. WANNA EAT.
GURGLE
OH, MY STOMACH.
"...I COULD WEAKEN EVERYONE IN NEIGHBORVILLE ENOUGH THAT THEY WOULD BE RIPE FOR CONQUEST, AND FOR BRAIN-EATING!"
SCOOP!
HUMAN COLLECTO
AAAAA?
MOAN.
OOOOO.
GROOOAN.
BUT... HOW TO DO IT?

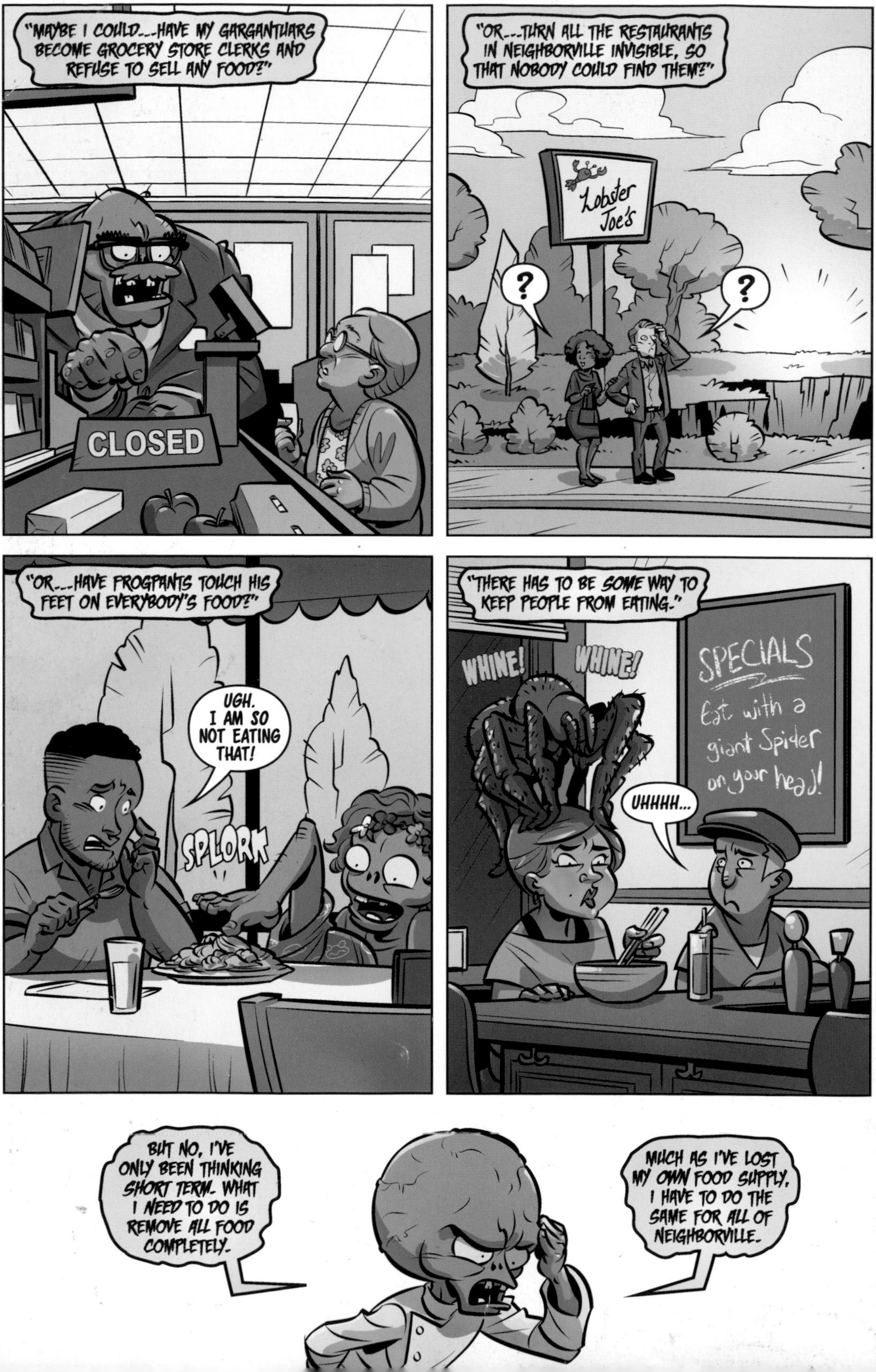
"MAYBE I COULD...HAVE MY GARGANTUARS BECOME GROCERY STORE CLERKS AND REFUSE TO SELL ANY FOOD?"
CLOSED
"OR...TURN ALL THE RESTAURANTS IN NEIGHBORVILLE INVISIBLE, SO THAT NOBODY COULD FIND THEM?"
Lobster Joe's
?
?
"OR...HAVE FROGPANTS TOUCH HIS FEET ON EVERYBODY'S FOOD?"
UGH. I AM SO NOT EATING THAT!
SPLORK
"THERE HAS TO BE SOME WAY TO KEEP PEOPLE FROM EATING."
WHINE!
WHINE!
SPECIALS
Eat with a giant Spider on your head!
UHHHH...
BUT NO, I'VE ONLY BEEN THINKING SHORT TERM. WHAT I NEED TO DO IS REMOVE ALL FOOD COMPLETELY.
MUCH AS I'VE LOST MY OWN FOOD SUPPLY, I HAVE TO DO THE SAME FOR ALL OF NEIGHBORVILLE.

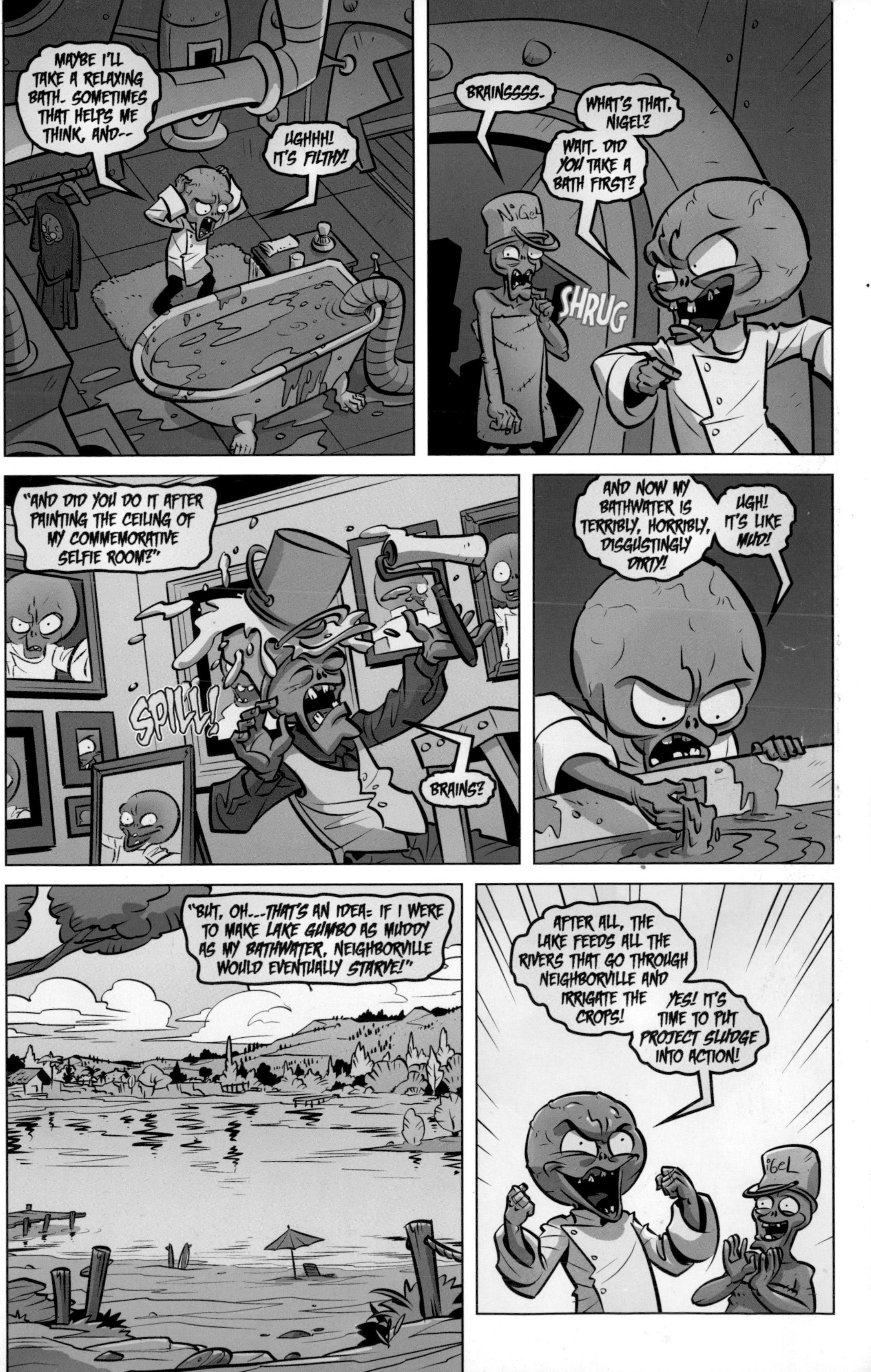
MAYBE I'LL TAKE A RELAXING BATH. SOMETIMES THAT HELPS ME THINK, AND--
UGHHH! IT'S FILTHY!
BRAINSSSS.
WHAT'S THAT, NIGEL?
WAIT. DID YOU TAKE A BATH FIRST?
NiGeL
SHRUG
"AND DID YOU DO IT AFTER PAINTING THE CEILING OF MY COMMEMORATIVE SELFIE ROOM?"
SPILL!
BRAINS?
AND NOW MY BATHWATER IS TERRIBLY, HORRIBLY, DISGUSTINGLY DIRTY!
UGH! IT'S LIKE MUD!
"BUT, OH...THAT'S AN IDEA: IF I WERE TO MAKE LAKE GUMBO AS MUDDY AS MY BATHWATER, NEIGHBORVILLE WOULD EVENTUALLY STARVE!"
AFTER ALL, THE LAKE FEEDS ALL THE RIVERS THAT GO THROUGH NEIGHBORVILLE AND IRRIGATE THE CROPS!
YES! IT'S TIME TO PUT PROJECT SLUDGE INTO ACTION!

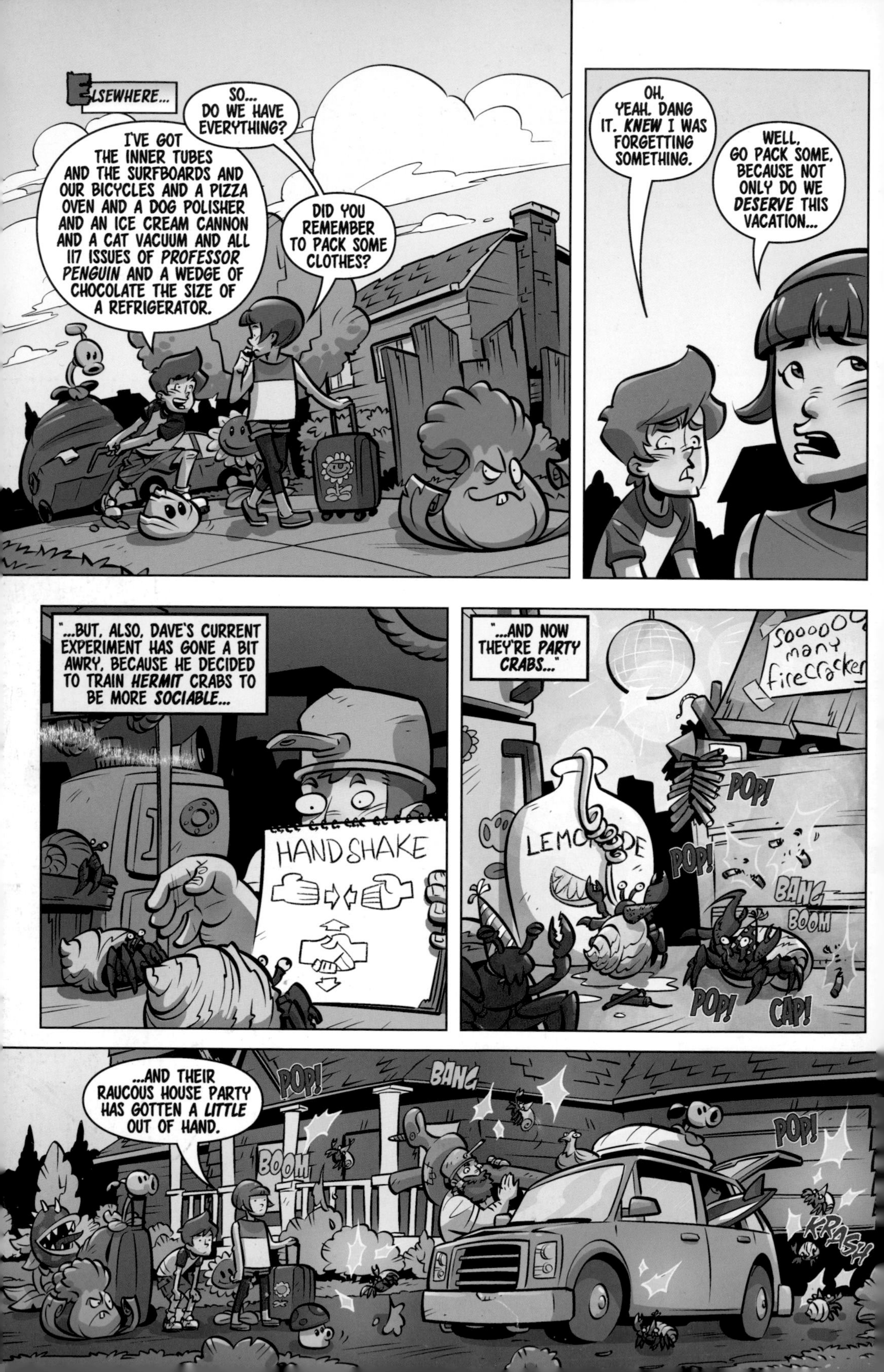
ELSEWHERE...
SO... DO WE HAVE EVERYTHING?
I'VE GOT THE INNER TUBES AND THE SURFBOARDS AND OUR BICYCLES AND A PIZZA OVEN AND A DOG POLISHER AND AN ICE CREAM CANNON AND A CAT VACUUM AND ALL 117 ISSUES OF *PROFESSOR PENGUIN* AND A WEDGE OF CHOCOLATE THE SIZE OF A REFRIGERATOR.
DID YOU REMEMBER TO PACK SOME CLOTHES?
OH, YEAH. DANG IT. *KNEW* I WAS FORGETTING SOMETHING.
WELL, GO PACK SOME, BECAUSE NOT ONLY DO WE *DESERVE* THIS VACATION...
"...BUT, ALSO, DAVE'S CURRENT EXPERIMENT HAS GONE A BIT AWRY, BECAUSE HE DECIDED TO TRAIN *HERMIT* CRABS TO BE MORE *SOCIABLE*...
HANDSHAKE
"...AND NOW THEY'RE *PARTY CRABS*..."
POP!
POP!
BANG
BOOM
POP!
CAP!
...AND THEIR RAUCOUS HOUSE PARTY HAS GOTTEN A *LITTLE* OUT OF HAND.
POP!
BANG
BOOM
POP!
KRASH

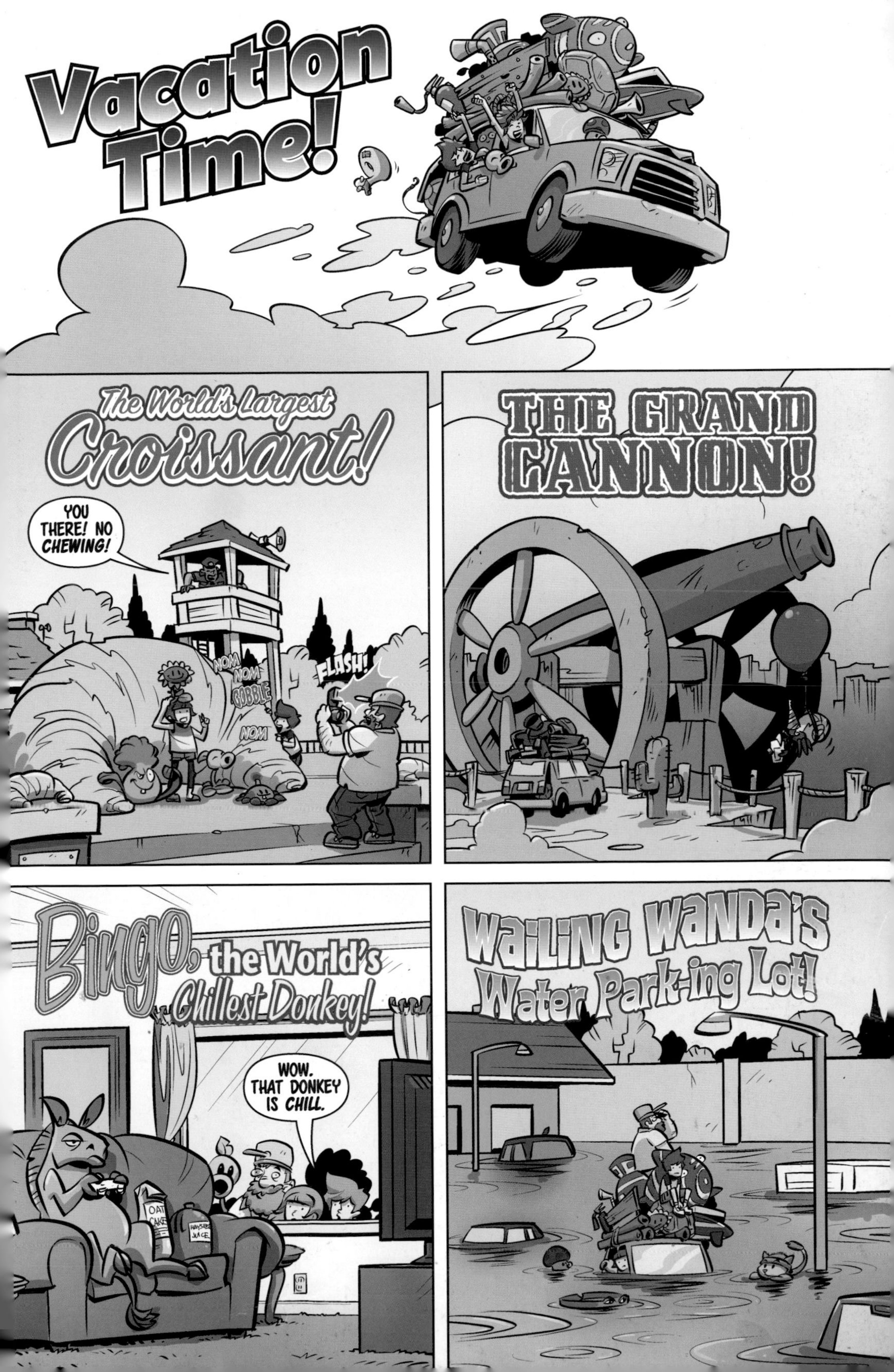
Vacation Time!
The World's Largest Croissant!
YOU THERE! NO CHEWING!
NOM NOM GOBBLE NOM
FLASH!
THE GRAND CANNON!
Bingo, the World's Chillest Donkey!
WOW. THAT DONKEY IS CHILL.
OAT CAKE
HAYSEED JUICE
WAILING WANDA'S Water Park-ing Lot!

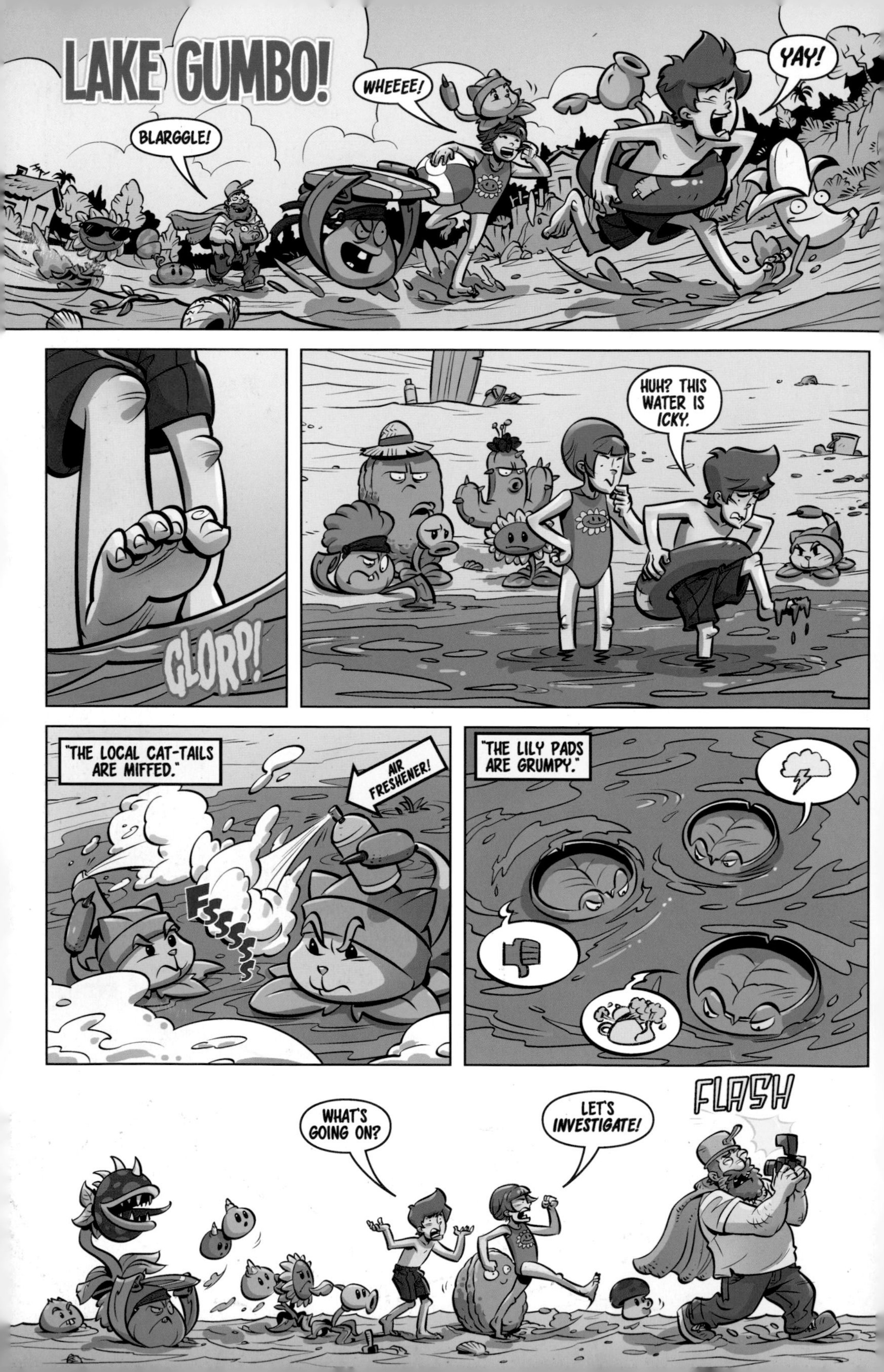
LAKE GUMBO!
BLARGGLE!
WHEEEE!
YAY!
GLORP!
HUH? THIS WATER IS ICKY.
"THE LOCAL CAT-TAILS ARE MIFFED."
AIR FRESHENER!
FSSSSS
"THE LILY PADS ARE GRUMPY."
WHAT'S GOING ON?
LET'S INVESTIGATE!
FLASH

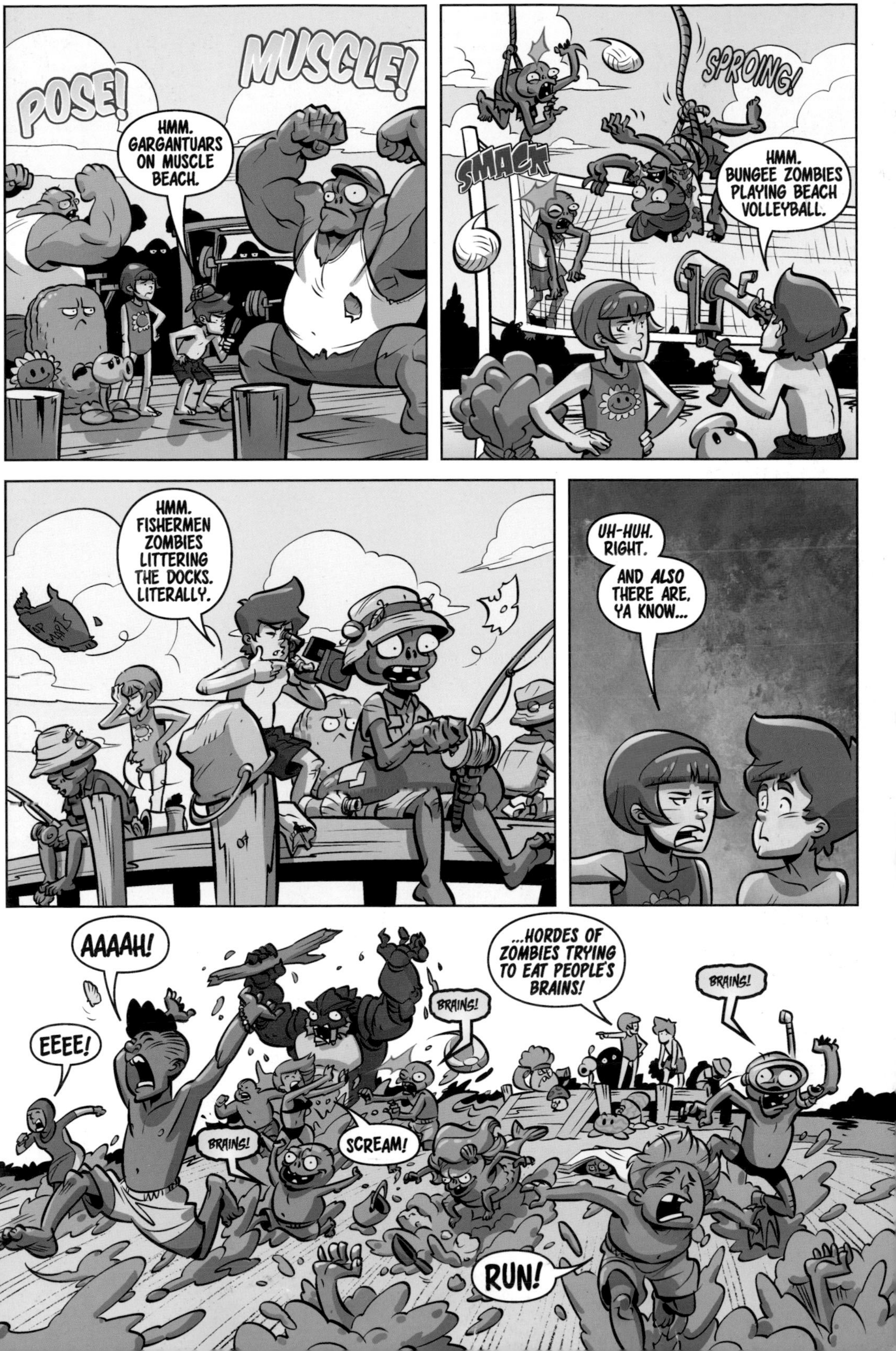
POSE!
MUSCLE!
HMM. GARGANTUARS ON MUSCLE BEACH.
SPROING!
SMACK
HMM. BUNGEE ZOMBIES PLAYING BEACH VOLLEYBALL.
HMM. FISHERMEN ZOMBIES LITTERING THE DOCKS. LITERALLY.
UH-HUH. RIGHT.
AND ALSO THERE ARE, YA KNOW...
AAAAH!
EEEE!
BRAINS!
...HORDES OF ZOMBIES TRYING TO EAT PEOPLE'S BRAINS!
BRAINS!
BRAINS!
SCREAM!
RUN!

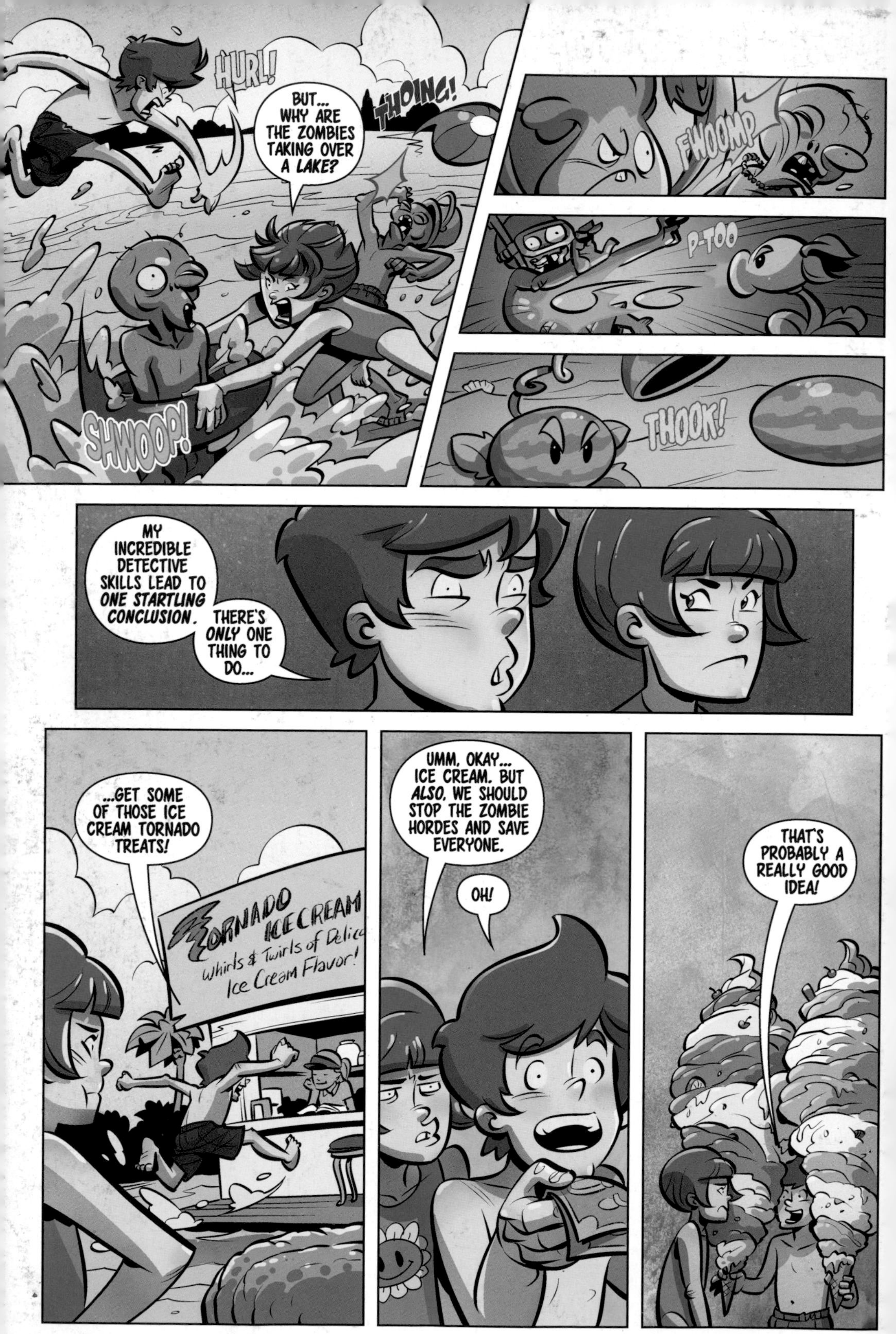
HURL!
BUT... WHY ARE THE ZOMBIES TAKING OVER A LAKE?
THOING!
SHWOOP!
FWOOMP
P-TOO
THOOK!
MY INCREDIBLE DETECTIVE SKILLS LEAD TO ONE STARTLING CONCLUSION.
THERE'S ONLY ONE THING TO DO...
...GET SOME OF THOSE ICE CREAM TORNADO TREATS!
TORNADO ICE CREAM
Whirls & Twirls of Delic
Ice Cream Flavor!
UMM, OKAY... ICE CREAM. BUT ALSO, WE SHOULD STOP THE ZOMBIE HORDES AND SAVE EVERYONE.
OH!
THAT'S PROBABLY A REALLY GOOD IDEA!

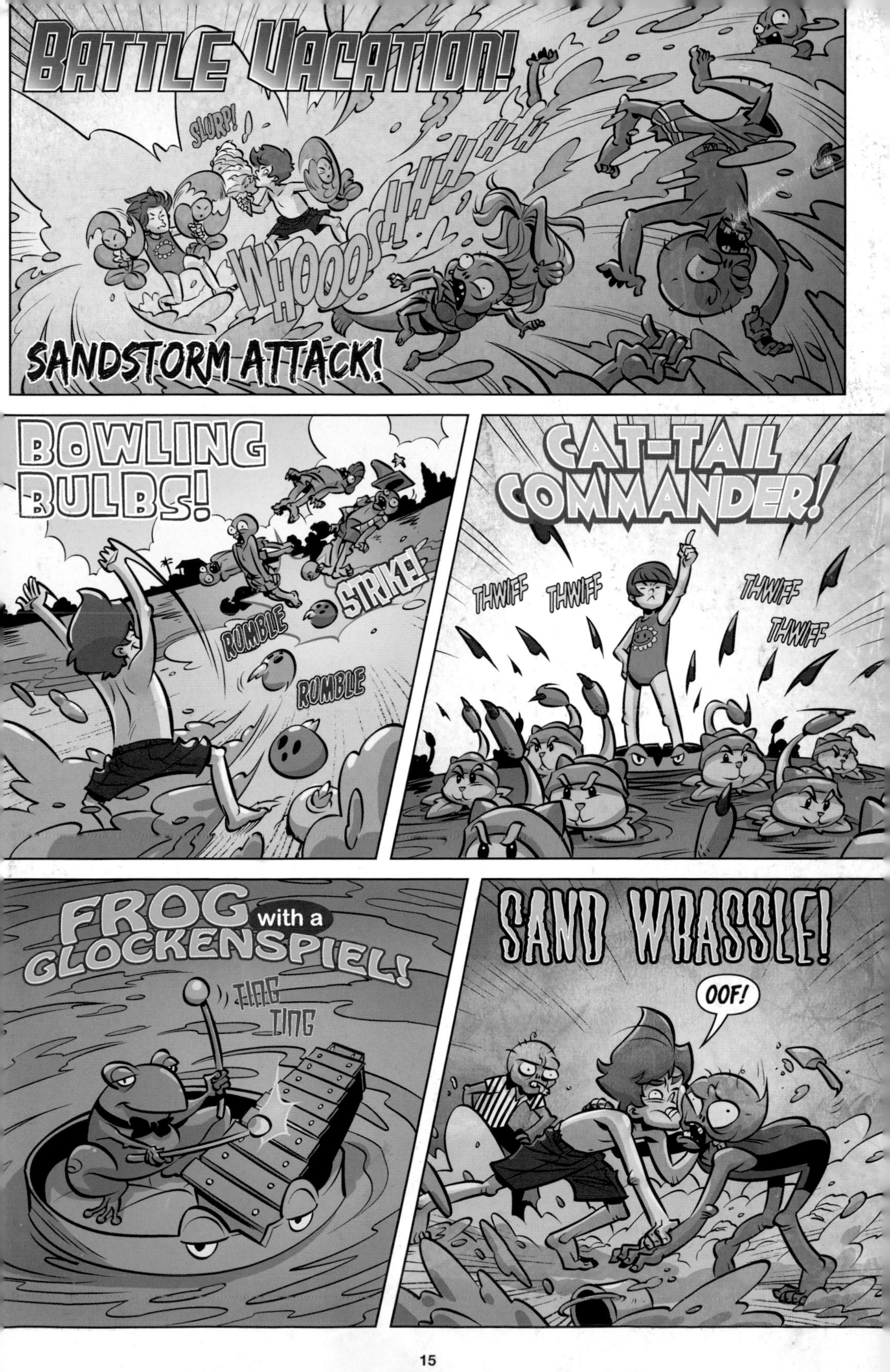
BATTLE VACATION!
SLORP!
WHOOOOSHHHHHH
SANDSTORM ATTACK!
BOWLING BULBS!
STRIKE!
RUMBLE
RUMBLE
CAT-TAIL COMMANDER!
THWIFF
THWIFF
THWIFF
THWIFF
FROG with a GLOCKENSPIEL!
TING
TING
SAND WRASSLE!
OOF!

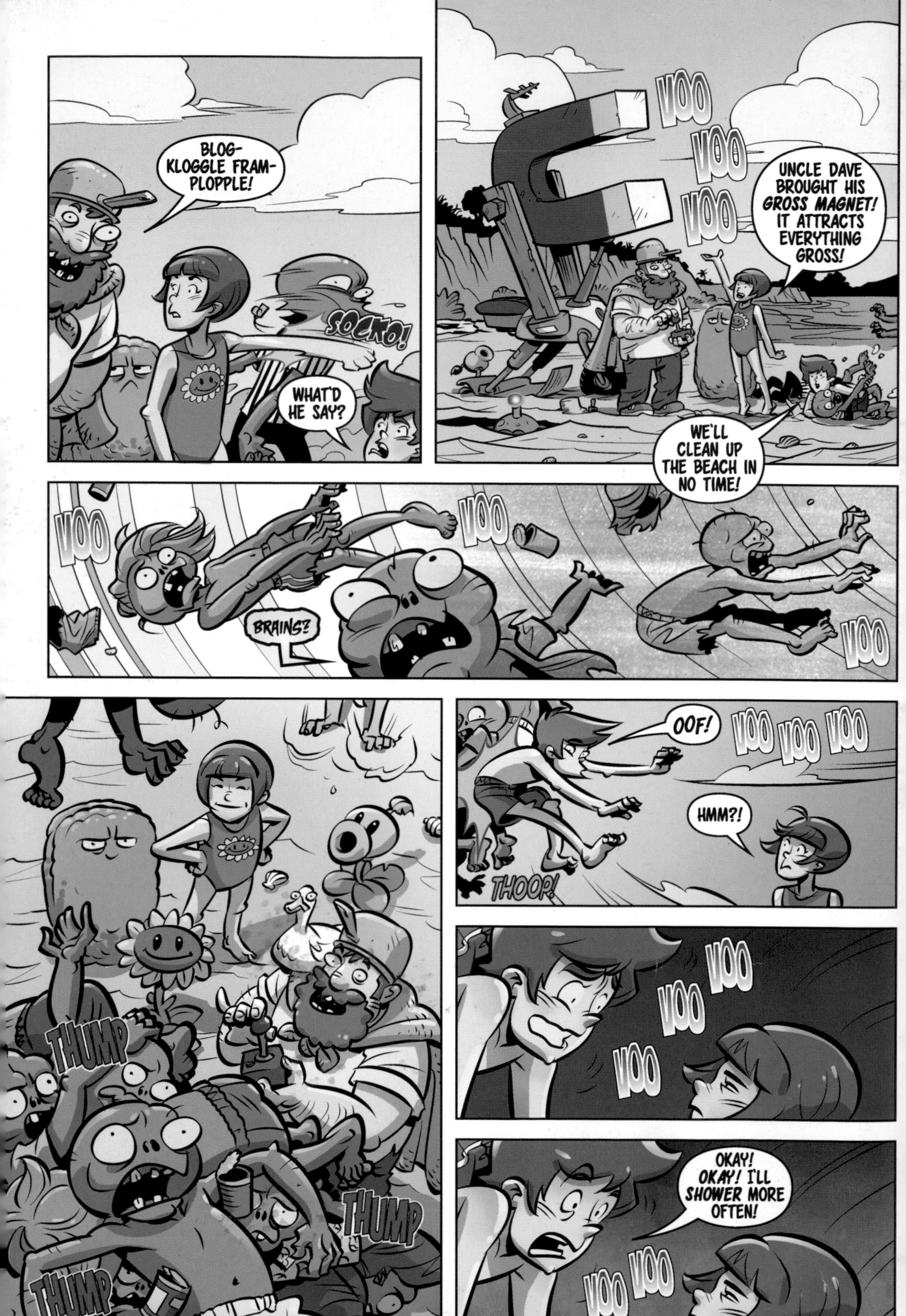
BLOG-KLOGGLE FRAM-PLOPPLE!
SOCKO!
WHAT'D HE SAY?
VOO
VOO
VOO
UNCLE DAVE BROUGHT HIS GROSS MAGNET! IT ATTRACTS EVERYTHING GROSS!
WE'LL CLEAN UP THE BEACH IN NO TIME!
VOO
VOO
BRAINS?
VOO
THUMP
THUMP
THUMP
OOF!
VOO VOO VOO
HMM?!
THOOP!
VOO
VOO
VOO
OKAY! OKAY! I'LL SHOWER MORE OFTEN!
VOO VOO

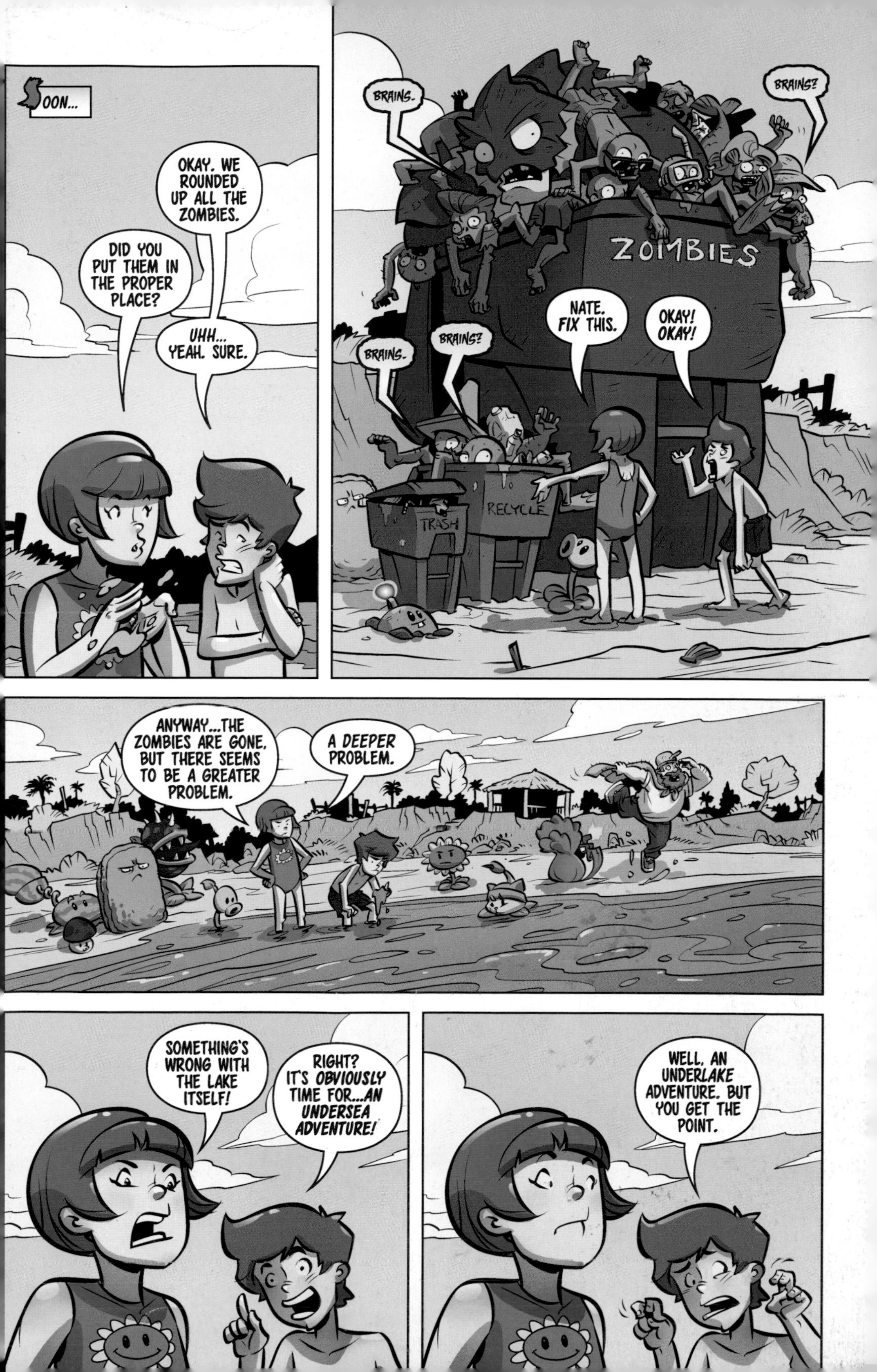
SOON...
OKAY. WE ROUNDED UP ALL THE ZOMBIES.
DID YOU PUT THEM IN THE PROPER PLACE?
UHH... YEAH. SURE.
BRAINS.
BRAINS?
ZOMBIES
NATE. FIX THIS.
OKAY! OKAY!
BRAINS.
BRAINS?
TRASH
RECYCLE
ANYWAY...THE ZOMBIES ARE GONE, BUT THERE SEEMS TO BE A GREATER PROBLEM.
A DEEPER PROBLEM.
SOMETHING'S WRONG WITH THE LAKE ITSELF!
RIGHT? IT'S *OBVIOUSLY* TIME FOR...*AN UNDERSEA ADVENTURE!*
WELL, AN UNDER*LAKE* ADVENTURE. BUT YOU GET THE POINT.

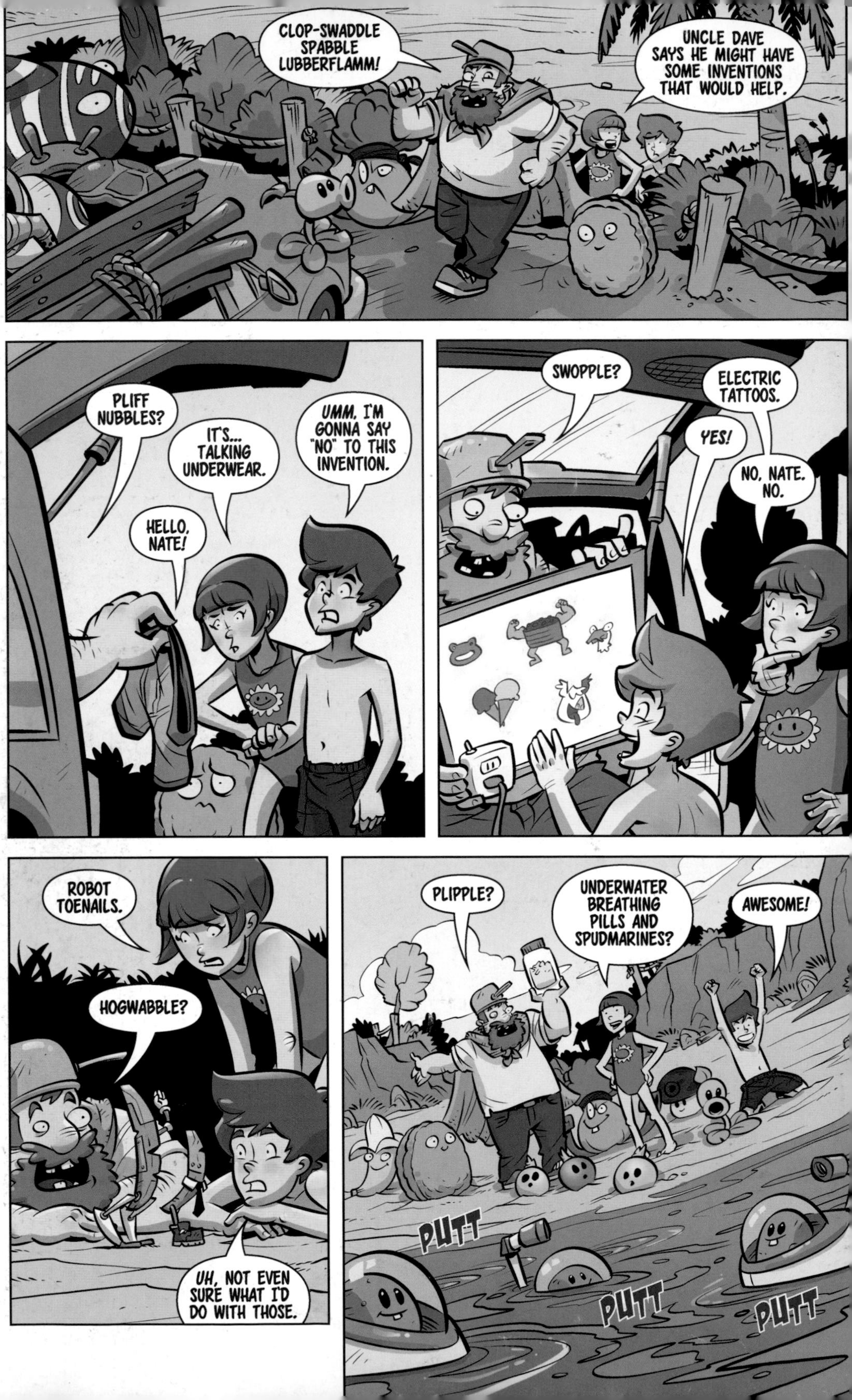
CLOP-SWADDLE SPABBLE LUBBERFLAMM!
UNCLE DAVE SAYS HE MIGHT HAVE SOME INVENTIONS THAT WOULD HELP.
PLIFF NUBBLES?
HELLO, NATE!
IT'S... TALKING UNDERWEAR.
UMM, I'M GONNA SAY "NO" TO THIS INVENTION.
SWOPPLE?
ELECTRIC TATTOOS.
YES!
NO, NATE. NO.
ROBOT TOENAILS.
HOGWABBLE?
UH, NOT EVEN SURE WHAT I'D DO WITH THOSE.
PLIPPLE?
UNDERWATER BREATHING PILLS AND SPUDMARINES?
AWESOME!
PUTT
PUTT
PUTT

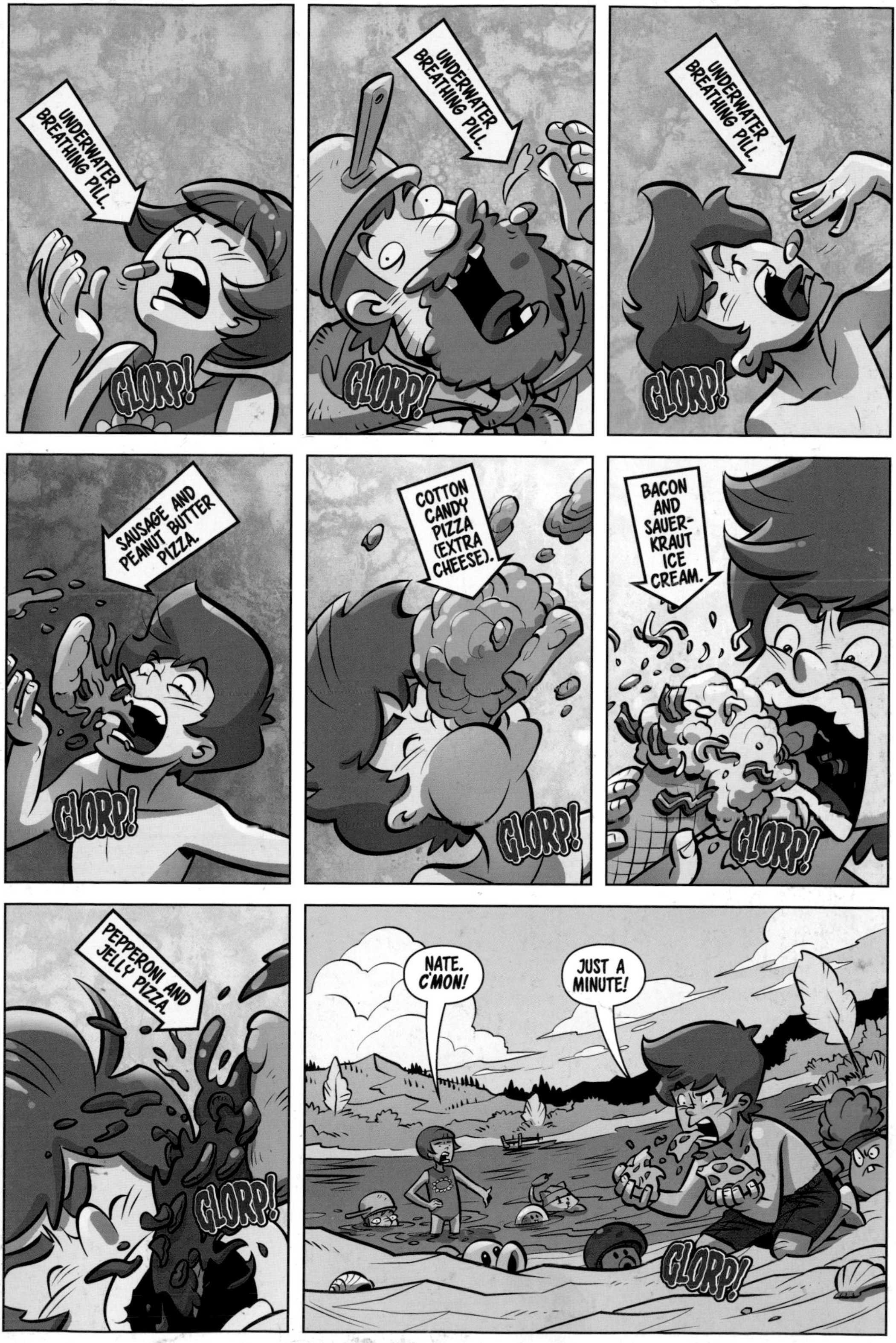
UNDERWATER BREATHING PILL.
GLORP!
UNDERWATER BREATHING PILL.
GLORP!
UNDERWATER BREATHING PILL.
GLORP!
SAUSAGE AND PEANUT BUTTER PIZZA.
GLORP!
COTTON CANDY PIZZA (EXTRA CHEESE).
GLORP!
BACON AND SAUER-KRAUT ICE CREAM.
GLORP!
PEPPERONI AND JELLY PIZZA.
GLORP!
NATE. C'MON!
JUST A MINUTE!
GLORP!

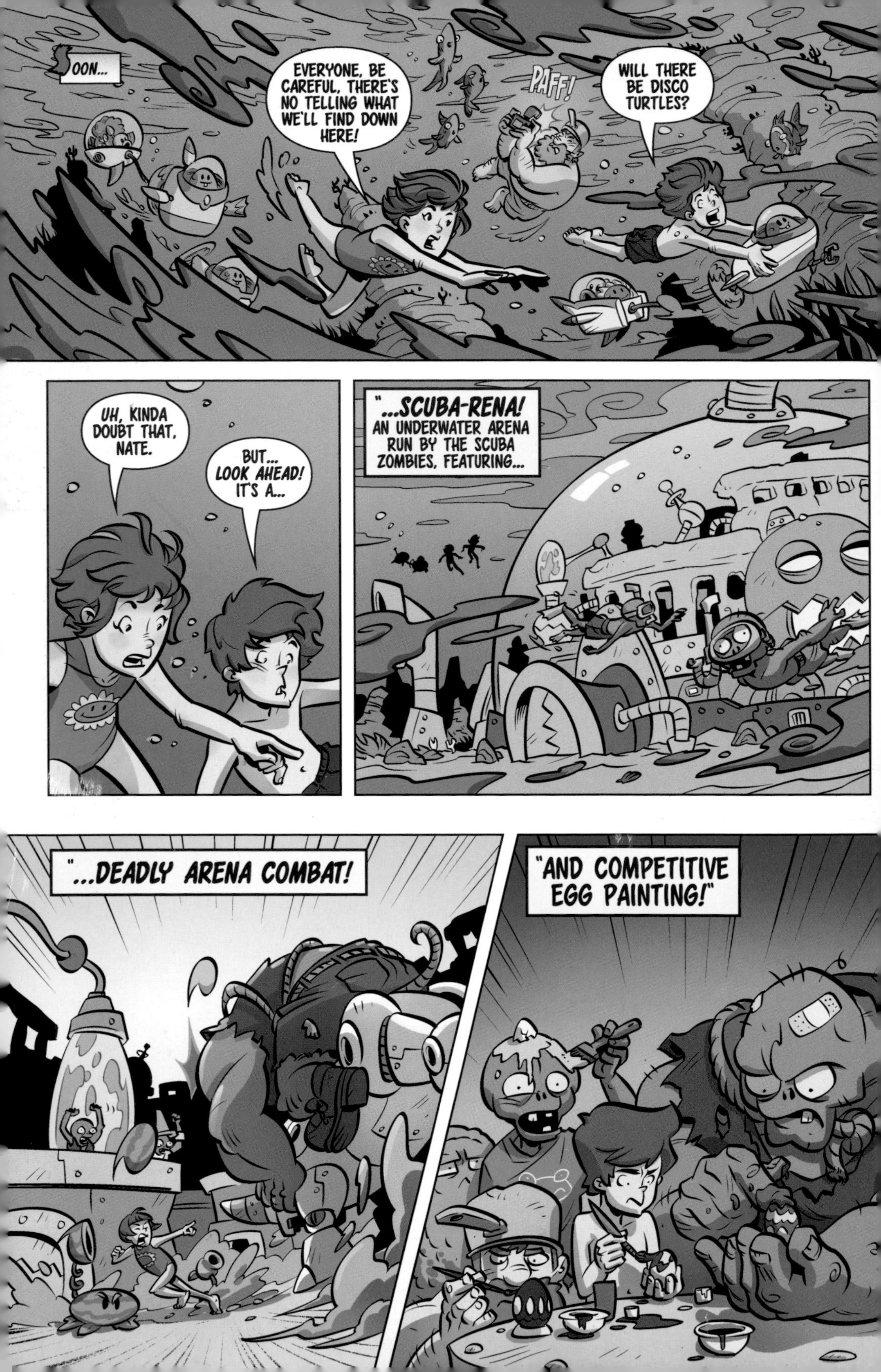
SOON...
EVERYONE, BE CAREFUL, THERE'S NO TELLING WHAT WE'LL FIND DOWN HERE!
PAFF!
WILL THERE BE DISCO TURTLES?
UH, KINDA DOUBT THAT, NATE.
BUT... LOOK AHEAD! IT'S A...
"...SCUBA-RENA! AN UNDERWATER ARENA RUN BY THE SCUBA ZOMBIES, FEATURING...
"...DEADLY ARENA COMBAT!
"AND COMPETITIVE EGG PAINTING!"

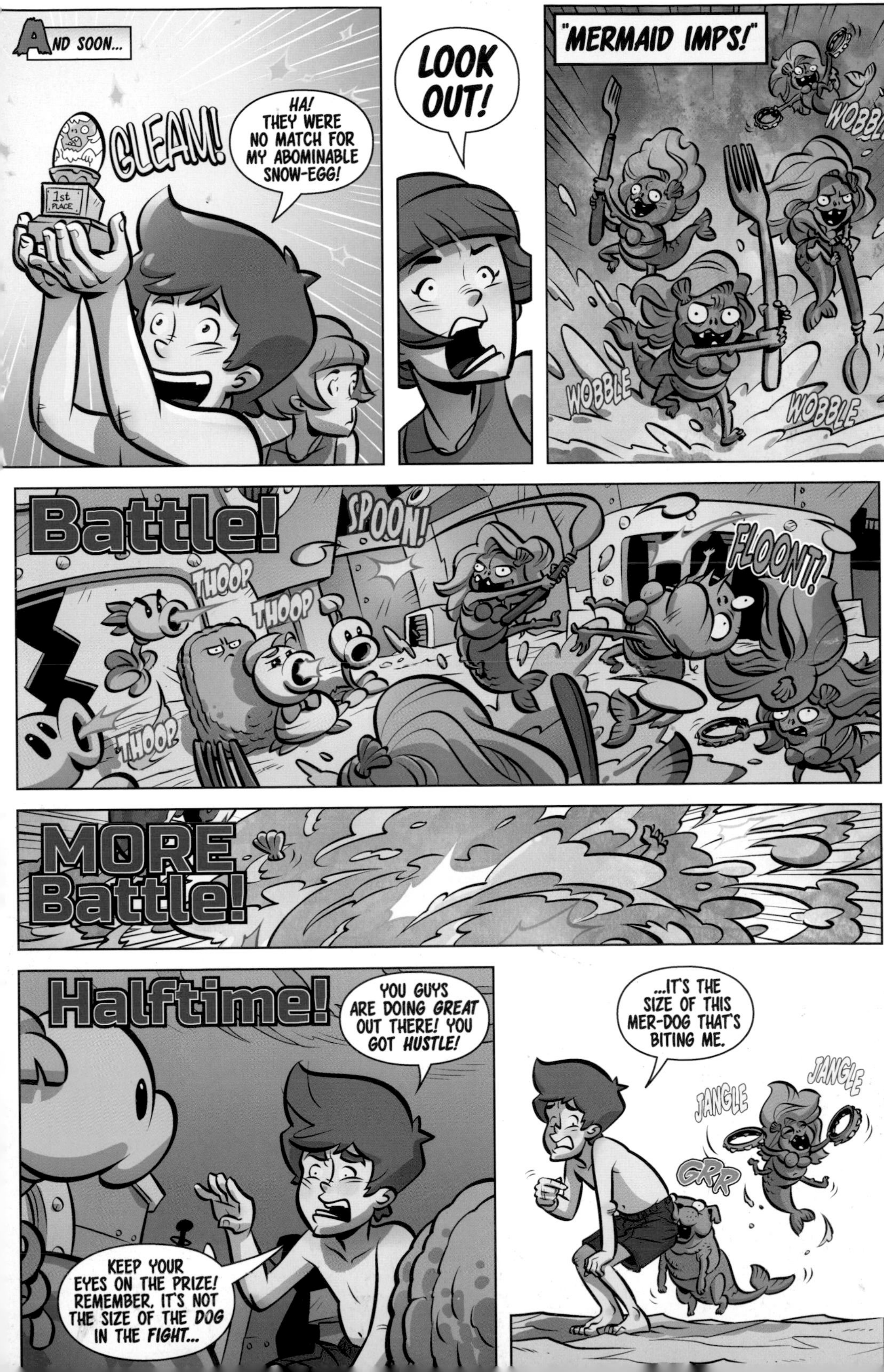
AND SOON...
GLEAM!
HA! THEY WERE NO MATCH FOR MY ABOMINABLE SNOW-EGG!
1st PLACE
LOOK OUT!
"MERMAID IMPS!"
WOBBLE
WOBBLE
WOBBLE
Battle!
SPOON!
THOOP
THOOP
THOOP
FLOONT!
MORE Battle!
Halftime!
YOU GUYS ARE DOING GREAT OUT THERE! YOU GOT HUSTLE!
KEEP YOUR EYES ON THE PRIZE! REMEMBER, IT'S NOT THE SIZE OF THE DOG IN THE FIGHT...
...IT'S THE SIZE OF THIS MER-DOG THAT'S BITING ME.
JANGLE
JANGLE
GRR

Second Half! BATTLE!

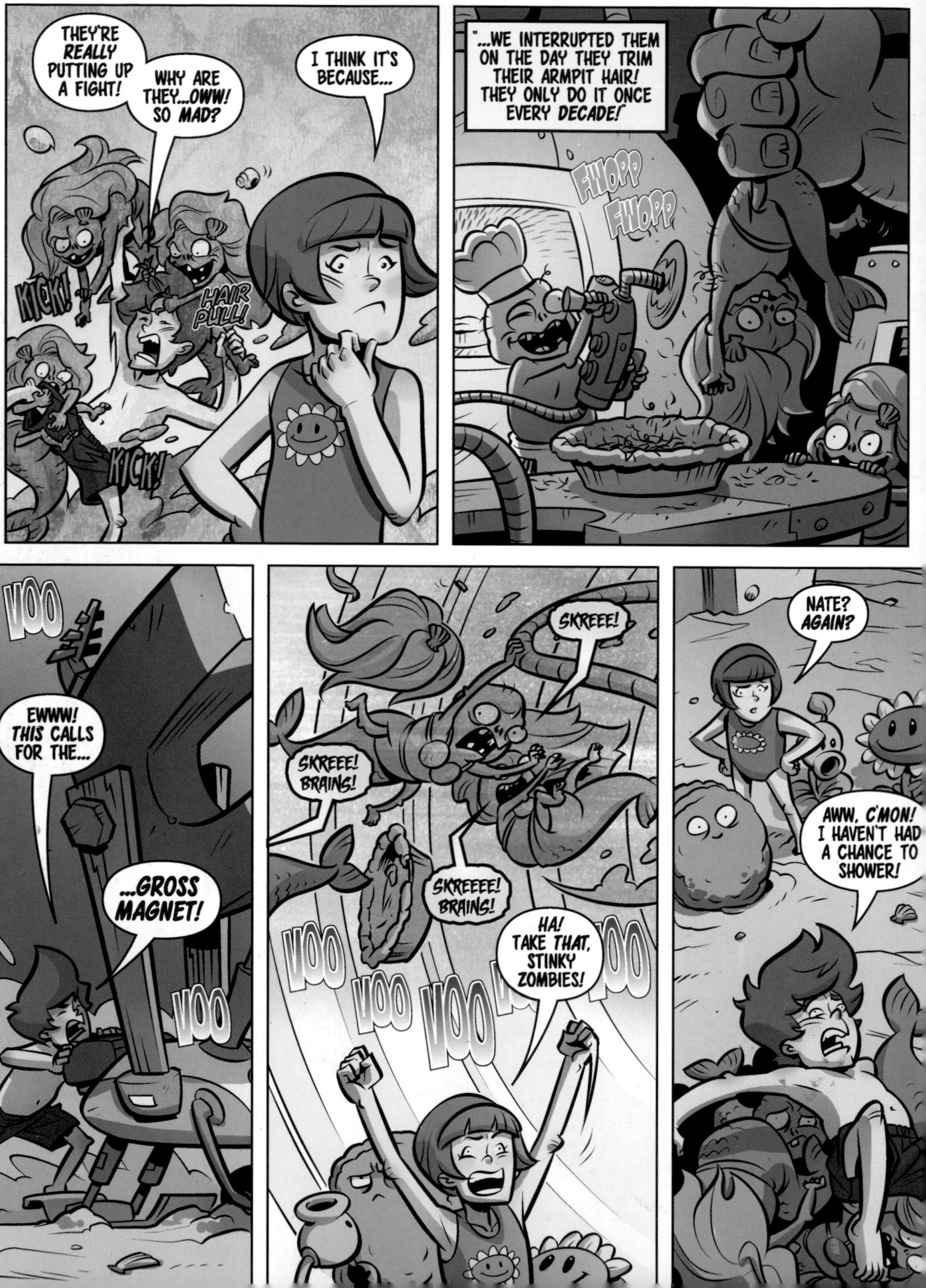
THEY'RE REALLY PUTTING UP A FIGHT!
WHY ARE THEY...OWW! SO MAD?
I THINK IT'S BECAUSE...
KICK!
HAIR PULL!
KICK!
"...WE INTERRUPTED THEM ON THE DAY THEY TRIM THEIR ARMPIT HAIR! THEY ONLY DO IT ONCE EVERY DECADE!"
FWOPP
FWOPP
VOO
EWWW! THIS CALLS FOR THE...
...GROSS MAGNET!
VOO
SKREEE!
SKREEE! BRAINS!
SKREEEE! BRAINS!
HA! TAKE THAT, STINKY ZOMBIES!
VOO
VOO
VOO
VOO
NATE? AGAIN?
AWW, C'MON! I HAVEN'T HAD A CHANCE TO SHOWER!

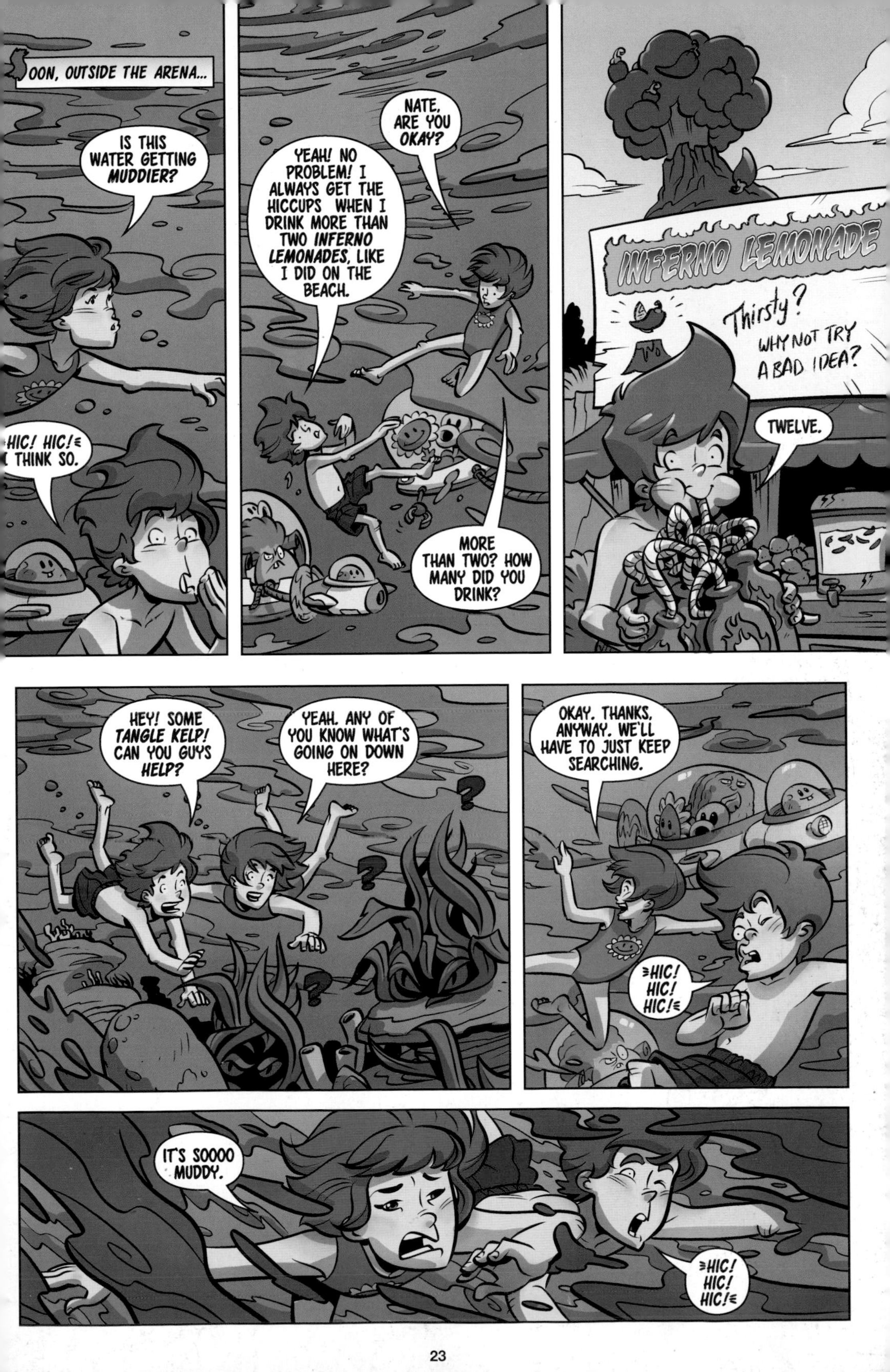

SOON, OUTSIDE THE ARENA...
IS THIS WATER GETTING MUDDIER?
HIC! HIC! I THINK SO.
NATE, ARE YOU OKAY?
YEAH! NO PROBLEM! I ALWAYS GET THE HICCUPS WHEN I DRINK MORE THAN TWO INFERNO LEMONADES, LIKE I DID ON THE BEACH.
MORE THAN TWO? HOW MANY DID YOU DRINK?
INFERNO LEMONADE
Thirsty? WHY NOT TRY A BAD IDEA?
TWELVE.
HEY! SOME TANGLE KELP! CAN YOU GUYS HELP?
YEAH. ANY OF YOU KNOW WHAT'S GOING ON DOWN HERE?
OKAY. THANKS, ANYWAY. WE'LL HAVE TO JUST KEEP SEARCHING.
HIC! HIC! HIC!
IT'S SOOOO MUDDY.
HIC! HIC! HIC!

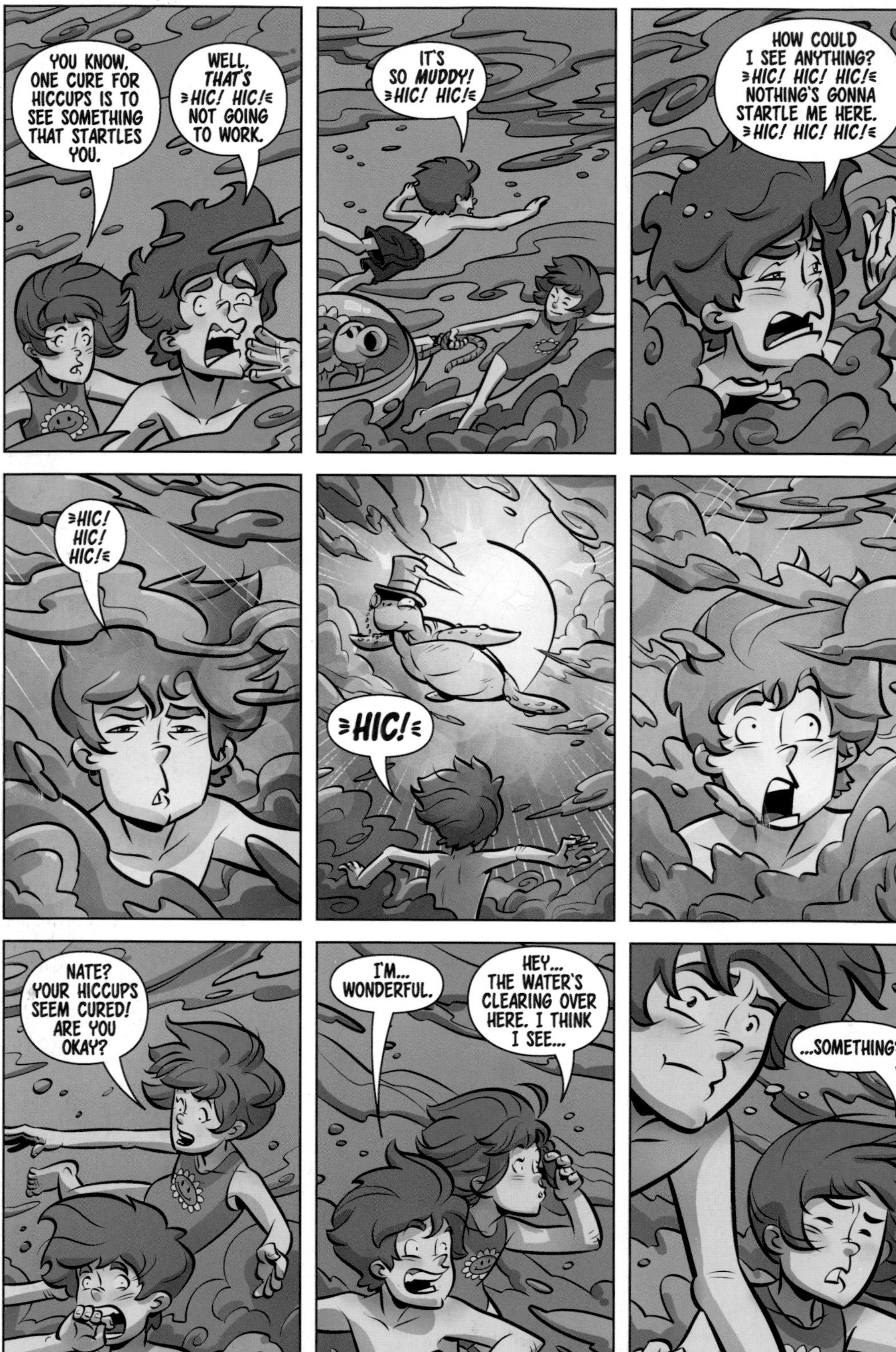

YOU KNOW, ONE CURE FOR HICCUPS IS TO SEE SOMETHING THAT STARTLES YOU.
WELL, THAT'S ≡HIC! HIC!≡ NOT GOING TO WORK.
IT'S SO MUDDY! ≡HIC! HIC!≡
HOW COULD I SEE ANYTHING? ≡HIC! HIC! HIC!≡ NOTHING'S GONNA STARTLE ME HERE. ≡HIC! HIC! HIC!≡
≡HIC! HIC! HIC!≡
≡HIC!≡
NATE? YOUR HICCUPS SEEM CURED! ARE YOU OKAY?
I'M... WONDERFUL.
HEY... THE WATER'S CLEARING OVER HERE. I THINK I SEE...
...SOMETHING?

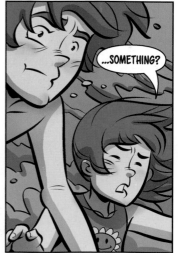

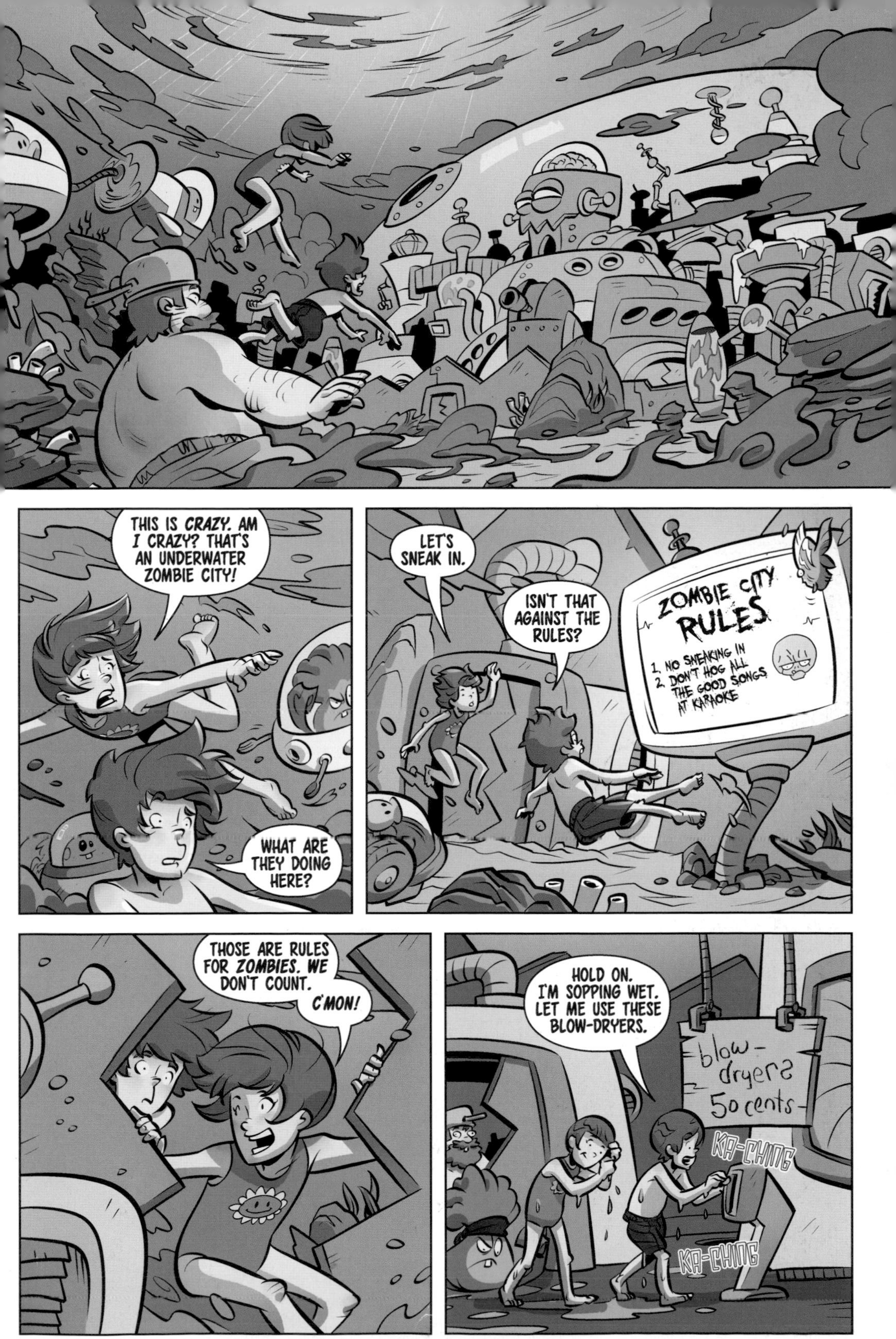

THIS IS CRAZY. AM I CRAZY? THAT'S AN UNDERWATER ZOMBIE CITY!
WHAT ARE THEY DOING HERE?
LET'S SNEAK IN.
ISN'T THAT AGAINST THE RULES?
ZOMBIE CITY RULES
1. NO SNEAKING IN
2. DON'T HOG ALL THE GOOD SONGS AT KARAOKE
THOSE ARE RULES FOR ZOMBIES. WE DON'T COUNT.
C'MON!
HOLD ON. I'M SOPPING WET. LET ME USE THESE BLOW-DRYERS.
blow-dryers 50 cents
KA-CHING
KA-CHING

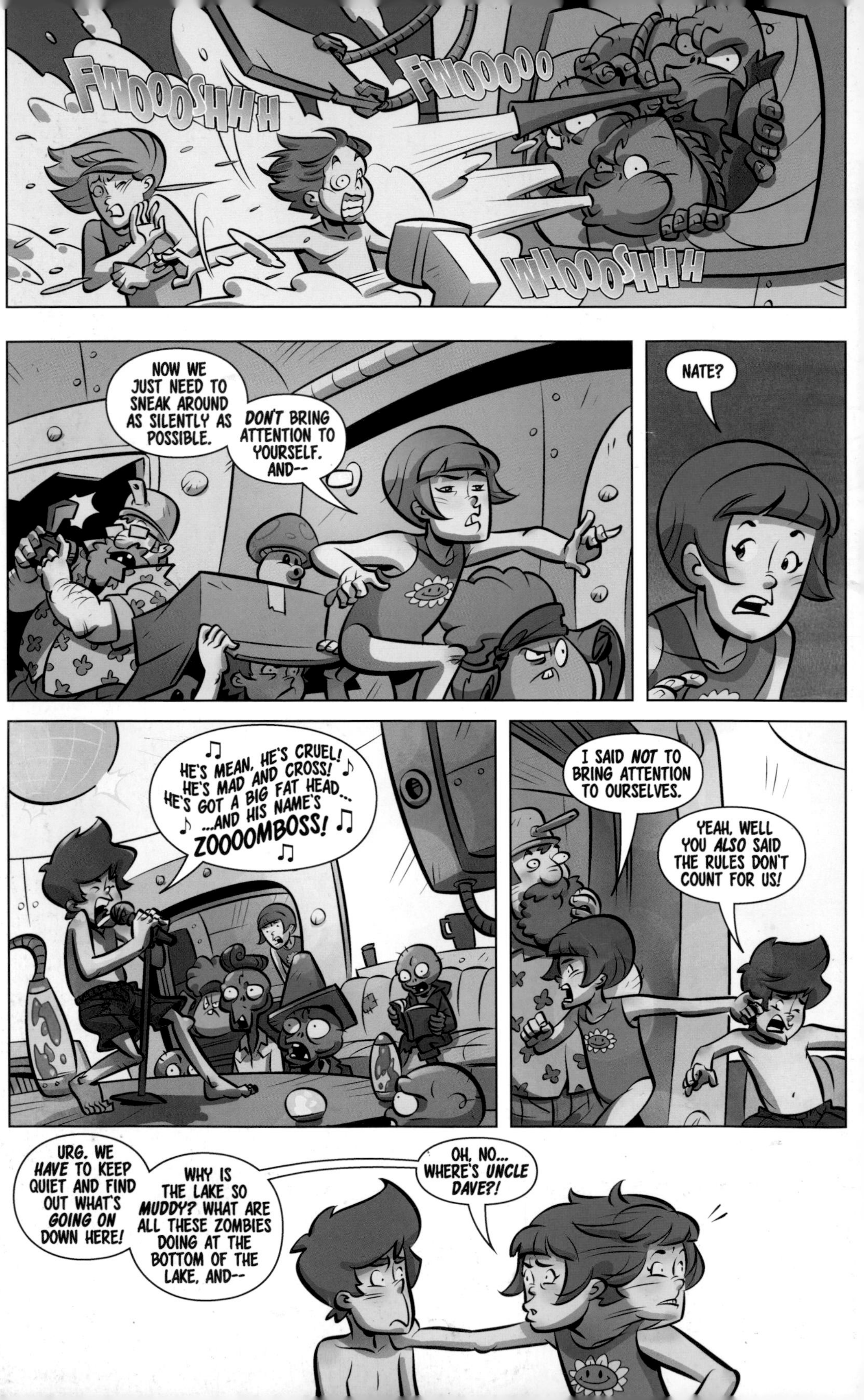
FWOOOSHHH
FWOOOOO
WHOOOSHHH
NOW WE JUST NEED TO SNEAK AROUND AS SILENTLY AS POSSIBLE.
DON'T BRING ATTENTION TO YOURSELF. AND--
NATE?
HE'S MEAN, HE'S CRUEL! HE'S MAD AND CROSS! HE'S GOT A BIG FAT HEAD... ...AND HIS NAME'S ZOOOOMBOSS!
I SAID NOT TO BRING ATTENTION TO OURSELVES.
YEAH, WELL YOU ALSO SAID THE RULES DON'T COUNT FOR US!
URG. WE HAVE TO KEEP QUIET AND FIND OUT WHAT'S GOING ON DOWN HERE!
WHY IS THE LAKE SO MUDDY? WHAT ARE ALL THESE ZOMBIES DOING AT THE BOTTOM OF THE LAKE, AND--
OH, NO... WHERE'S UNCLE DAVE?!

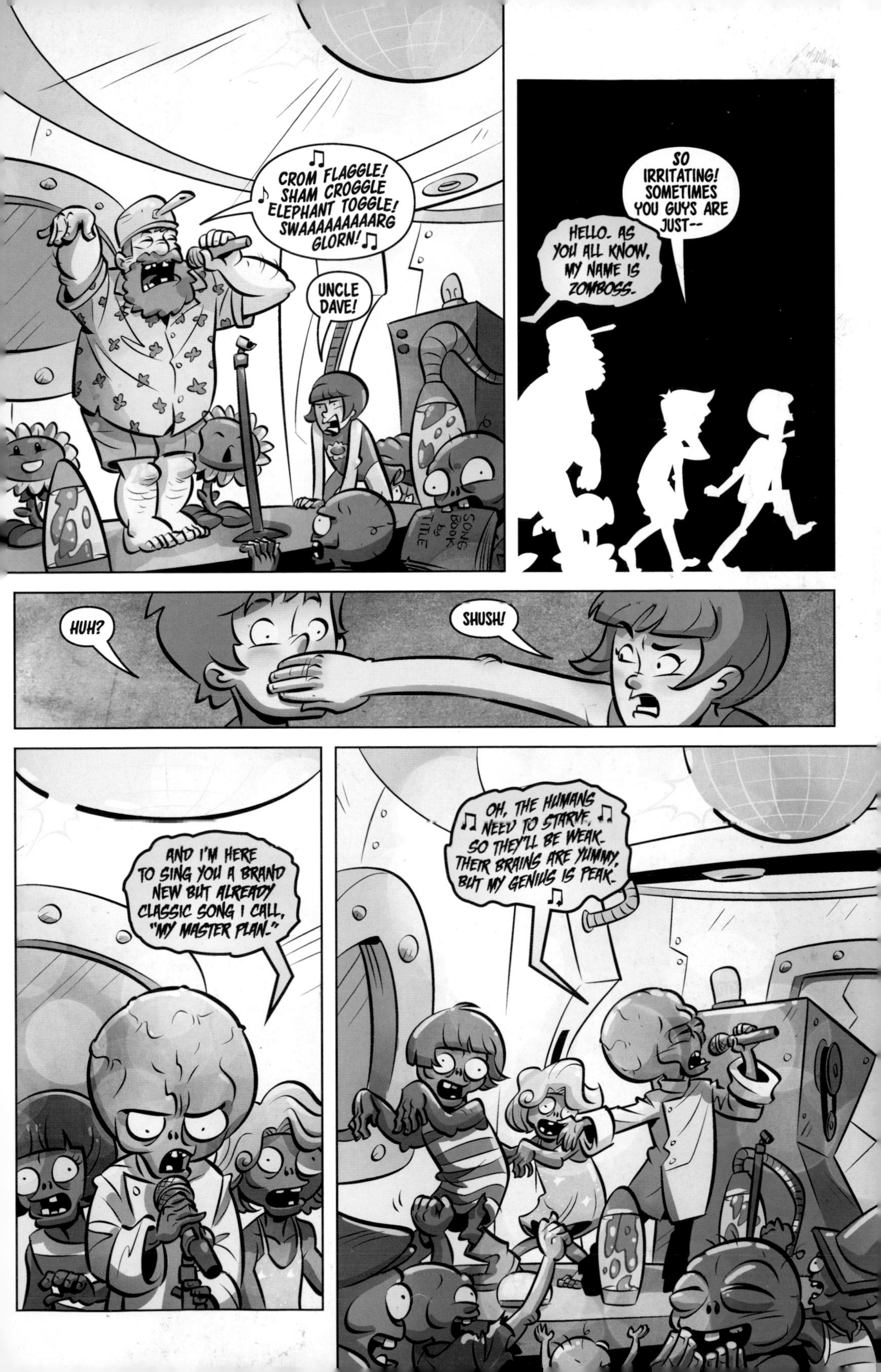
♪ CROM FLAGGLE! SHAM CROGGLE ELEPHANT TOGGLE! SWAAAAAAAAARG GLORN! ♫
UNCLE DAVE!
SONG BOOK by TITLE
HELLO. AS YOU ALL KNOW, MY NAME IS ZOMBOSS.
SO IRRITATING! SOMETIMES YOU GUYS ARE JUST--
HUH?
SHUSH!
AND I'M HERE TO SING YOU A BRAND NEW BUT ALREADY CLASSIC SONG I CALL, "MY MASTER PLAN."
♫ OH, THE HUMANS NEED TO STARVE, ♫ SO THEY'LL BE WEAK. THEIR BRAINS ARE YUMMY, BUT MY GENIUS IS PEAK. ♫

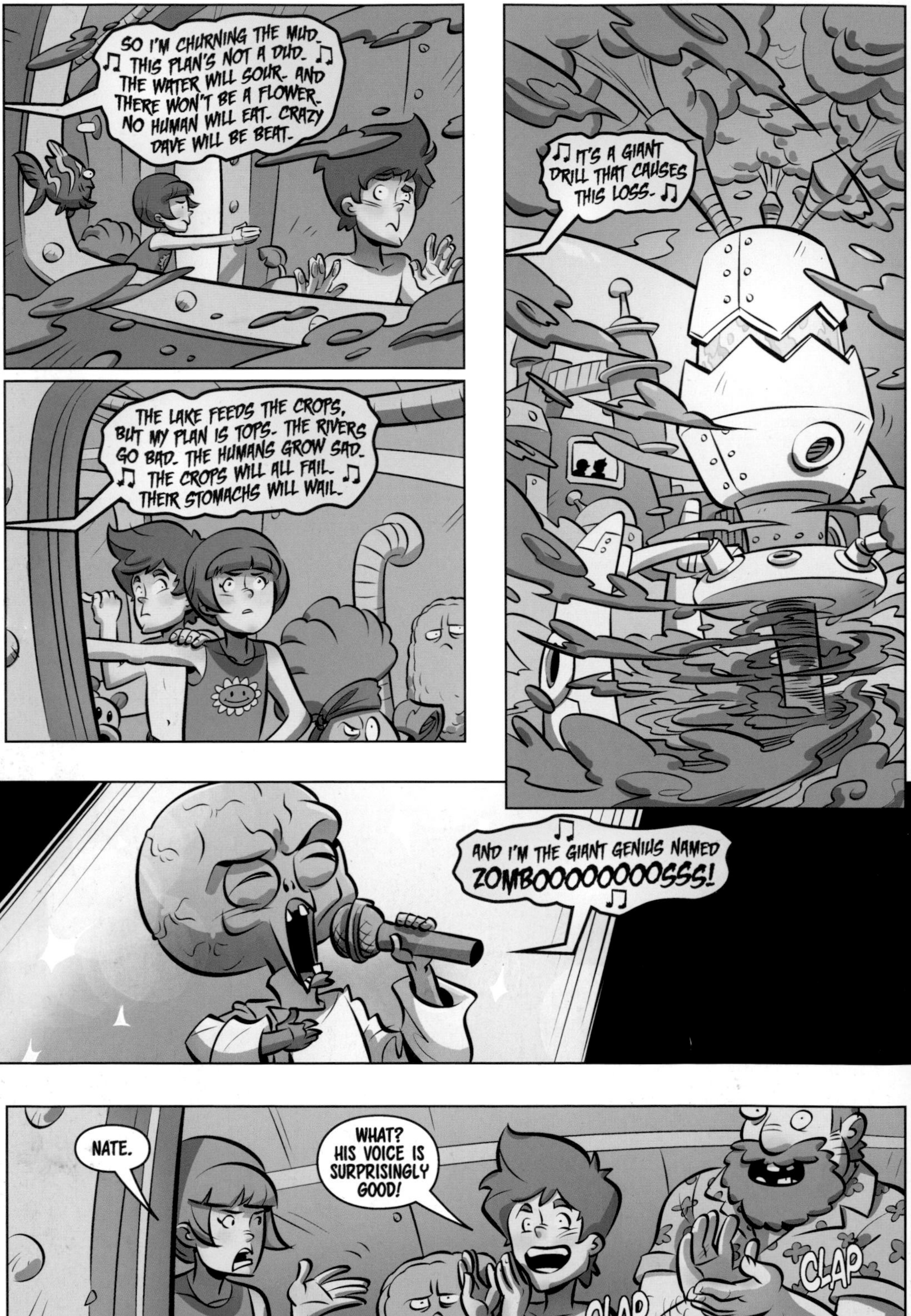
SO I'M CHURNING THE MUD. ♫ THIS PLAN'S NOT A DUD. ♫ THE WATER WILL SOUR. AND THERE WON'T BE A FLOWER. NO HUMAN WILL EAT. CRAZY DAVE WILL BE BEAT.
THE LAKE FEEDS THE CROPS, BUT MY PLAN IS TOPS. THE RIVERS GO BAD. THE HUMANS GROW SAD. ♫ THE CROPS WILL ALL FAIL. ♫ THEIR STOMACHS WILL WAIL.
♫ IT'S A GIANT DRILL THAT CAUSES THIS LOSS. ♫
♫ AND I'M THE GIANT GENIUS NAMED ZOMBOOOOOOOOSSS! ♫
NATE.
WHAT? HIS VOICE IS SURPRISINGLY GOOD!
CLAP
CLAP

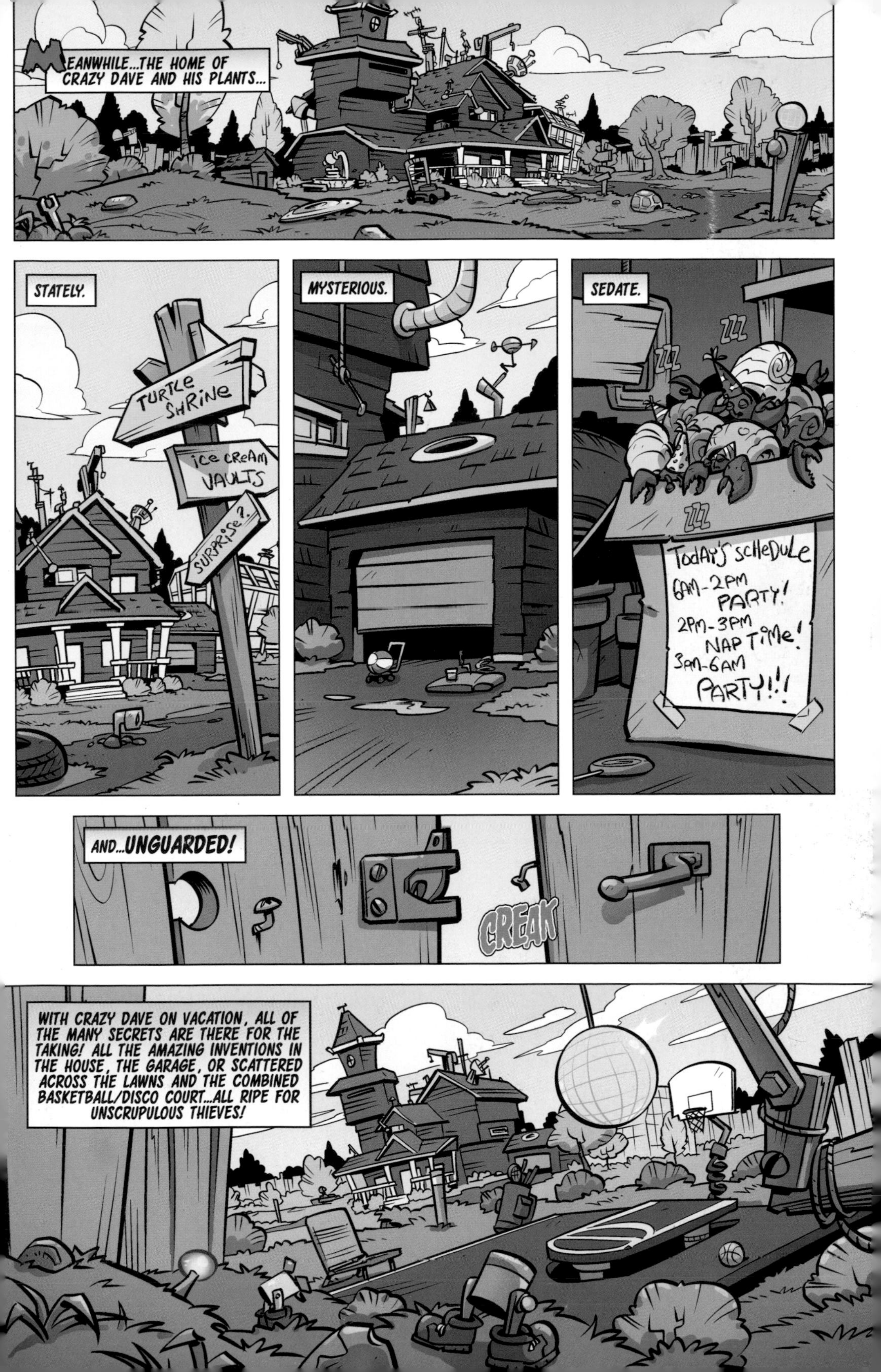
MEANWHILE...THE HOME OF CRAZY DAVE AND HIS PLANTS...
STATELY.
TURTLE SHRINE
ICE CREAM VAULTS
SURPRISE?
MYSTERIOUS.
SEDATE.
ZZZ
ZZZ
ZZZ
TODAY'S SCHEDULE
6AM-2PM PARTY!
2PM-3PM NAP TIME!
3PM-6AM PARTY!!!
AND...UNGUARDED!
CREAK
WITH CRAZY DAVE ON VACATION, ALL OF THE MANY SECRETS ARE THERE FOR THE TAKING! ALL THE AMAZING INVENTIONS IN THE HOUSE, THE GARAGE, OR SCATTERED ACROSS THE LAWNS AND THE COMBINED BASKETBALL/DISCO COURT...ALL RIPE FOR UNSCRUPULOUS THIEVES!

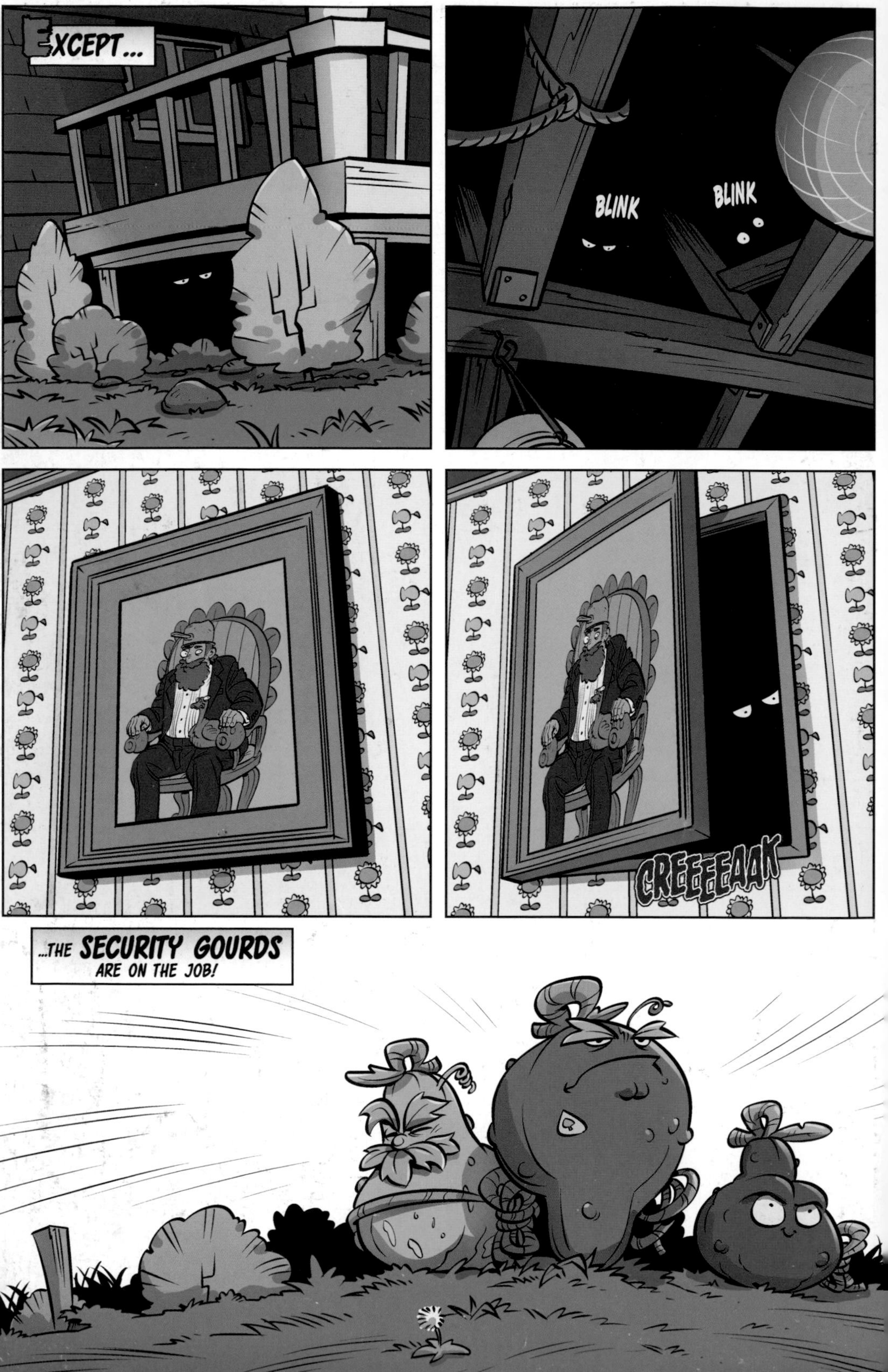
EXCEPT...
BLINK
BLINK
CREEEEAAK
...THE SECURITY GOURDS ARE ON THE JOB!

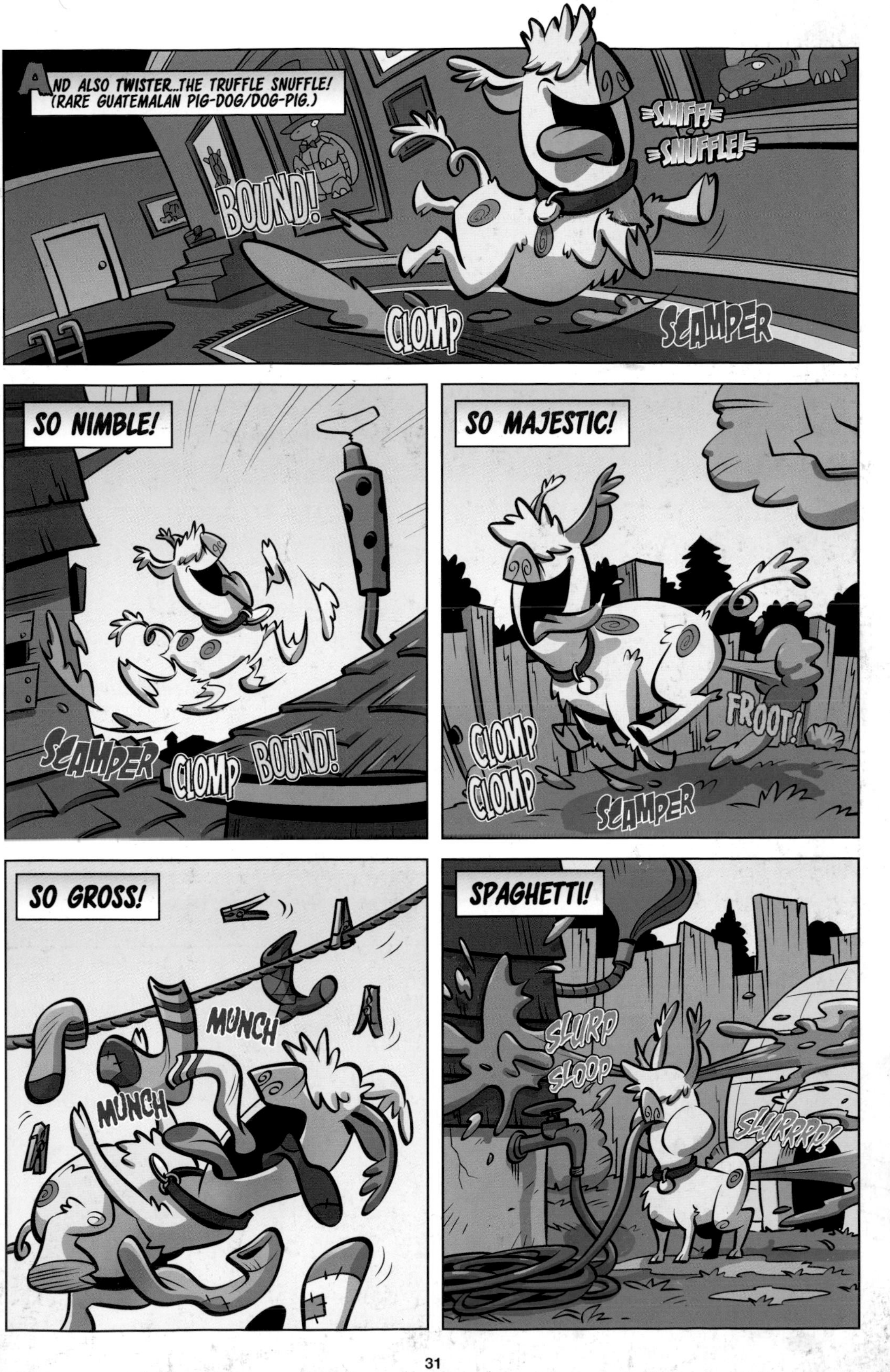
AND ALSO TWISTER...THE TRUFFLE SNUFFLE!
(RARE GUATEMALAN PIG-DOG/DOG-PIG.)
SNIFF!
SNUFFLE!
BOUND!
CLOMP
SCAMPER
SO NIMBLE!
SCAMPER
CLOMP
BOUND!
SO MAJESTIC!
FROOT!
CLOMP
CLOMP
SCAMPER
SO GROSS!
MUNCH
MUNCH
SPAGHETTI!
SLURP
SLOOP
SLURRRP!

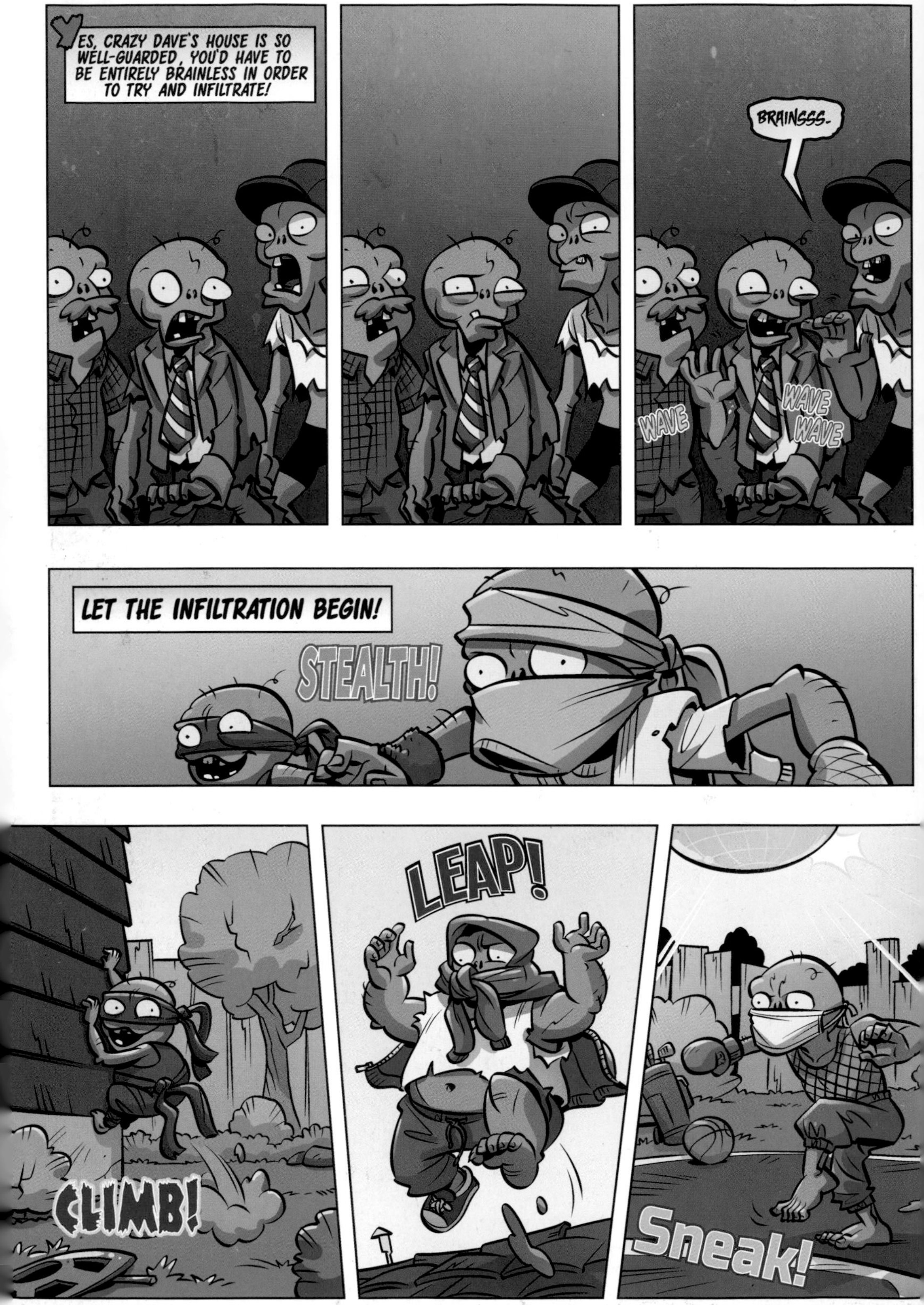
YES, CRAZY DAVE'S HOUSE IS SO WELL-GUARDED, YOU'D HAVE TO BE ENTIRELY BRAINLESS IN ORDER TO TRY AND INFILTRATE!
BRAINSSS-
WAVE
WAVE
WAVE
LET THE INFILTRATION BEGIN!
STEALTH!
CLIMB!
LEAP!
Sneak!

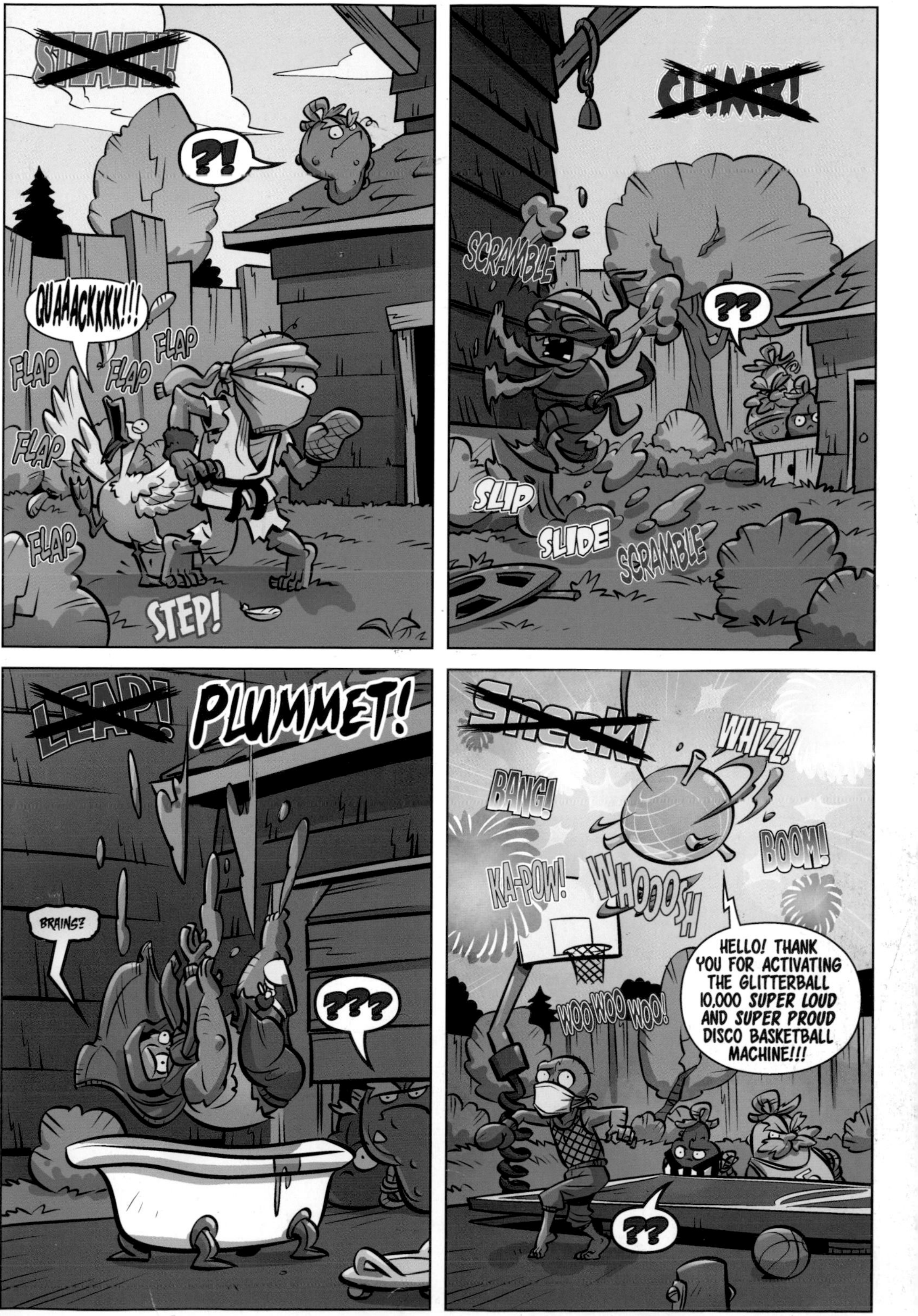

STEALTH!
?!
QUAAACKKKK!!!
FLAP
FLAP
FLAP
FLAP
FLAP
STEP!
CLIMB!
SCRAMBLE
??
SLIP
SLIDE
SCRAMBLE
LEAP!
PLUMMET!
BRAINS?
???
Sneak!
WHIZZ!
BANG!
BOOM!
KA-POW!
WHOOOSH
HELLO! THANK YOU FOR ACTIVATING THE GLITTERBALL 10,000 SUPER LOUD AND SUPER PROUD DISCO BASKETBALL MACHINE!!!
WOO WOO WOO!
??

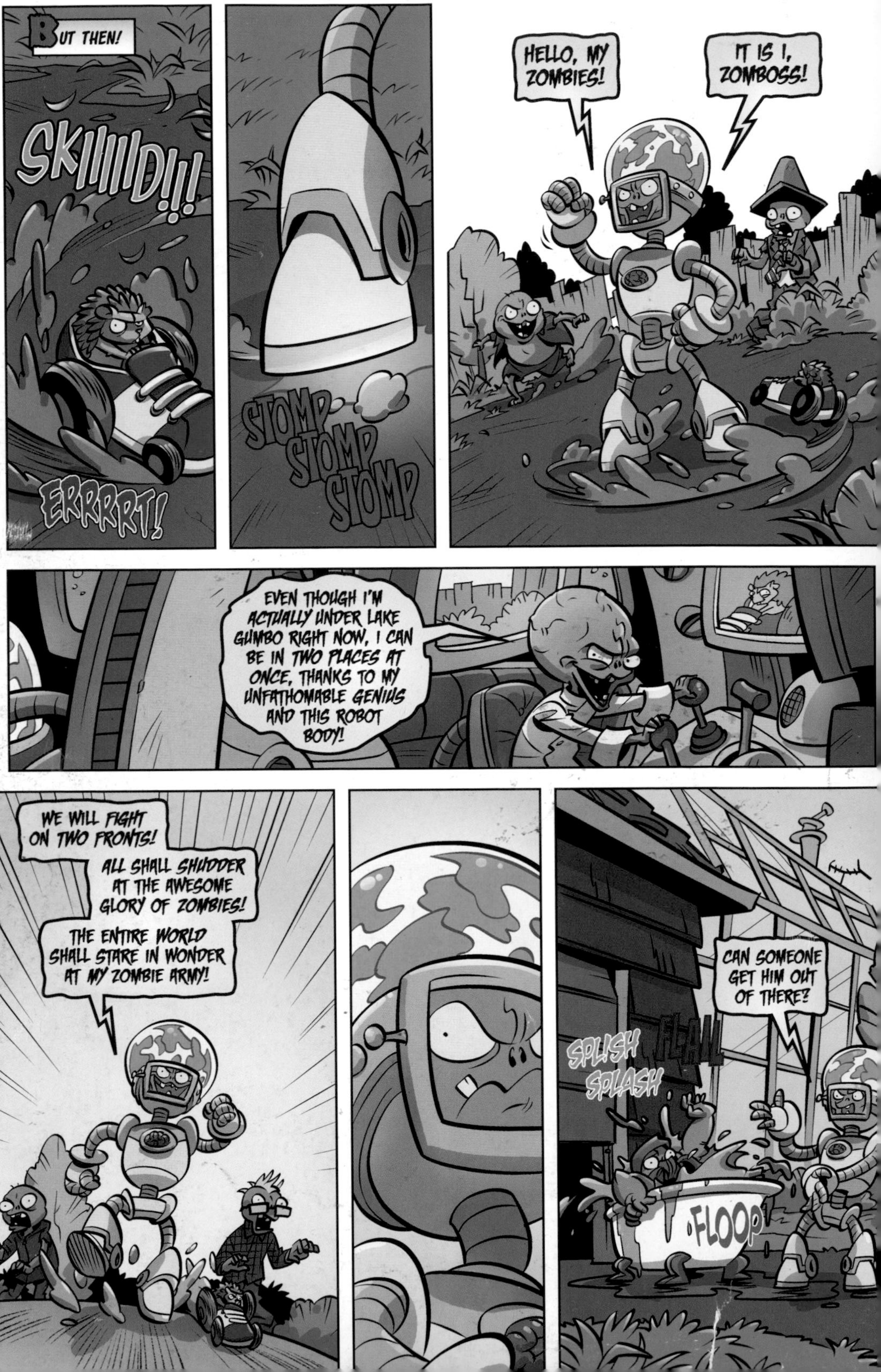
BUT THEN!
SKIIIIID!!!
ERRRRT!
STOMP STOMP STOMP
HELLO, MY ZOMBIES!
IT IS I, ZOMBOSS!
EVEN THOUGH I'M ACTUALLY UNDER LAKE GUMBO RIGHT NOW, I CAN BE IN TWO PLACES AT ONCE, THANKS TO MY UNFATHOMABLE GENIUS AND THIS ROBOT BODY!
WE WILL FIGHT ON TWO FRONTS!
ALL SHALL SHUDDER AT THE AWESOME GLORY OF ZOMBIES!
THE ENTIRE WORLD SHALL STARE IN WONDER AT MY ZOMBIE ARMY!
CAN SOMEONE GET HIM OUT OF THERE?
SPLISH SPLASH
FLAIL
FLOOP

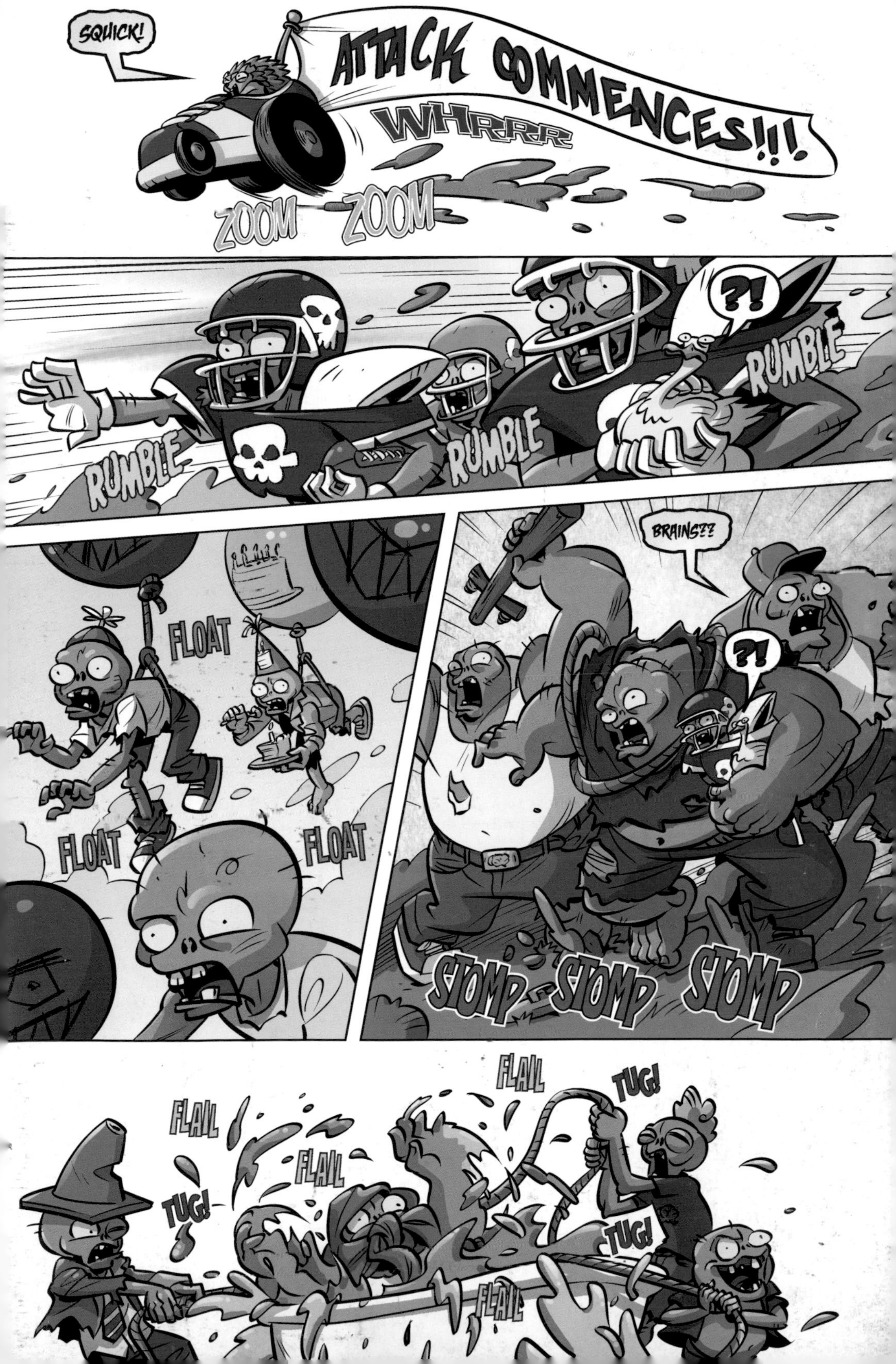
SQUICK!
ATTACK COMMENCES!!!
WHRRR
ZOOM ZOOM
RUMBLE
RUMBLE
?!
RUMBLE
FLOAT
FLOAT
FLOAT
BRAINS??
?!
STOMP STOMP STOMP
FLAIL
FLAIL
TUG!
FLAIL
TUG!
TUG!
FLAIL

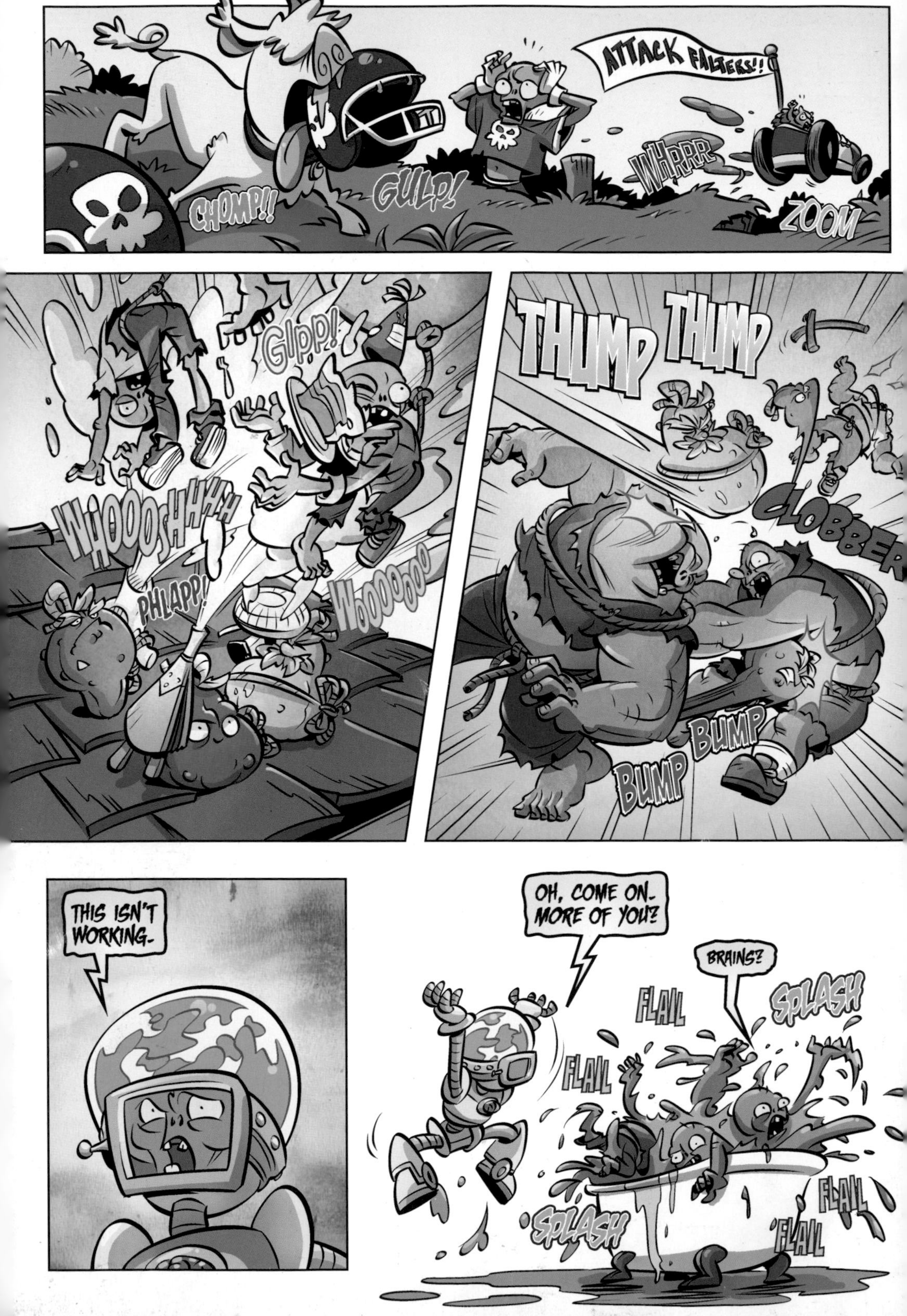
CHOMP!!
GULP!
ATTACK FALTERS!!
WHRRR
ZOOM
GIPP!
WHOOOSHHHH
PHLAPP!
WOOOOOO
THUMP
THUMP
CLOBBER
BUMP
BUMP
THIS ISN'T WORKING.
OH, COME ON. MORE OF YOU?
BRAINS?
FLAIL
FLAIL
SPLASH
SPLASH
FLAIL
FLAIL

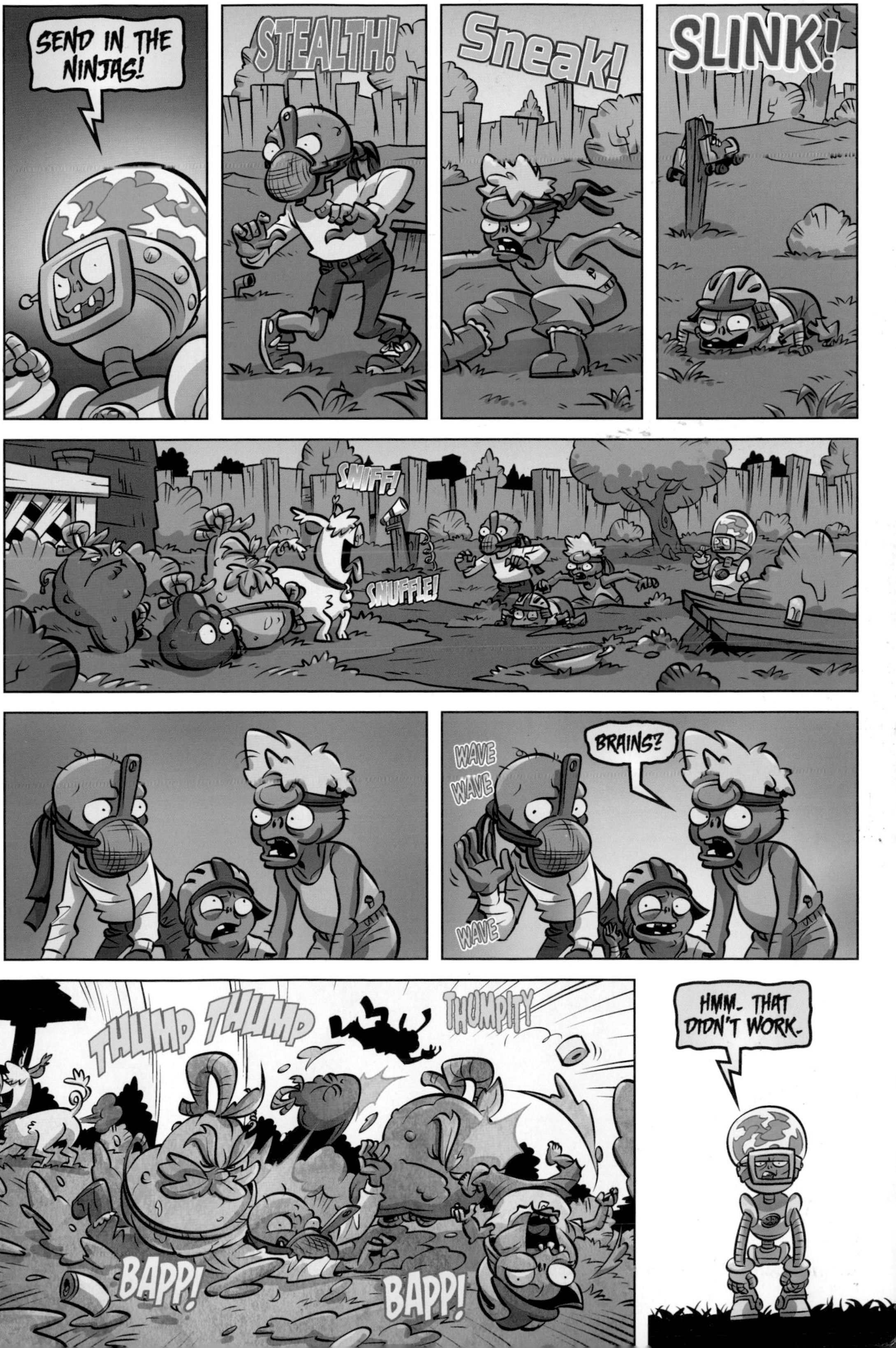
SEND IN THE NINJAS!
STEALTH!
Sneak!
SLINK!
SNIFF!
SNUFFLE!
WAVE
WAVE
WAVE
BRAINS?
THUMP THUMP
THUMPITY
BAPP!
BAPP!
HMM. THAT DIDN'T WORK.

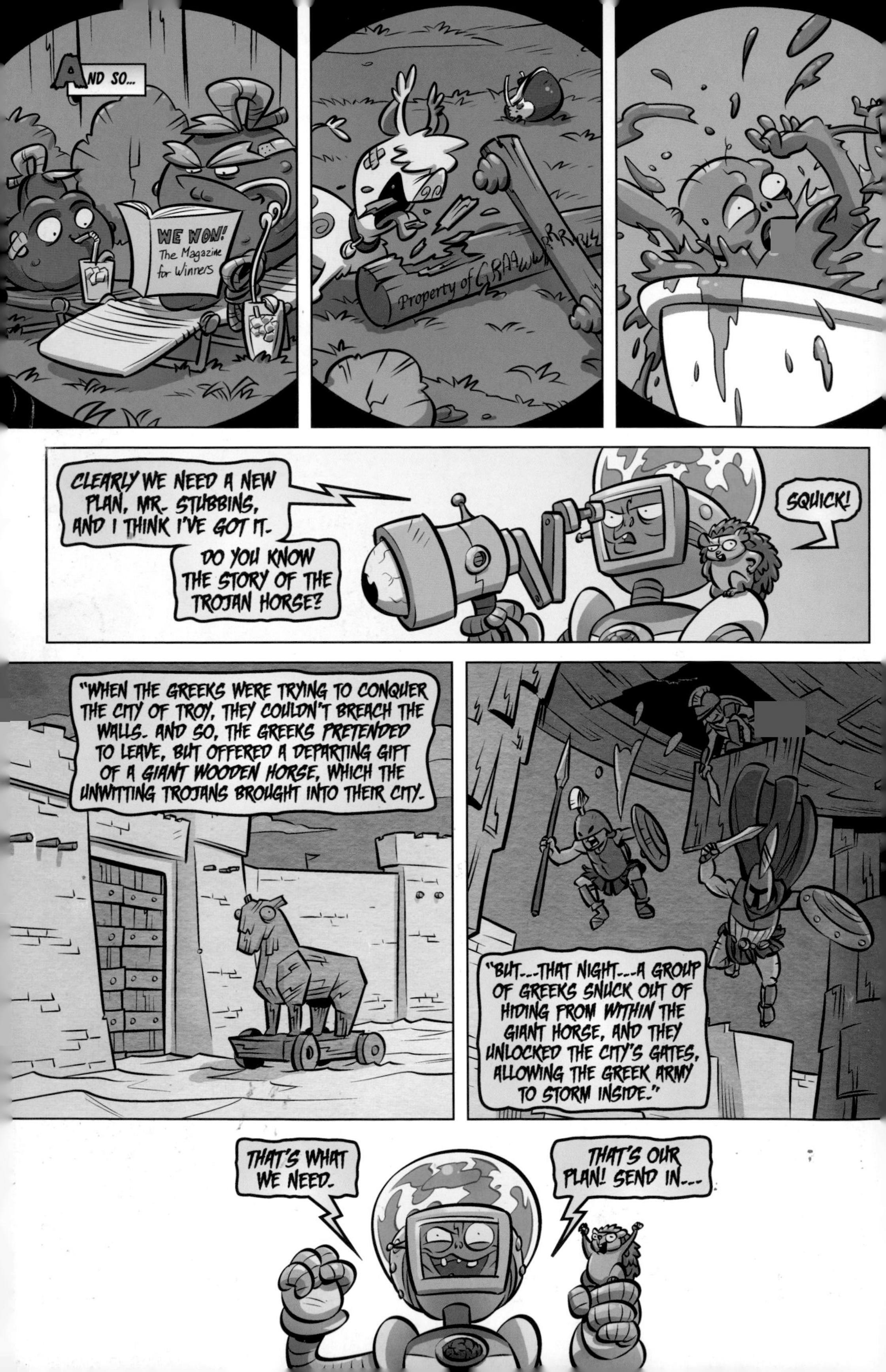
AND SO...
WE WON! The Magazine for Winners
Property of
CLEARLY WE NEED A NEW PLAN, MR. STUBBINS, AND I THINK I'VE GOT IT.
DO YOU KNOW THE STORY OF THE TROJAN HORSE?
SQUICK!
"WHEN THE GREEKS WERE TRYING TO CONQUER THE CITY OF TROY, THEY COULDN'T BREACH THE WALLS. AND SO, THE GREEKS PRETENDED TO LEAVE, BUT OFFERED A DEPARTING GIFT OF A GIANT WOODEN HORSE, WHICH THE UNWITTING TROJANS BROUGHT INTO THEIR CITY.
"BUT...THAT NIGHT...A GROUP OF GREEKS SNUCK OUT OF HIDING FROM WITHIN THE GIANT HORSE, AND THEY UNLOCKED THE CITY'S GATES, ALLOWING THE GREEK ARMY TO STORM INSIDE."
THAT'S WHAT WE NEED.
THAT'S OUR PLAN! SEND IN...

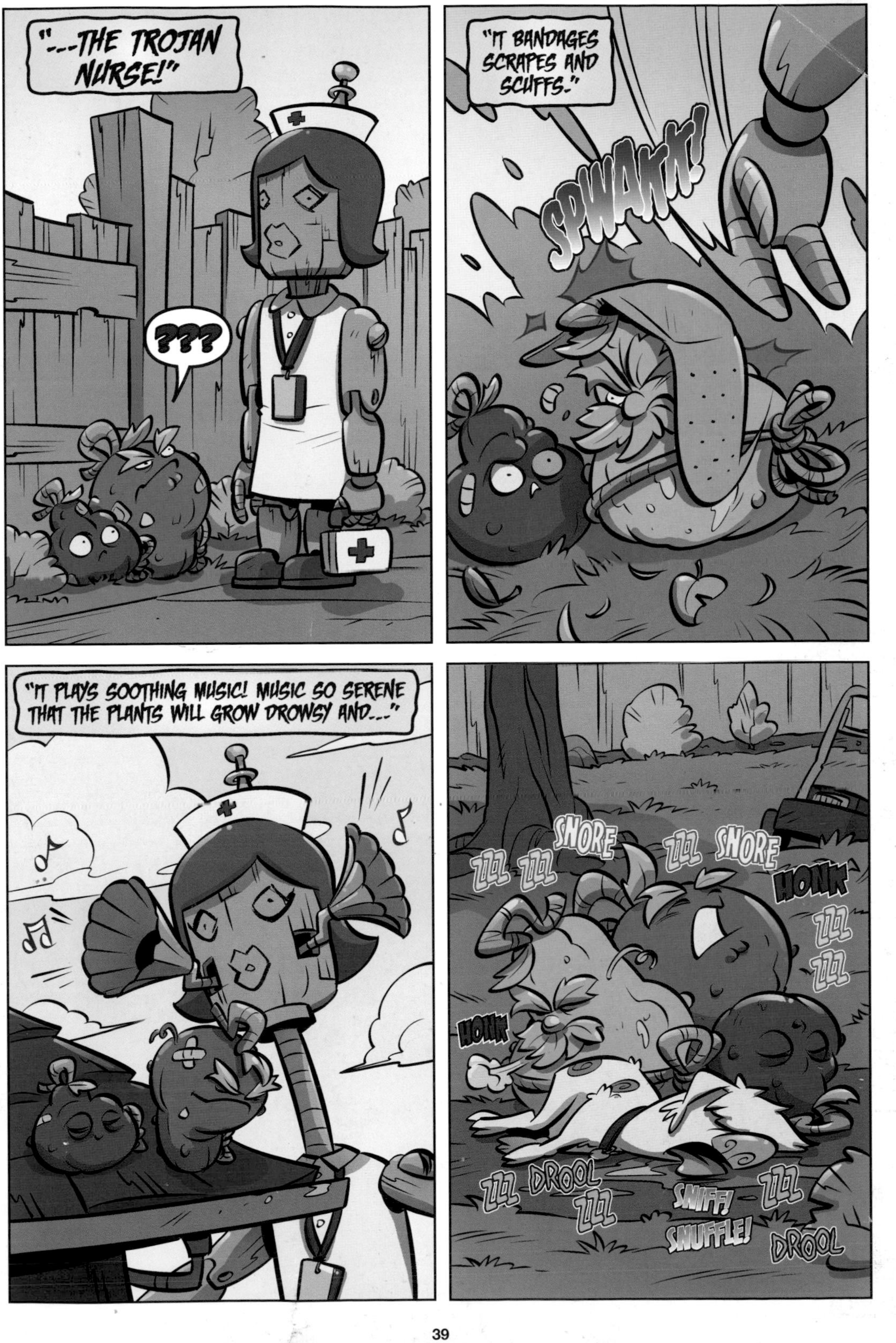
"---THE TROJAN NURSE!"
???
"IT BANDAGES SCRAPES AND SCUFFS."
SPWANK!
"IT PLAYS SOOTHING MUSIC! MUSIC SO SERENE THAT THE PLANTS WILL GROW DROWSY AND..."
SNORE
ZZZ ZZZ
ZZZ SNORE
HONK
ZZZ
ZZZ
HONK
ZZZ DROOL
ZZZ
SNIFF!
SNUFFLE!
ZZZ
DROOL

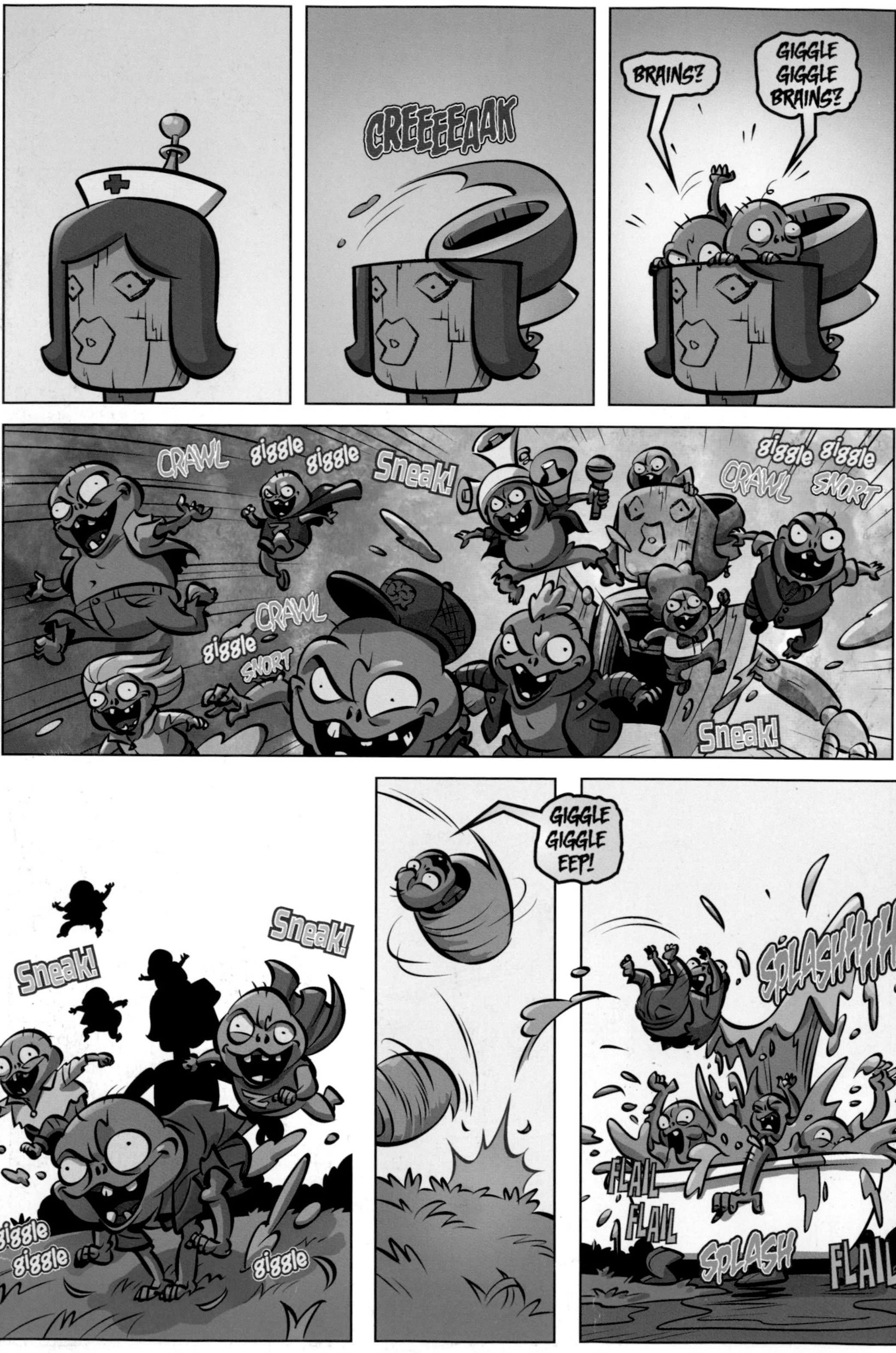
CREEEEAAK
BRAINS?
GIGGLE GIGGLE BRAINS?
CRAWL
giggle giggle
Sneak!
giggle giggle
CRAWL
SNORT
CRAWL
giggle
SNORT
Sneak!
Sneak!
Sneak!
giggle giggle
giggle
GIGGLE GIGGLE EEP!
SPLASHHHH
FLAIL
FLAIL
SPLASH
FLAIL

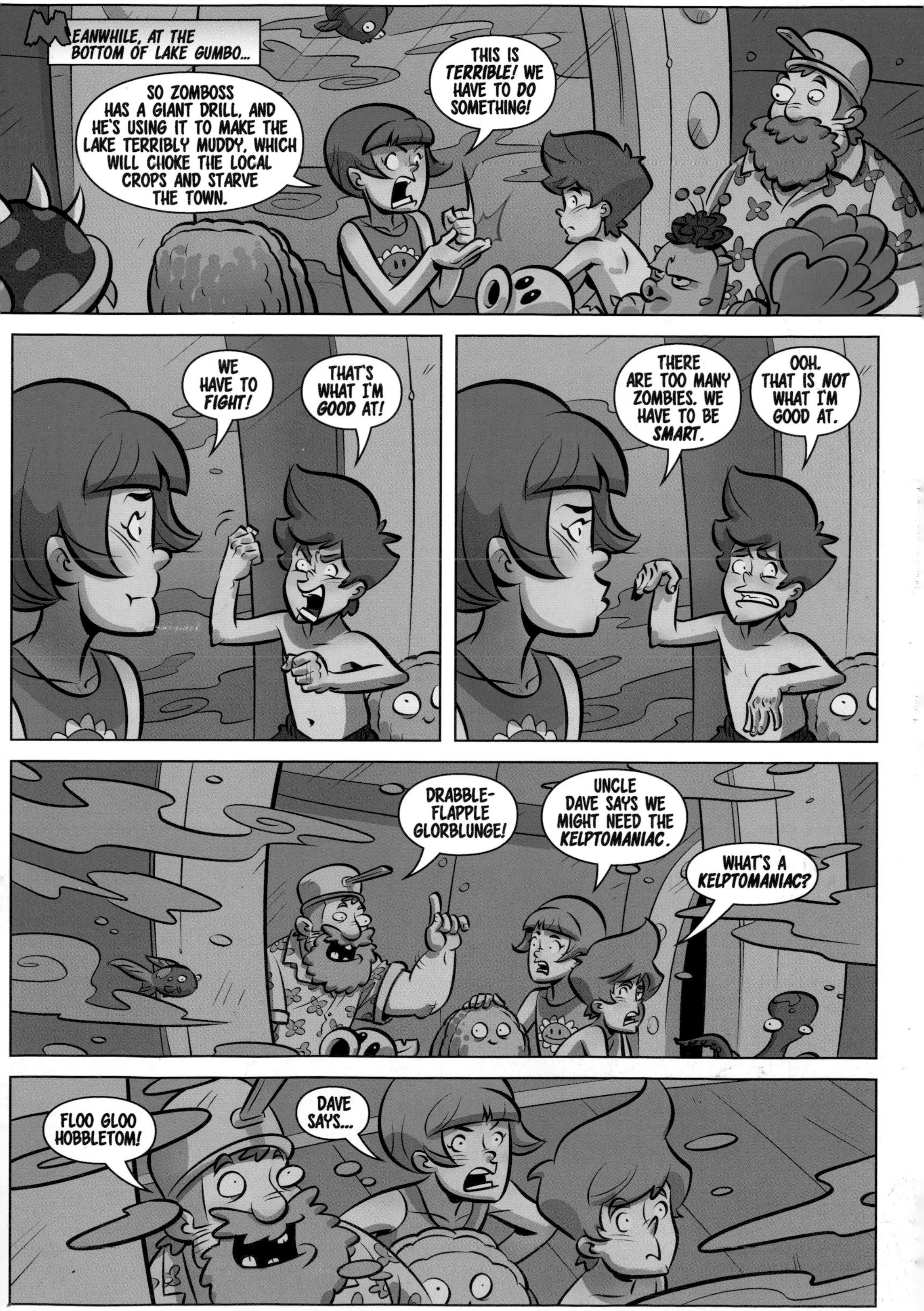
MEANWHILE, AT THE BOTTOM OF LAKE GUMBO...
SO ZOMBOSS HAS A GIANT DRILL, AND HE'S USING IT TO MAKE THE LAKE TERRIBLY MUDDY, WHICH WILL CHOKE THE LOCAL CROPS AND STARVE THE TOWN.
THIS IS TERRIBLE! WE HAVE TO DO SOMETHING!
WE HAVE TO FIGHT!
THAT'S WHAT I'M GOOD AT!
THERE ARE TOO MANY ZOMBIES. WE HAVE TO BE SMART.
OOH. THAT IS NOT WHAT I'M GOOD AT.
DRABBLE-FLAPPLE GLORBLUNGE!
UNCLE DAVE SAYS WE MIGHT NEED THE KELPTOMANIAC.
WHAT'S A KELPTOMANIAC?
FLOO GLOO HOBBLETOM!
DAVE SAYS...

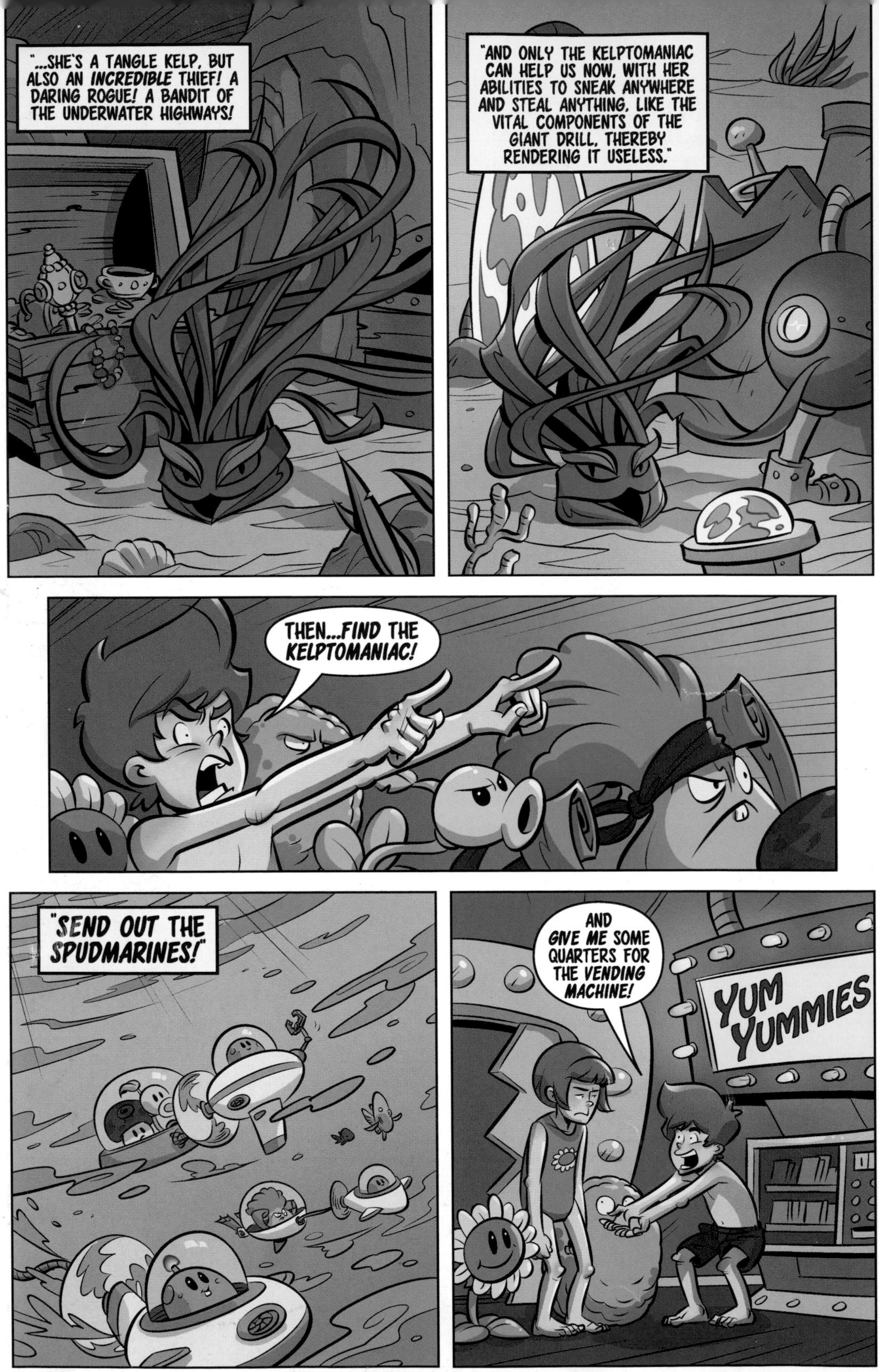
"...SHE'S A TANGLE KELP, BUT ALSO AN *INCREDIBLE* THIEF! A DARING ROGUE! A BANDIT OF THE UNDERWATER HIGHWAYS!
"AND ONLY THE KELPTOMANIAC CAN HELP US NOW, WITH HER ABILITIES TO SNEAK ANYWHERE AND STEAL ANYTHING, LIKE THE VITAL COMPONENTS OF THE GIANT DRILL, THEREBY RENDERING IT USELESS."
THEN...*FIND* THE KELPTOMANIAC!
"*SEND OUT THE SPUDMARINES!*"
AND *GIVE ME* SOME QUARTERS FOR THE *VENDING* MACHINE!
YUM YUMMIES

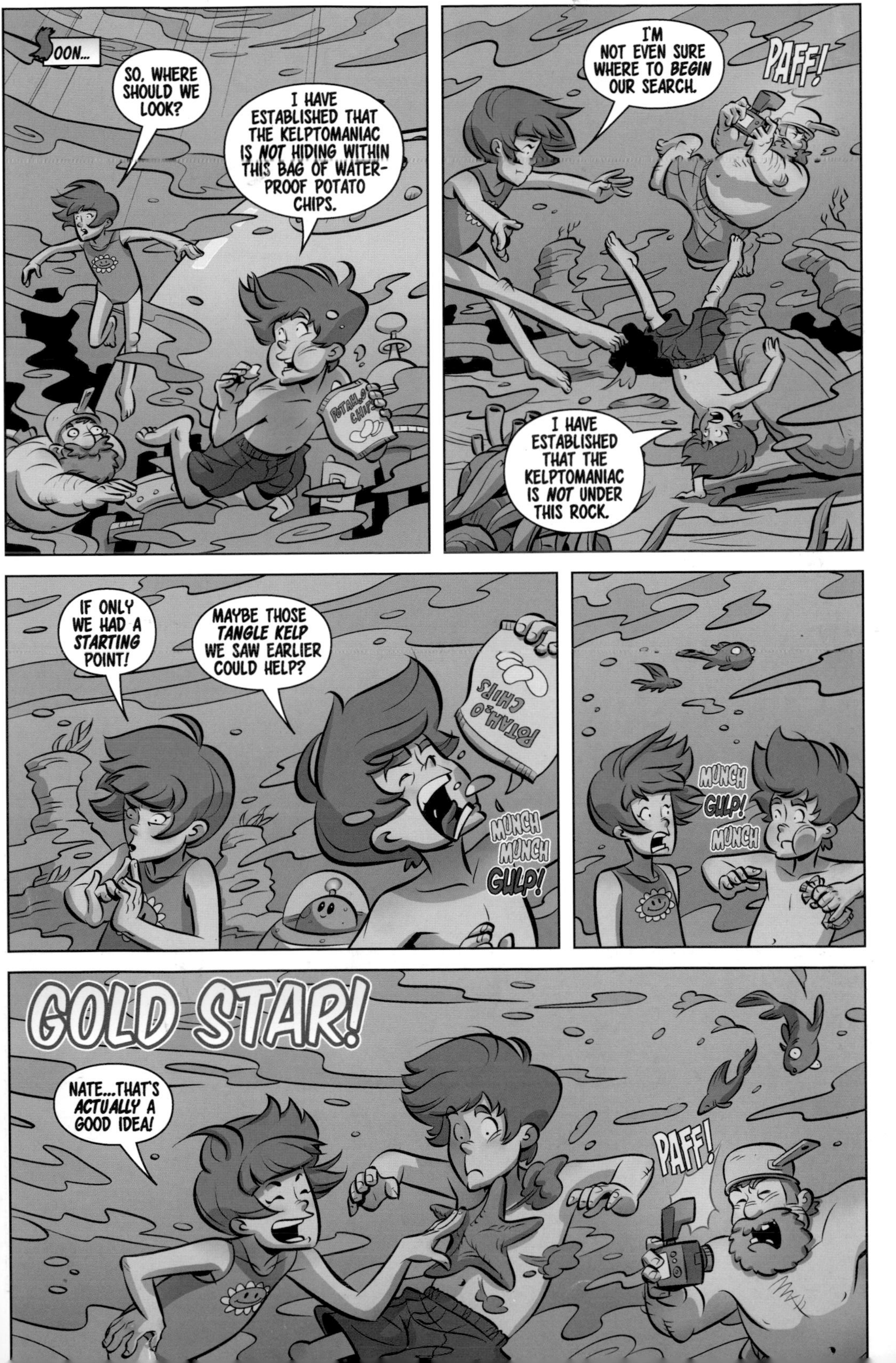
SOON...
SO, WHERE SHOULD WE LOOK?
I HAVE ESTABLISHED THAT THE KELPTOMANIAC IS NOT HIDING WITHIN THIS BAG OF WATER-PROOF POTATO CHIPS.
POTAH2O CHIPS
I'M NOT EVEN SURE WHERE TO BEGIN OUR SEARCH.
PAFF!
I HAVE ESTABLISHED THAT THE KELPTOMANIAC IS NOT UNDER THIS ROCK.
IF ONLY WE HAD A STARTING POINT!
MAYBE THOSE TANGLE KELP WE SAW EARLIER COULD HELP?
POTAH2O CHIPS
MUNCH
MUNCH
GULP!
MUNCH
GULP!
MUNCH
GOLD STAR!
NATE...THAT'S ACTUALLY A GOOD IDEA!
PAFF!

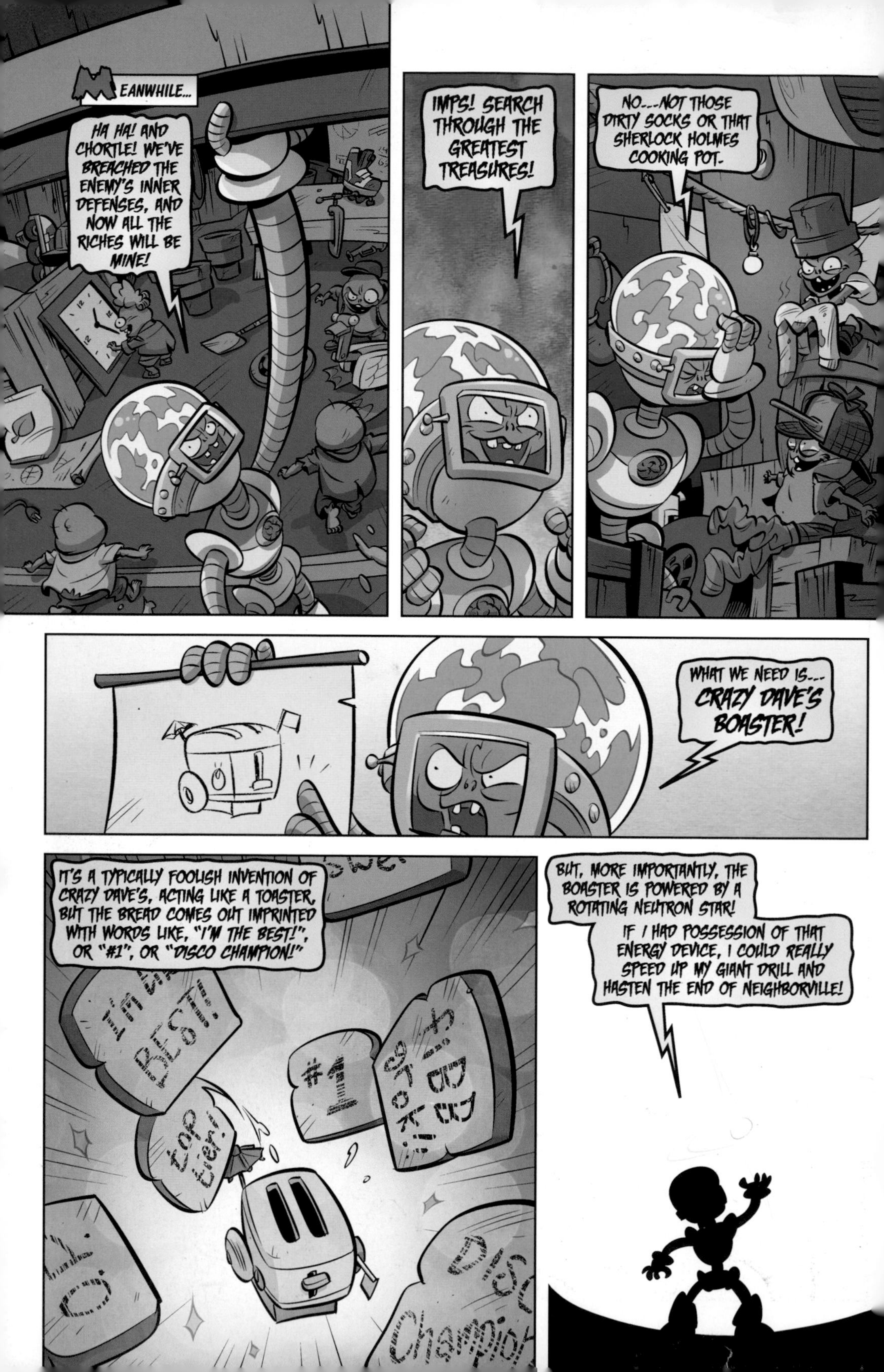
MEANWHILE...
HA HA! AND CHORTLE! WE'VE BREACHED THE ENEMY'S INNER DEFENSES, AND NOW ALL THE RICHES WILL BE MINE!
IMPS! SEARCH THROUGH THE GREATEST TREASURES!
NO...NOT THOSE DIRTY SOCKS OR THAT SHERLOCK HOLMES COOKING POT.
WHAT WE NEED IS... CRAZY DAVE'S BOASTER!
IT'S A TYPICALLY FOOLISH INVENTION OF CRAZY DAVE'S, ACTING LIKE A TOASTER, BUT THE BREAD COMES OUT IMPRINTED WITH WORDS LIKE, "I'M THE BEST!", OR "#1", OR "DISCO CHAMPION!"
I'M THE BEST!
#1
top tier!
Champion
BUT, MORE IMPORTANTLY, THE BOASTER IS POWERED BY A ROTATING NEUTRON STAR!
IF I HAD POSSESSION OF THAT ENERGY DEVICE, I COULD REALLY SPEED UP MY GIANT DRILL AND HASTEN THE END OF NEIGHBORVILLE!

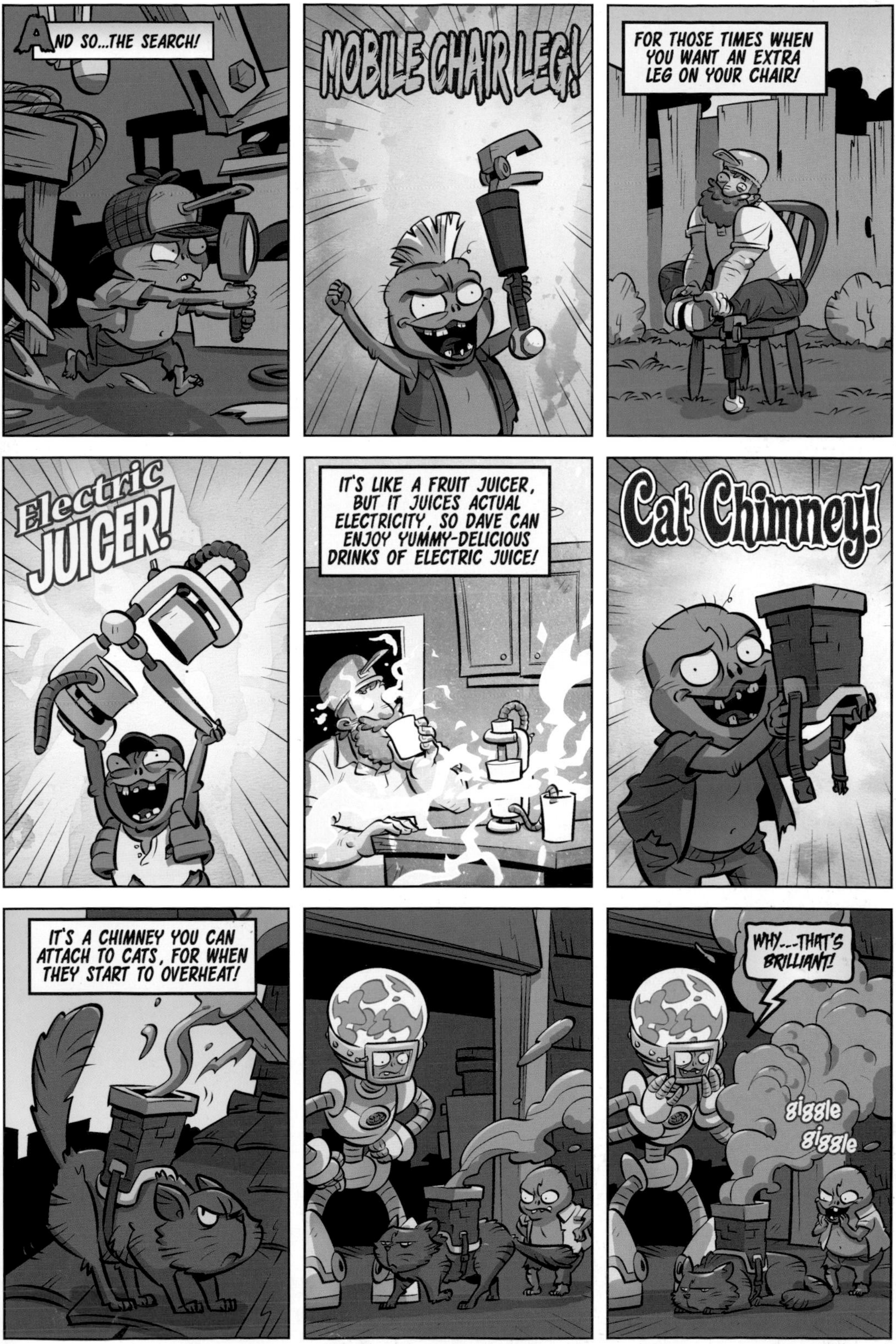
AND SO...THE SEARCH!
MOBILE CHAIR LEG!
FOR THOSE TIMES WHEN YOU WANT AN EXTRA LEG ON YOUR CHAIR!
Electric JUICER!
IT'S LIKE A FRUIT JUICER, BUT IT JUICES ACTUAL ELECTRICITY, SO DAVE CAN ENJOY YUMMY-DELICIOUS DRINKS OF ELECTRIC JUICE!
Cat Chimney!
IT'S A CHIMNEY YOU CAN ATTACH TO CATS, FOR WHEN THEY START TO OVERHEAT!
WHY...THAT'S BRILLIANT!
giggle
giggle

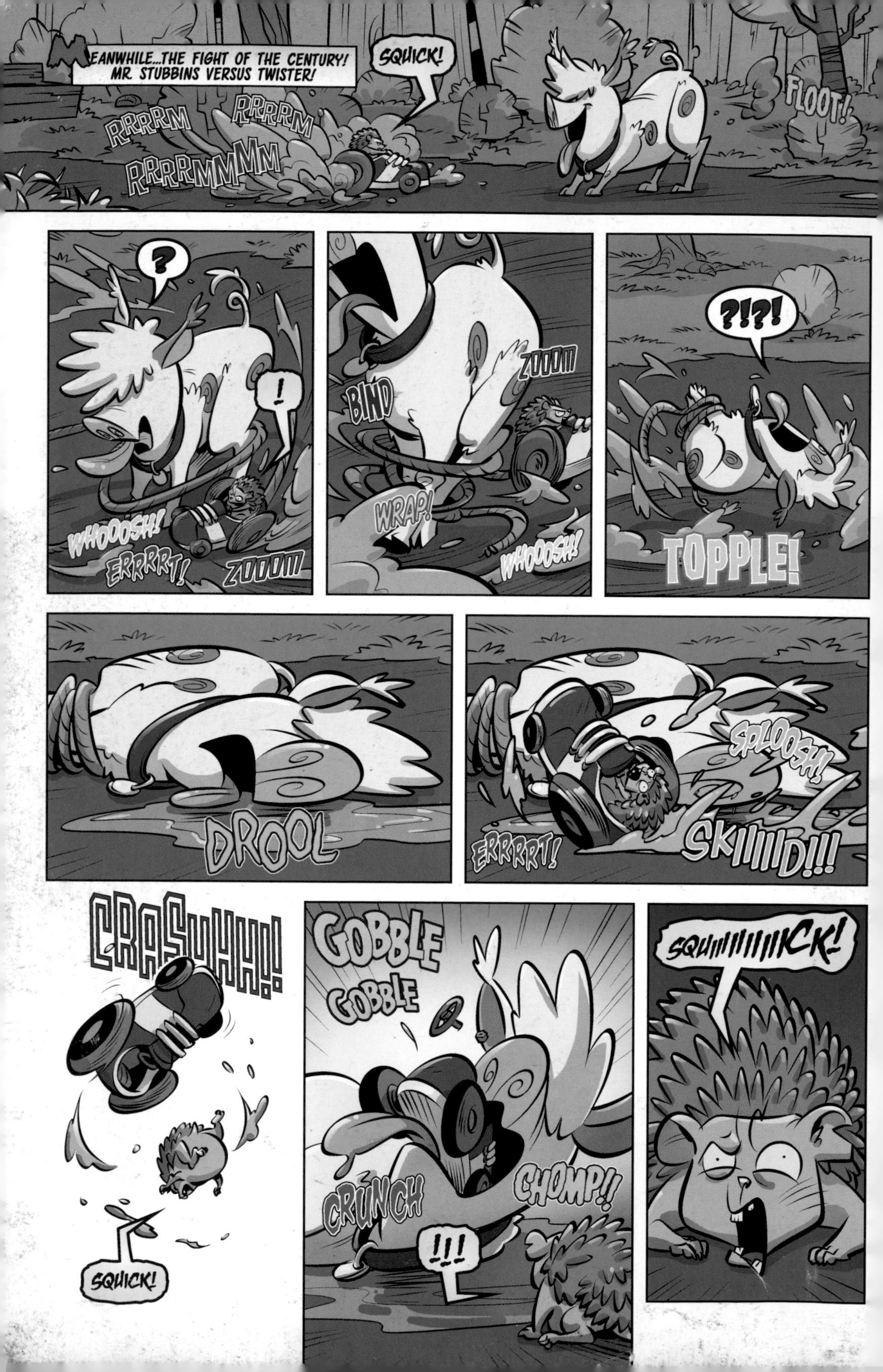
MEANWHILE...THE FIGHT OF THE CENTURY! MR. STUBBINS VERSUS TWISTER!
SQUICK!
RRRRM
RRRRM
RRRRMMMM
FLOOT!
?
!
WHOOOSH!
ERRRRT!
ZOOOM
BIND
ZOOOM
WRAP!
WHOOOSH!
?!?!
TOPPLE!
DROOL
SPLOOSH!
ERRRRT!
SKIIIID!!!
CRASHHH!
SQUICK!
GOBBLE
GOBBLE
CRUNCH
CHOMP!!
!!!
SQUIIIIIIIICK!

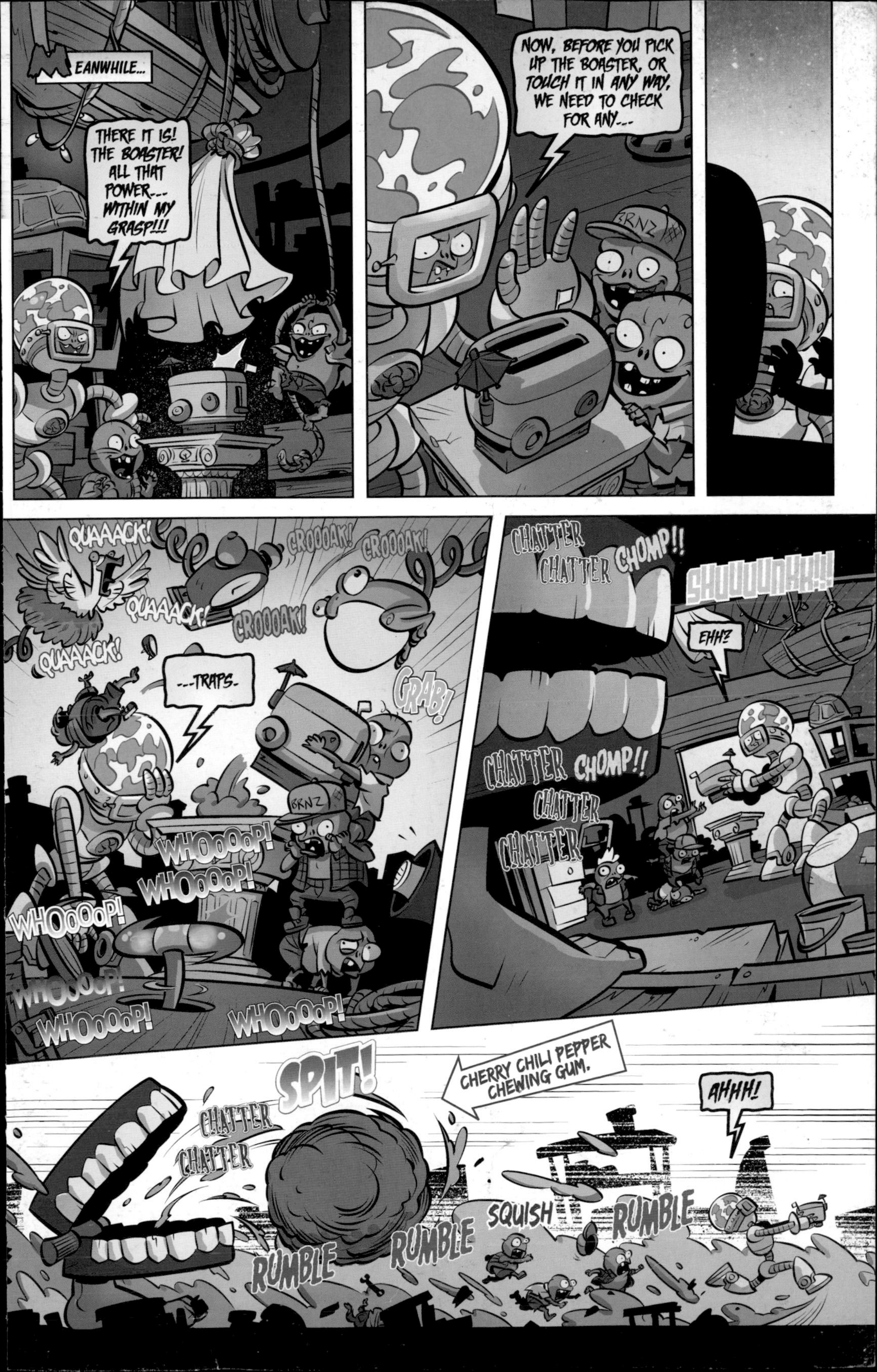
MEANWHILE...
THERE IT IS! THE BOASTER! ALL THAT POWER... WITHIN MY GRASP!!!
NOW, BEFORE YOU PICK UP THE BOASTER, OR TOUCH IT IN ANY WAY, WE NEED TO CHECK FOR ANY...
BRNZ
QUAAACK!
CROOOAK!
CROOOAK!
QUAAACK!
CROOOAK!
QUAAACK!
...TRAPS.
GRAB!
BRNZ
WHOOOOP!
WHOOOOP!
WHOOOOP!
WHOOOOP!
WHOOOOP!
WHOOOOP!
CHATTER
CHATTER
CHOMP!!
SHUUUUNKK!!!
EHH?
CHATTER
CHOMP!!
CHATTER
CHATTER
CHERRY CHILI PEPPER CHEWING GUM.
SPIT!
CHATTER
CHATTER
AHHH!
SQUISH
RUMBLE
RUMBLE
RUMBLE

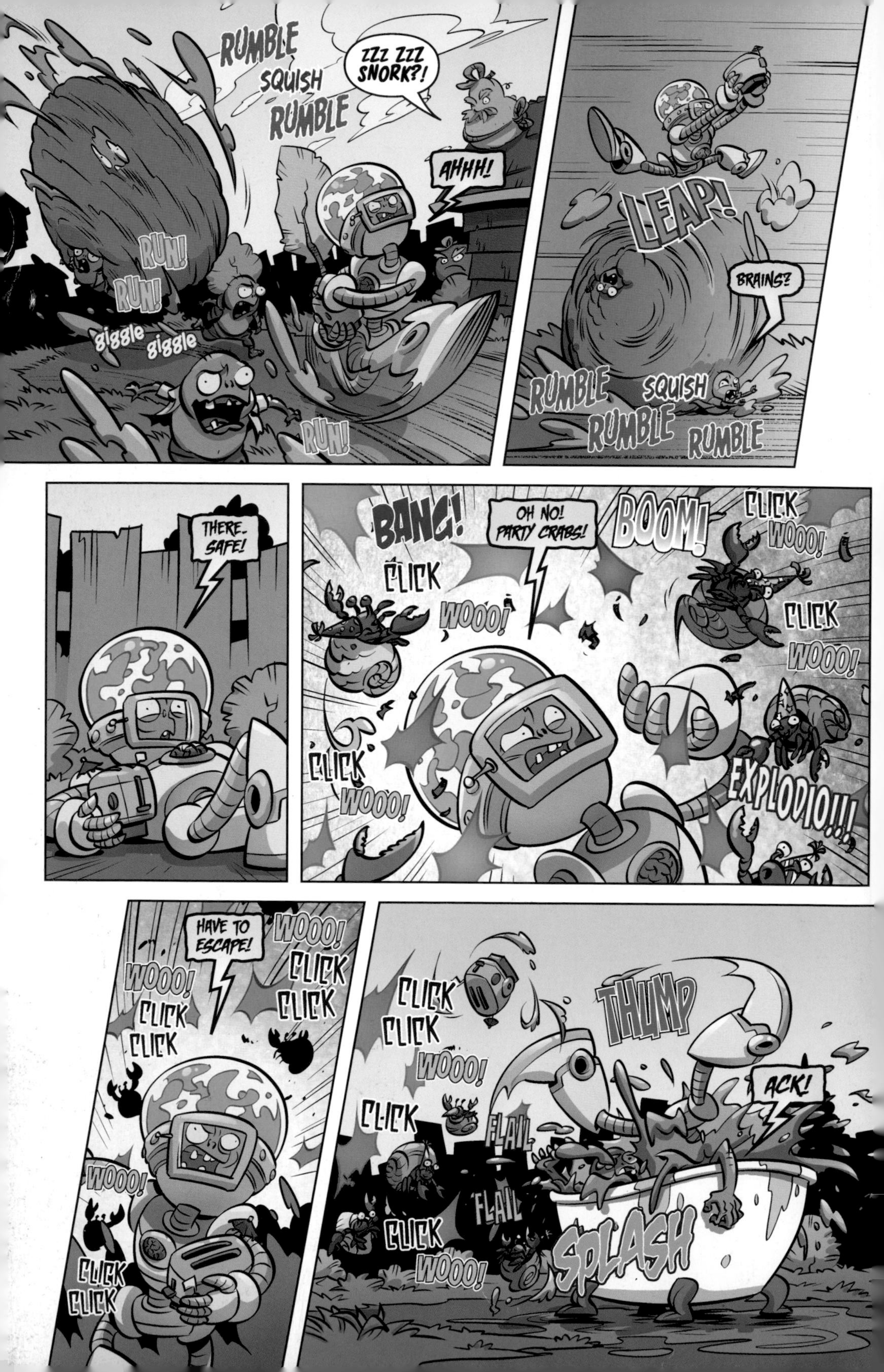
RUMBLE
SQUISH
RUMBLE
ZZZ ZZZ SNORK?!
AHHH!
RUN!
RUN!
giggle giggle
RUN!
LEAP!
BRAINS?
RUMBLE
SQUISH
RUMBLE
RUMBLE
THERE. SAFE!
BANG!
OH NO! PARTY CRABS!
BOOM!
CLICK
WOOO!
CLICK
WOOO!
CLICK
WOOO!
CLICK
WOOO!
EXPLODIO!!!
HAVE TO ESCAPE!
WOOO!
WOOO!
CLICK
CLICK
CLICK
CLICK
WOOO!
CLICK
CLICK
CLICK
CLICK
WOOO!
THUMP
CLICK
FLAIL
FLAIL
ACK!
CLICK
WOOO!
SPLASH

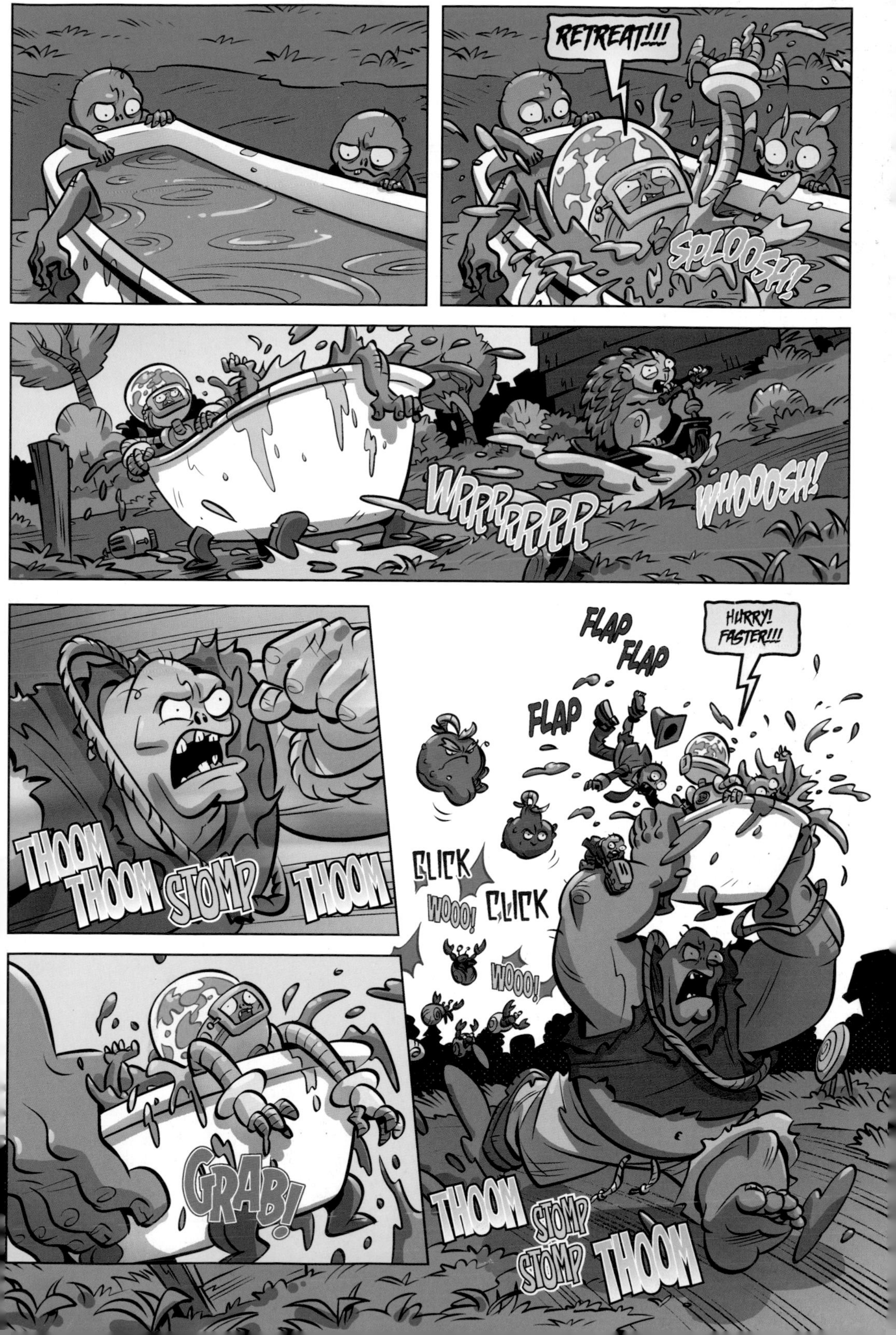

RETREAT!!!
SPLOOSH!
WRRRRRRRR
WHOOOSH!
THOOM
THOOM
STOMP
THOOM
FLAP
FLAP
FLAP
HURRY! FASTER!!!
CLICK
CLICK
WOOO!
WOOO!
GRAB!
THOOM
STOMP
STOMP
THOOM

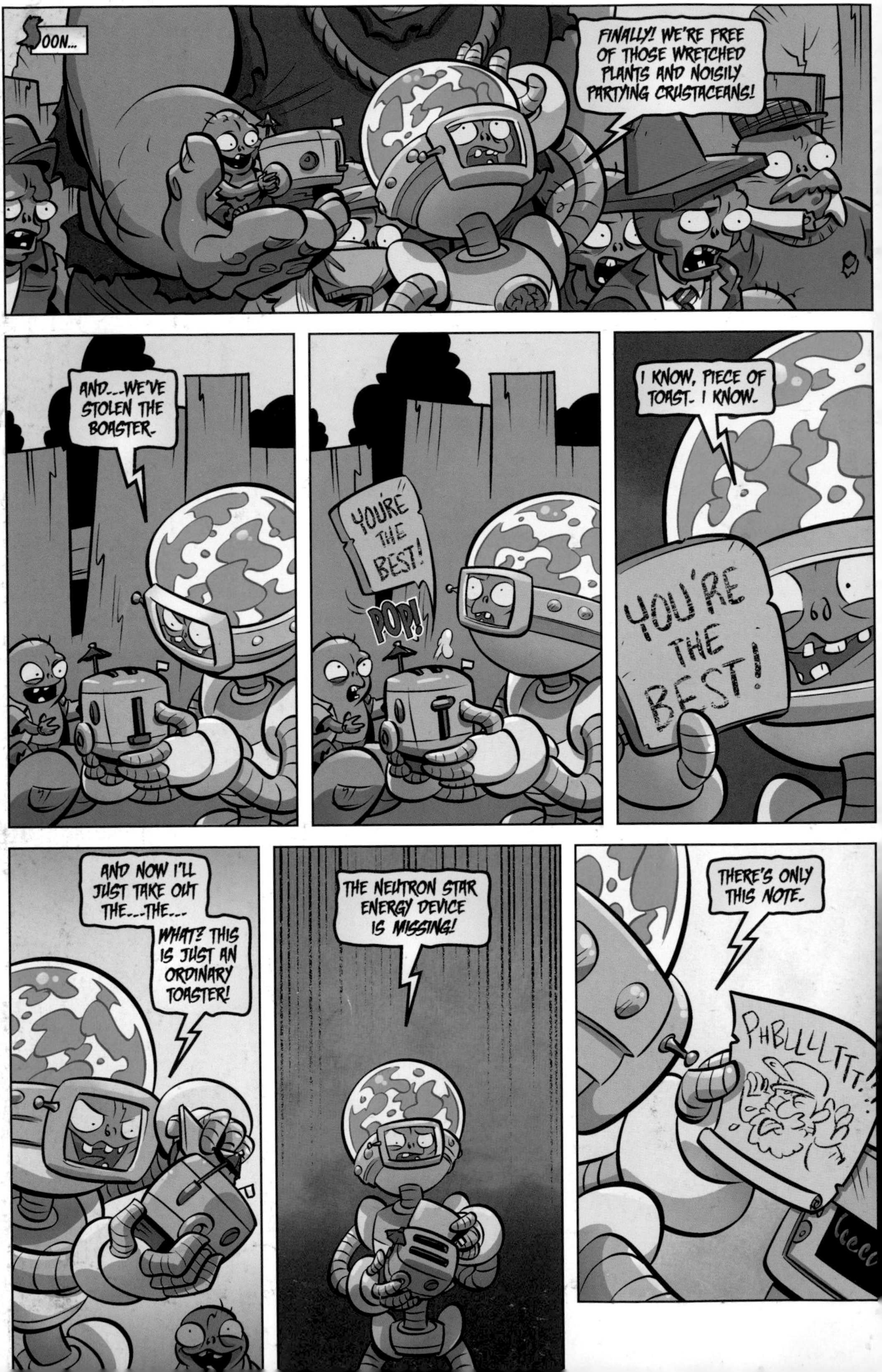
SOON...
FINALLY! WE'RE FREE OF THOSE WRETCHED PLANTS AND NOISILY PARTYING CRUSTACEANS!
AND...WE'VE STOLEN THE BOASTER.
YOU'RE THE BEST!
POP!
I KNOW, PIECE OF TOAST. I KNOW.
YOU'RE THE BEST!
AND NOW I'LL JUST TAKE OUT THE...THE...
WHAT? THIS IS JUST AN ORDINARY TOASTER!
THE NEUTRON STAR ENERGY DEVICE IS MISSING!
THERE'S ONLY THIS NOTE.
PHBLLLLTTT.

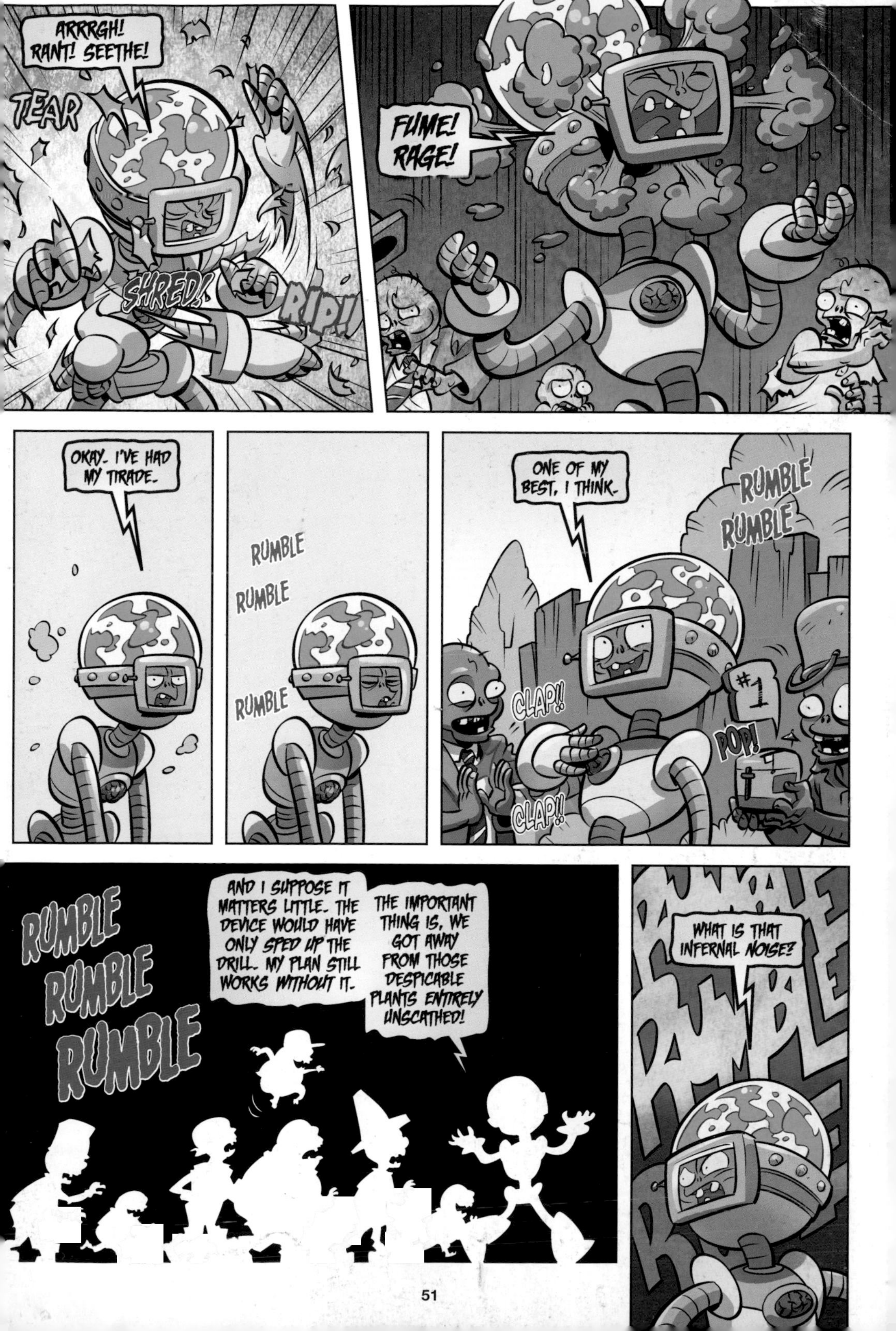
ARRRGH! RANT! SEETHE!
TEAR
SHRED!
RIP!!
FUME! RAGE!
OKAY. I'VE HAD MY TIRADE.
RUMBLE
RUMBLE
RUMBLE
ONE OF MY BEST, I THINK.
RUMBLE
RUMBLE
CLAP!!
CLAP!!
#1
POP!
RUMBLE
RUMBLE
RUMBLE
AND I SUPPOSE IT MATTERS LITTLE. THE DEVICE WOULD HAVE ONLY SPED UP THE DRILL. MY PLAN STILL WORKS WITHOUT IT.
THE IMPORTANT THING IS, WE GOT AWAY FROM THOSE DESPICABLE PLANTS ENTIRELY UNSCATHED!
WHAT IS THAT INFERNAL NOISE?

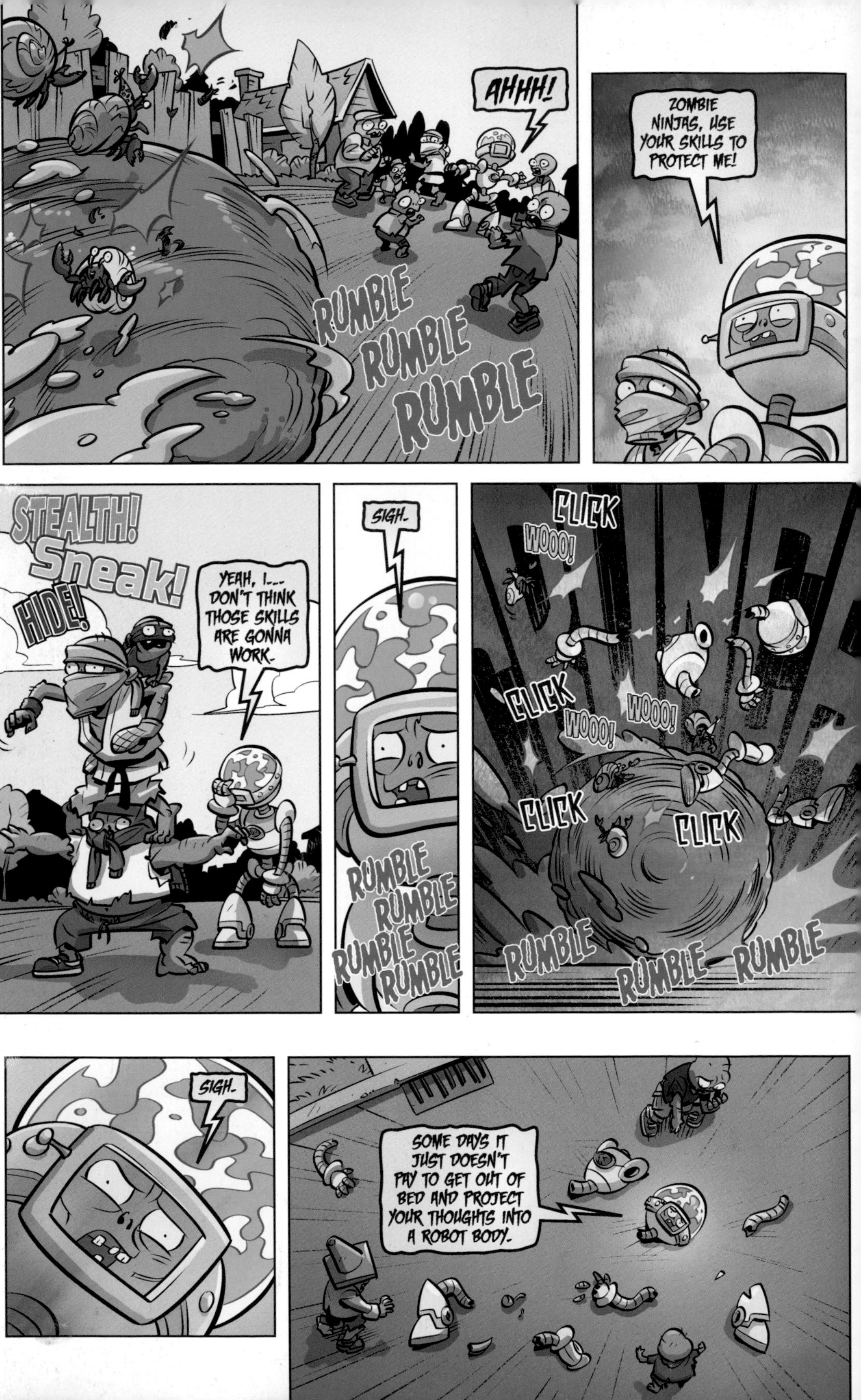

AHHH!
RUMBLE
RUMBLE
RUMBLE
ZOMBIE NINJAS, USE YOUR SKILLS TO PROTECT ME!
STEALTH!
Sneak!
HIDE!
YEAH, I... DON'T THINK THOSE SKILLS ARE GONNA WORK.
SIGH.
RUMBLE
RUMBLE
RUMBLE
RUMBLE
CLICK
WOOO!
CLICK
WOOO!
WOOO!
CLICK
CLICK
RUMBLE
RUMBLE
RUMBLE
SIGH.
SOME DAYS IT JUST DOESN'T PAY TO GET OUT OF BED AND PROJECT YOUR THOUGHTS INTO A ROBOT BODY.

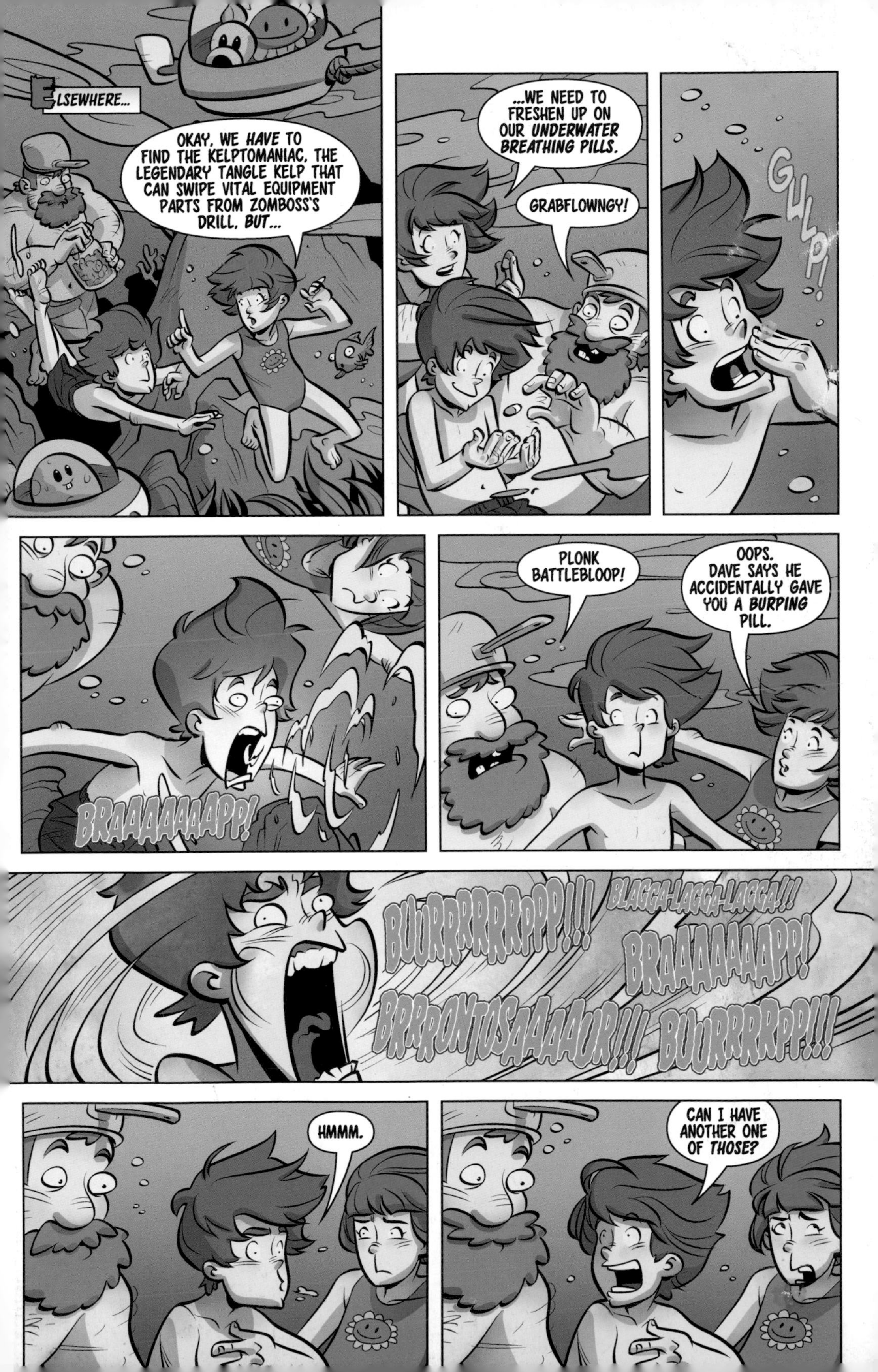
ELSEWHERE...
OKAY, WE HAVE TO FIND THE KELPTOMANIAC, THE LEGENDARY TANGLE KELP THAT CAN SWIPE VITAL EQUIPMENT PARTS FROM ZOMBOSS'S DRILL, BUT...
...WE NEED TO FRESHEN UP ON OUR UNDERWATER BREATHING PILLS.
GRABFLOWNGY!
GULP!
BRAAAAAAAPP!
PLONK BATTLEBLOOP!
OOPS. DAVE SAYS HE ACCIDENTALLY GAVE YOU A BURPING PILL.
BUURRRRRRPPP!!!
BLAGGA-LAGGA-LAGGA!!!
BRAAAAAAAPP!
BRRRONTOSAAAAUR!!!
BUURRRRPP!!!
HMMM.
CAN I HAVE ANOTHER ONE OF THOSE?

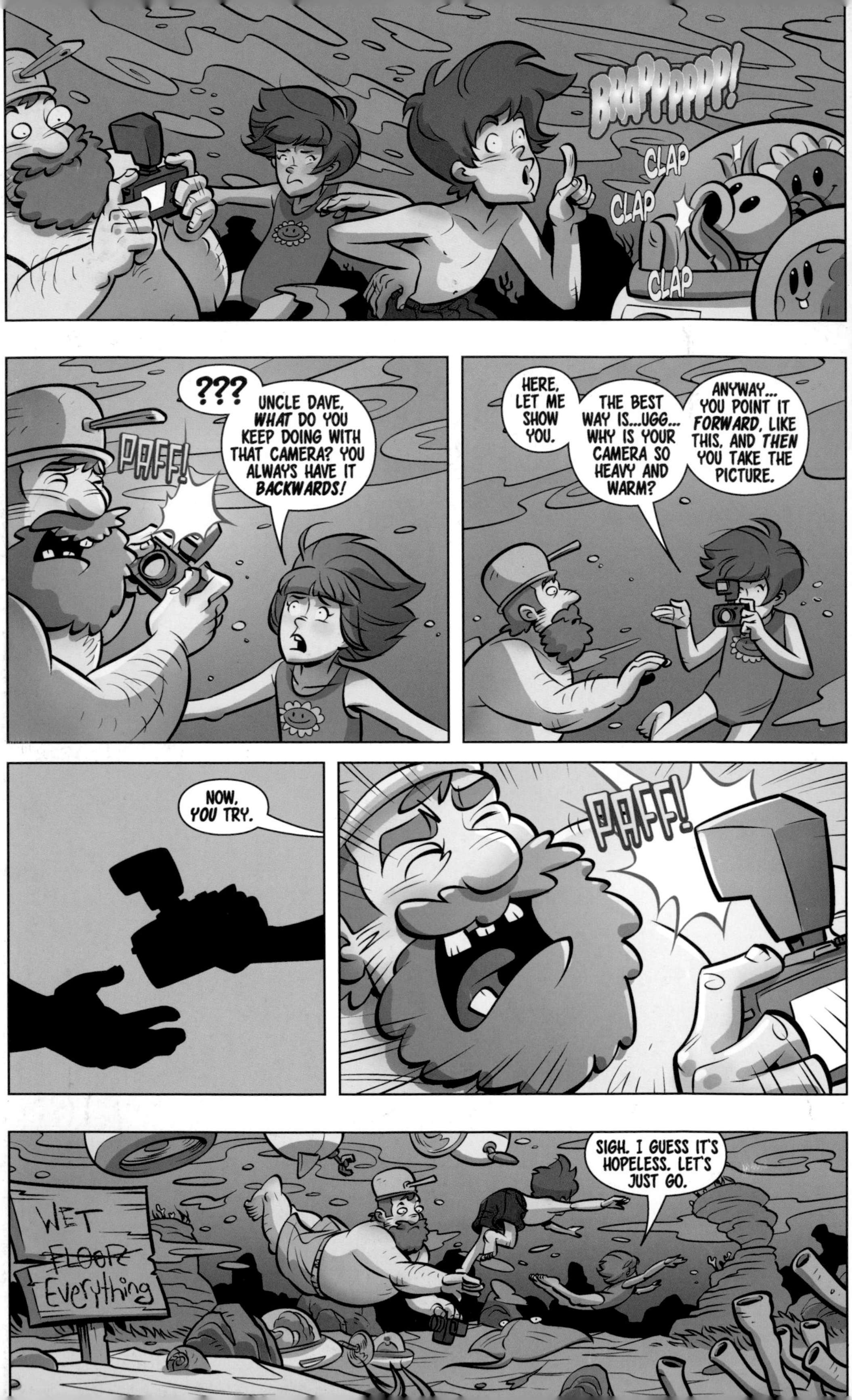
BRAPPPPPP!
CLAP
CLAP
CLAP
???
UNCLE DAVE, WHAT DO YOU KEEP DOING WITH THAT CAMERA? YOU ALWAYS HAVE IT BACKWARDS!
PAFF!
HERE, LET ME SHOW YOU.
THE BEST WAY IS...UGG... WHY IS YOUR CAMERA SO HEAVY AND WARM?
ANYWAY... YOU POINT IT FORWARD, LIKE THIS, AND THEN YOU TAKE THE PICTURE.
NOW, YOU TRY.
PAFF!
WET FLOOR Everything
SIGH. I GUESS IT'S HOPELESS. LET'S JUST GO.

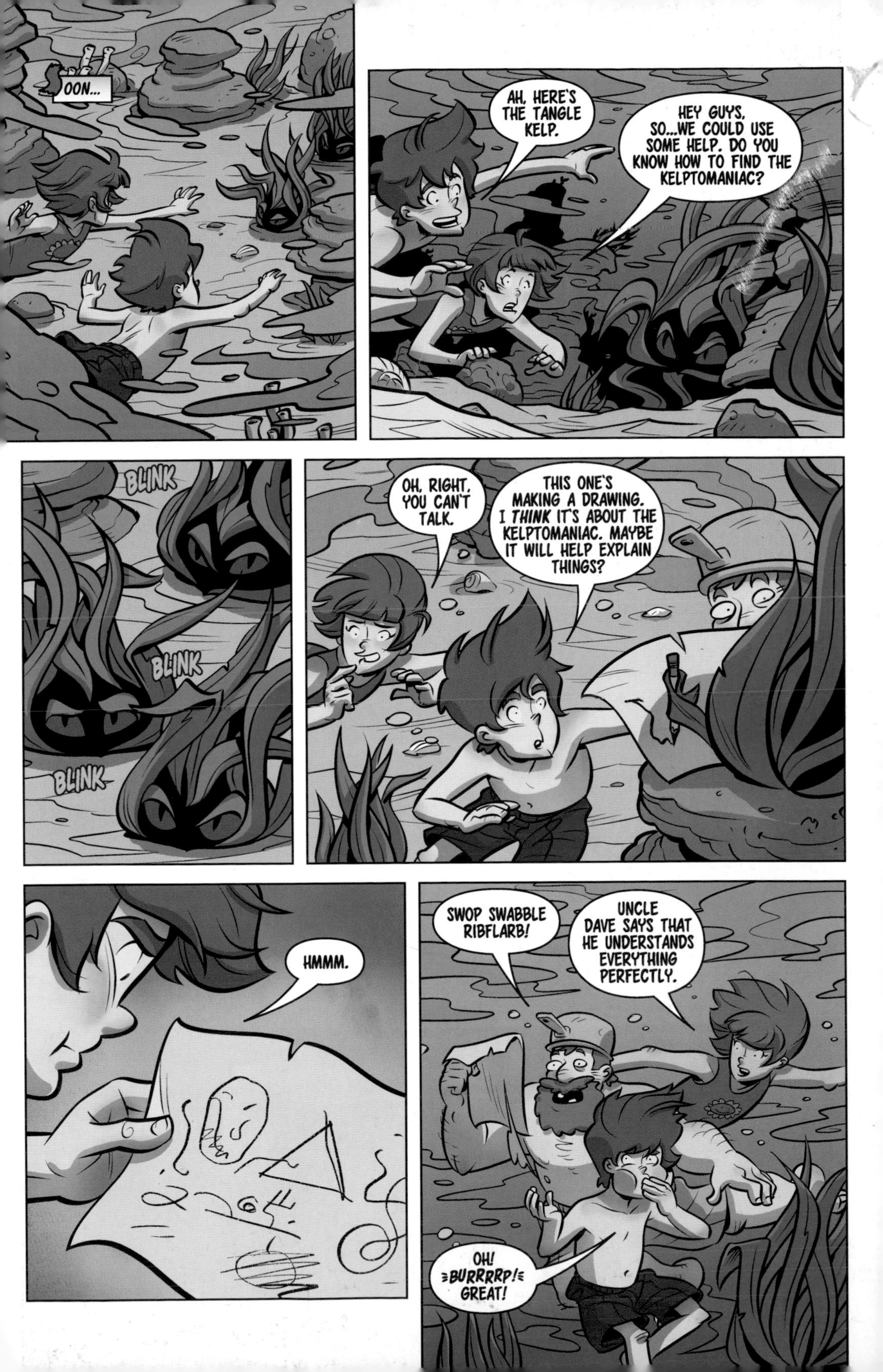
OON...
AH, HERE'S THE TANGLE KELP.
HEY GUYS, SO...WE COULD USE SOME HELP. DO YOU KNOW HOW TO FIND THE KELPTOMANIAC?
BLINK
BLINK
BLINK
OH, RIGHT, YOU CAN'T TALK.
THIS ONE'S MAKING A DRAWING. I *THINK* IT'S ABOUT THE KELPTOMANIAC. MAYBE IT WILL HELP EXPLAIN THINGS?
HMMM.
SWOP SWABBLE RIBFLARB!
UNCLE DAVE SAYS THAT HE UNDERSTANDS EVERYTHING PERFECTLY.
OH! *BURRRRP!* GREAT!

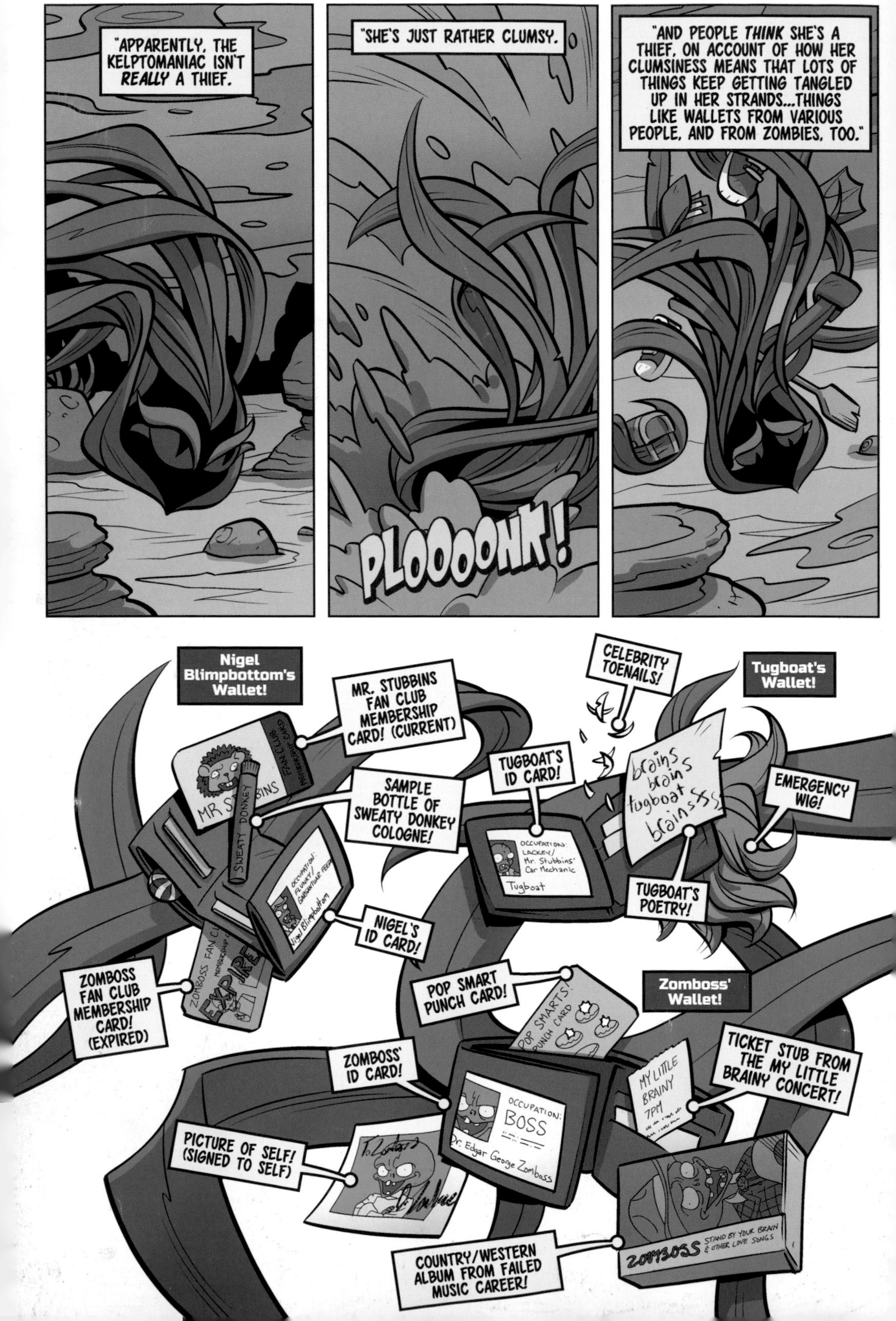

"APPARENTLY, THE KELPTOMANIAC ISN'T REALLY A THIEF.
"SHE'S JUST RATHER CLUMSY.
PLOOOONK!
"AND PEOPLE THINK SHE'S A THIEF, ON ACCOUNT OF HOW HER CLUMSINESS MEANS THAT LOTS OF THINGS KEEP GETTING TANGLED UP IN HER STRANDS...THINGS LIKE WALLETS FROM VARIOUS PEOPLE, AND FROM ZOMBIES, TOO."
Nigel Blimpbottom's Wallet!
MR. STUBBINS FAN CLUB MEMBERSHIP CARD! (CURRENT)
MR STUBBINS
FAN CLUB MEMBERSHIP CARD
SWEATY DONKEY
SAMPLE BOTTLE OF SWEATY DONKEY COLOGNE!
NIGEL'S ID CARD!
Nigel Blimpbottom
ZOMBOSS FAN CLUB MEMBERSHIP CARD! (EXPIRED)
EXPIRED
CELEBRITY TOENAILS!
Tugboat's Wallet!
TUGBOAT'S ID CARD!
OCCUPATION: LACKEY/ Mr. Stubbins' Car Mechanic
Tugboat
brains brain tugboat brainsss
EMERGENCY WIG!
TUGBOAT'S POETRY!
POP SMART PUNCH CARD!
POP SMARTS! PUNCH CARD
Zomboss' Wallet!
ZOMBOSS' ID CARD!
OCCUPATION: BOSS
Dr. Edgar George Zomboss
TICKET STUB FROM THE MY LITTLE BRAINY CONCERT!
MY LITTLE BRAINY 7PM
PICTURE OF SELF! (SIGNED TO SELF)
ZOMBOSS
STAND BY YOUR BRAIN & OTHER LOVE SONGS
COUNTRY/WESTERN ALBUM FROM FAILED MUSIC CAREER!

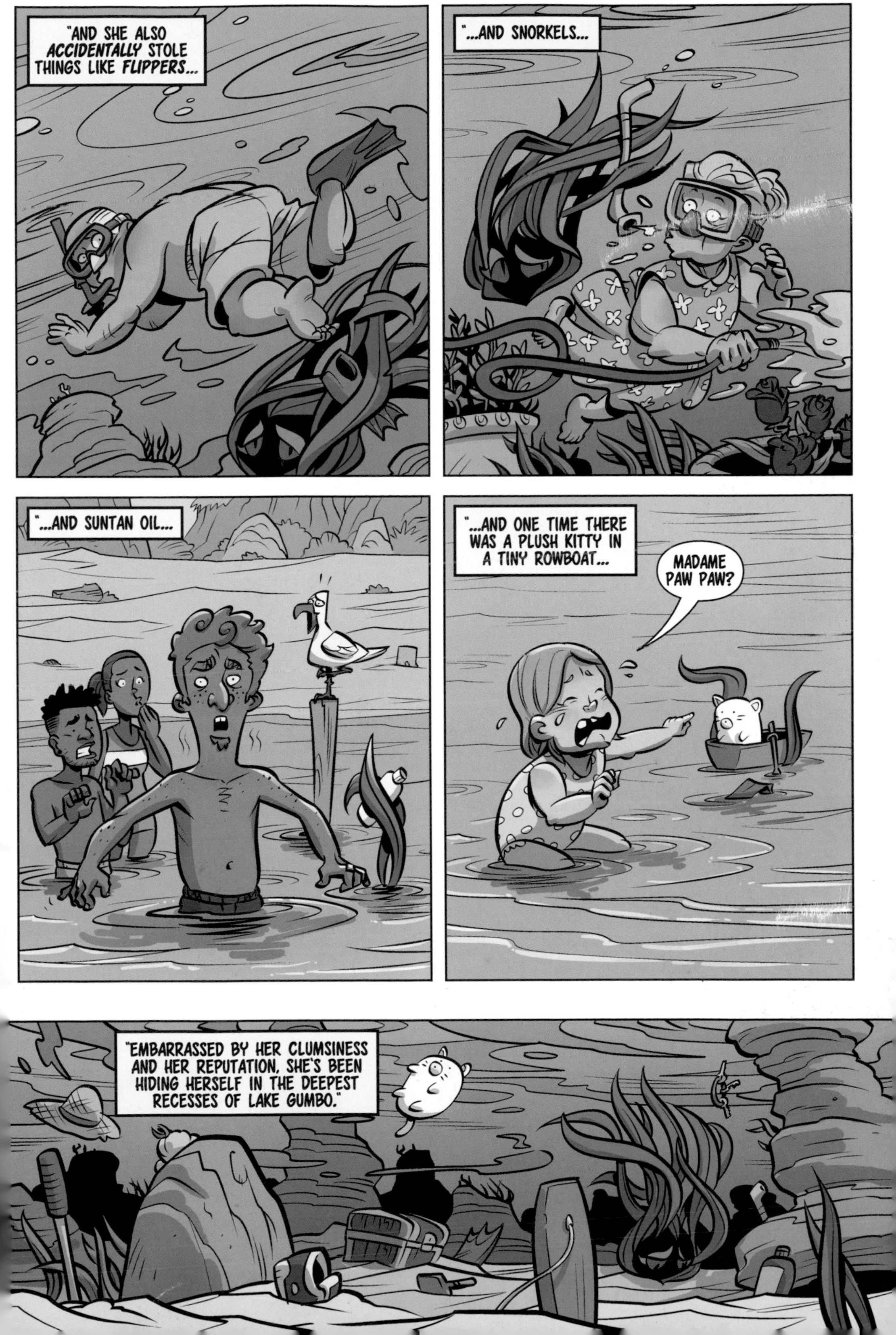
"AND SHE ALSO *ACCIDENTALLY* STOLE THINGS LIKE *FLIPPERS*...
"...AND SNORKELS...
"...AND SUNTAN OIL...
"...AND ONE TIME THERE WAS A PLUSH KITTY IN A TINY ROWBOAT...
MADAME PAW PAW?
"EMBARRASSED BY HER CLUMSINESS AND HER REPUTATION, SHE'S BEEN HIDING HERSELF IN THE DEEPEST RECESSES OF LAKE GUMBO."

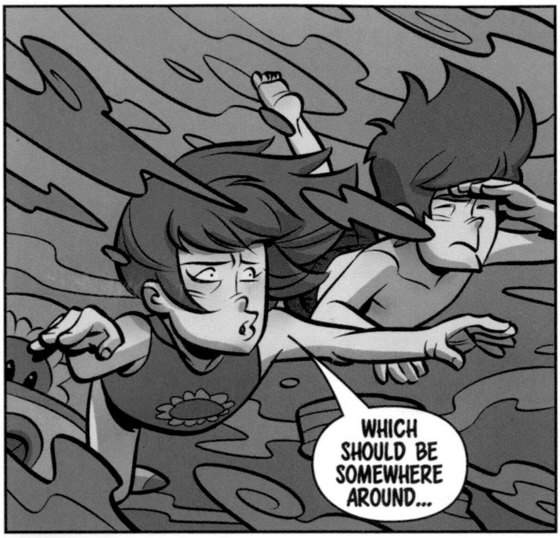
WHICH SHOULD BE SOMEWHERE AROUND...

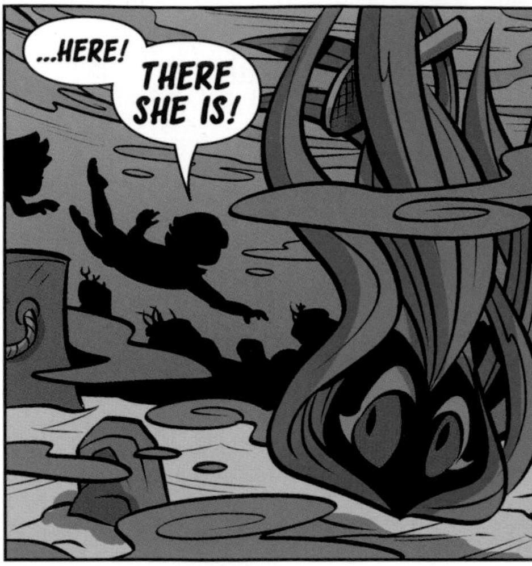
...HERE!
THERE SHE IS!

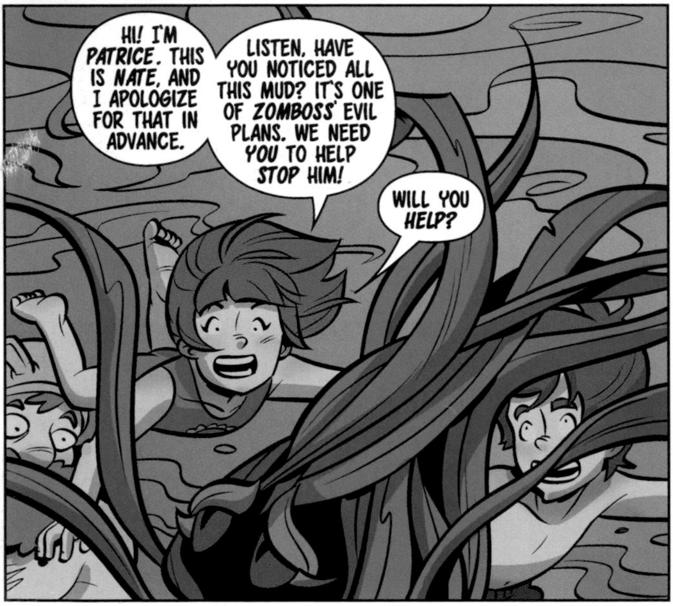
HI! I'M PATRICE. THIS IS NATE, AND I APOLOGIZE FOR THAT IN ADVANCE.
LISTEN, HAVE YOU NOTICED ALL THIS MUD? IT'S ONE OF ZOMBOSS' EVIL PLANS. WE NEED YOU TO HELP STOP HIM!
WILL YOU HELP?

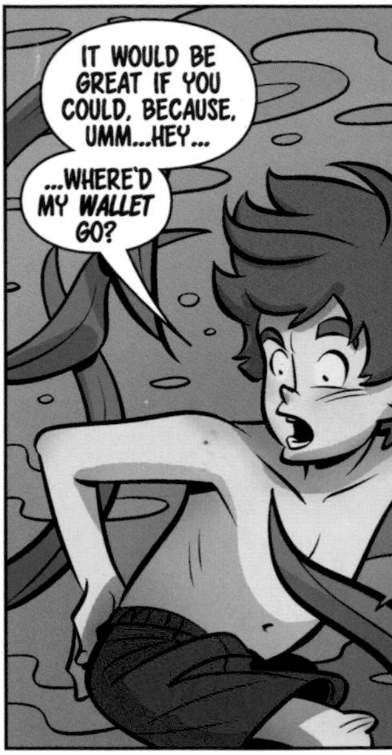
IT WOULD BE GREAT IF YOU COULD, BECAUSE, UMM...HEY...
...WHERE'D MY WALLET GO?

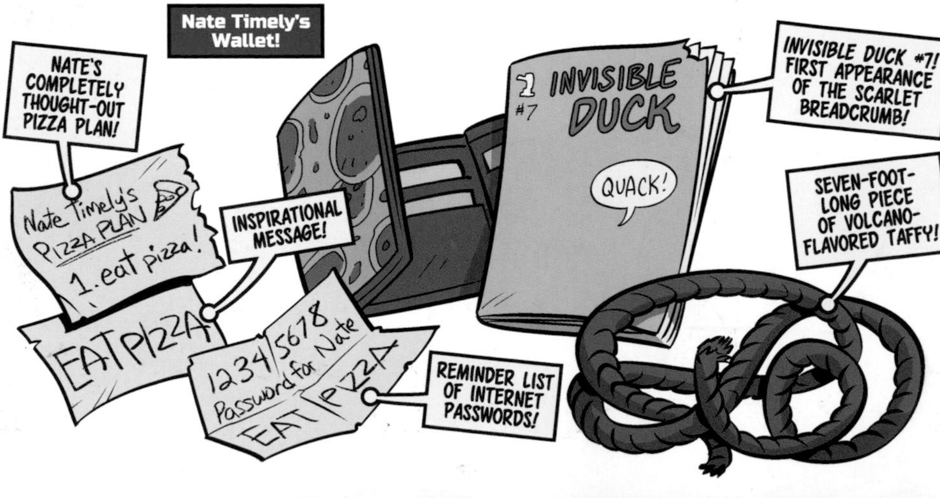
Nate Timely's Wallet!
NATE'S COMPLETELY THOUGHT-OUT PIZZA PLAN!
Nate Timely's PIZZA PLAN
1. eat pizza!
INSPIRATIONAL MESSAGE!
EAT PIZZA
1234/5678 Password for Nate
EAT PIZZA
REMINDER LIST OF INTERNET PASSWORDS!
INVISIBLE DUCK
#7
QUACK!
INVISIBLE DUCK #7! FIRST APPEARANCE OF THE SCARLET BREADCRUMB!
SEVEN-FOOT-LONG PIECE OF VOLCANO-FLAVORED TAFFY!

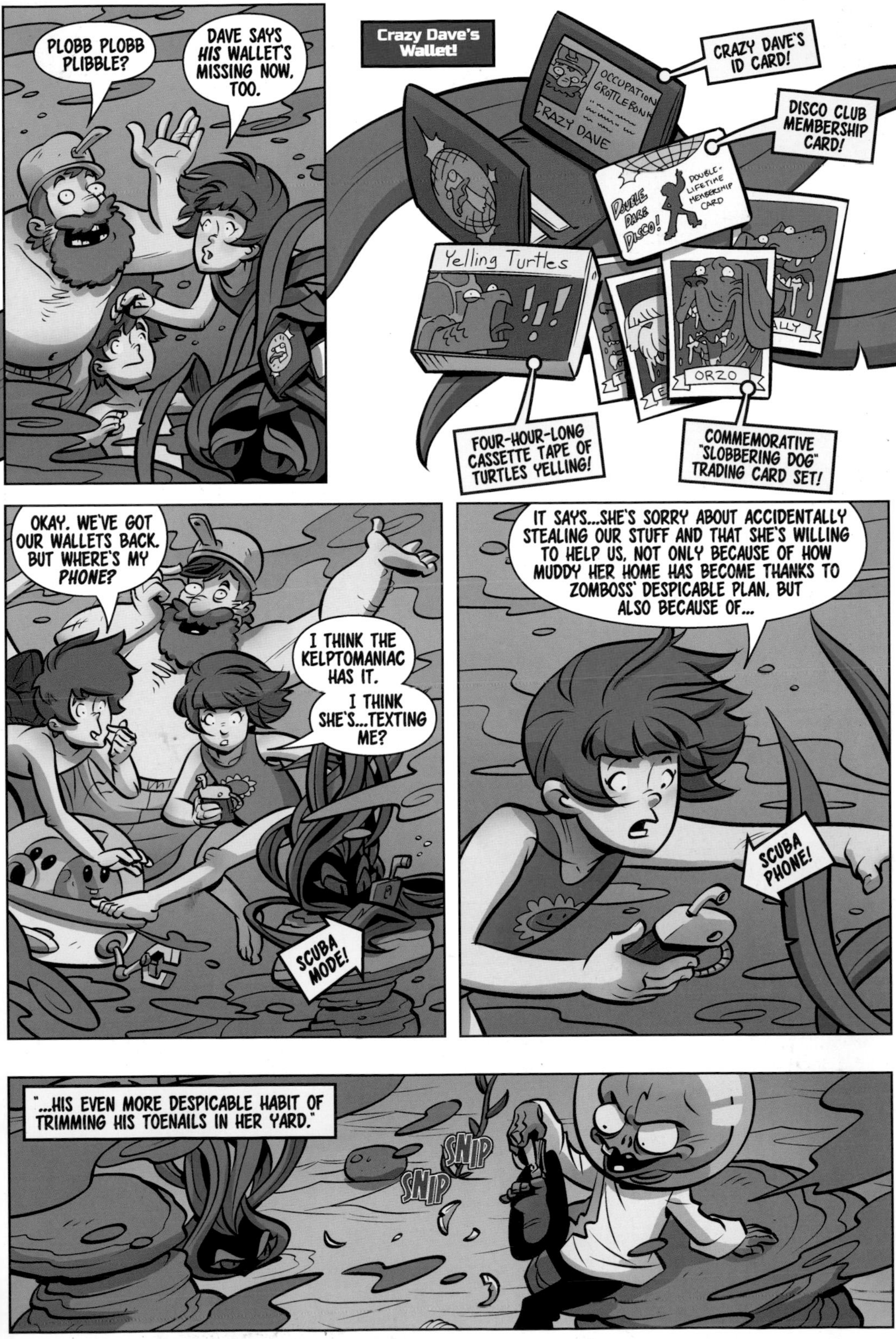
PLOBB PLOBB PLIBBLE?
DAVE SAYS HIS WALLET'S MISSING NOW, TOO.
Crazy Dave's Wallet!
OCCUPATION GROTTLEBONK
CRAZY DAVE
CRAZY DAVE'S ID CARD!
DOUBLE-LIFETIME MEMBERSHIP CARD
DOUBLE DARE DISCO!
DISCO CLUB MEMBERSHIP CARD!
Yelling Turtles
ORZO
FOUR-HOUR-LONG CASSETTE TAPE OF TURTLES YELLING!
COMMEMORATIVE "SLOBBERING DOG" TRADING CARD SET!
OKAY. WE'VE GOT OUR WALLETS BACK. BUT WHERE'S MY PHONE?
I THINK THE KELPTOMANIAC HAS IT.
I THINK SHE'S...TEXTING ME?
SCUBA MODE!
IT SAYS...SHE'S SORRY ABOUT ACCIDENTALLY STEALING OUR STUFF AND THAT SHE'S WILLING TO HELP US, NOT ONLY BECAUSE OF HOW MUDDY HER HOME HAS BECOME THANKS TO ZOMBOSS' DESPICABLE PLAN, BUT ALSO BECAUSE OF...
SCUBA PHONE!
"...HIS EVEN MORE DESPICABLE HABIT OF TRIMMING HIS TOENAILS IN HER YARD."
SNIP
SNIP

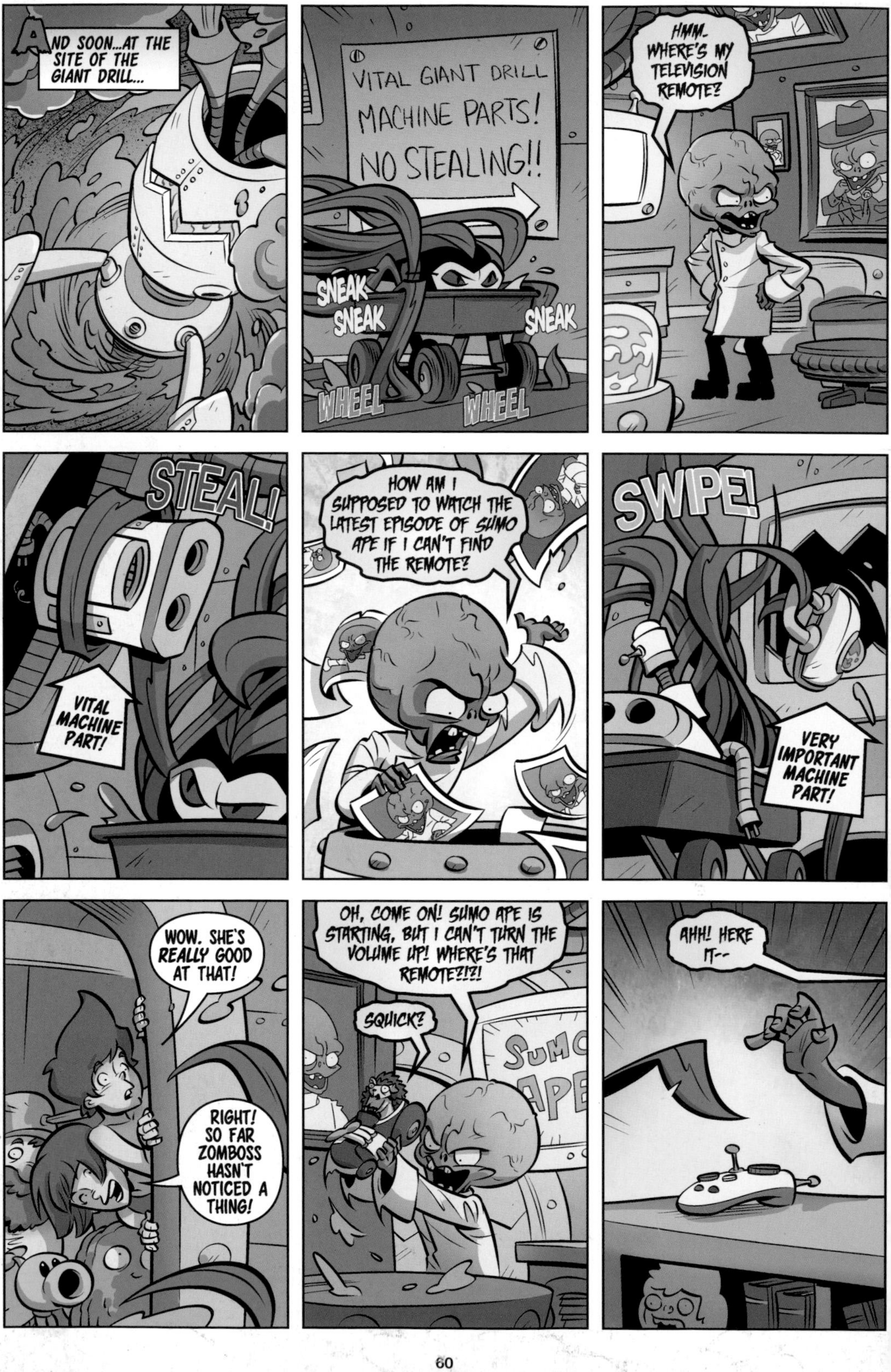
AND SOON...AT THE SITE OF THE GIANT DRILL...
VITAL GIANT DRILL MACHINE PARTS! NO STEALING!!
SNEAK
SNEAK
SNEAK
WHEEL
WHEEL
HMM. WHERE'S MY TELEVISION REMOTE?
STEAL!
VITAL MACHINE PART!
HOW AM I SUPPOSED TO WATCH THE LATEST EPISODE OF SUMO APE IF I CAN'T FIND THE REMOTE?
SWIPE!
VERY IMPORTANT MACHINE PART!
WOW. SHE'S REALLY GOOD AT THAT!
RIGHT! SO FAR ZOMBOSS HASN'T NOTICED A THING!
OH, COME ON! SUMO APE IS STARTING, BUT I CAN'T TURN THE VOLUME UP! WHERE'S THAT REMOTE?!?!
SQUICK?
SUMO APE
AHH! HERE IT--

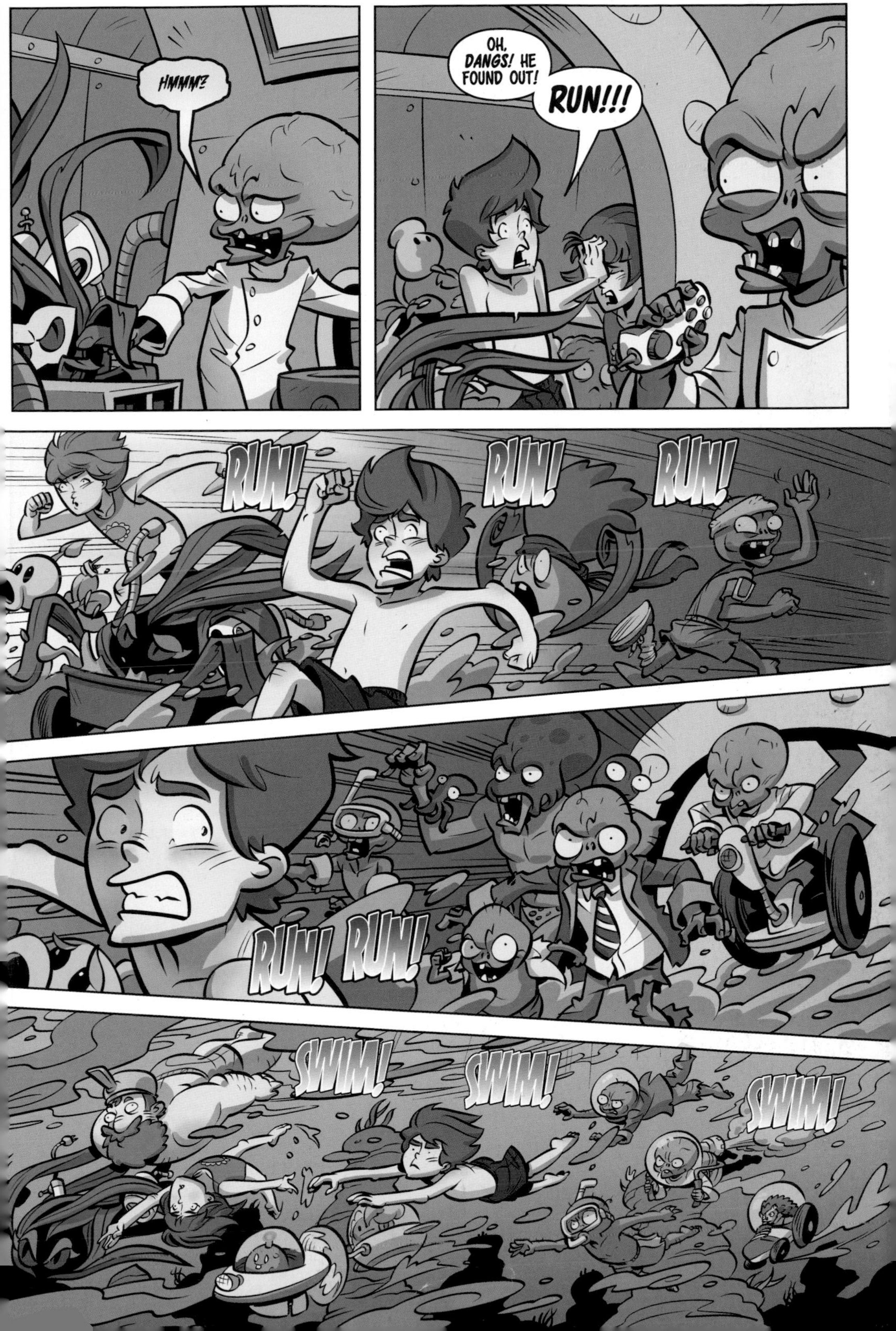
HMMM?
OH, DANGS! HE FOUND OUT!
RUN!!!
RUN!
RUN!
RUN!
RUN!
RUN!
SWIM!
SWIM!
SWIM!

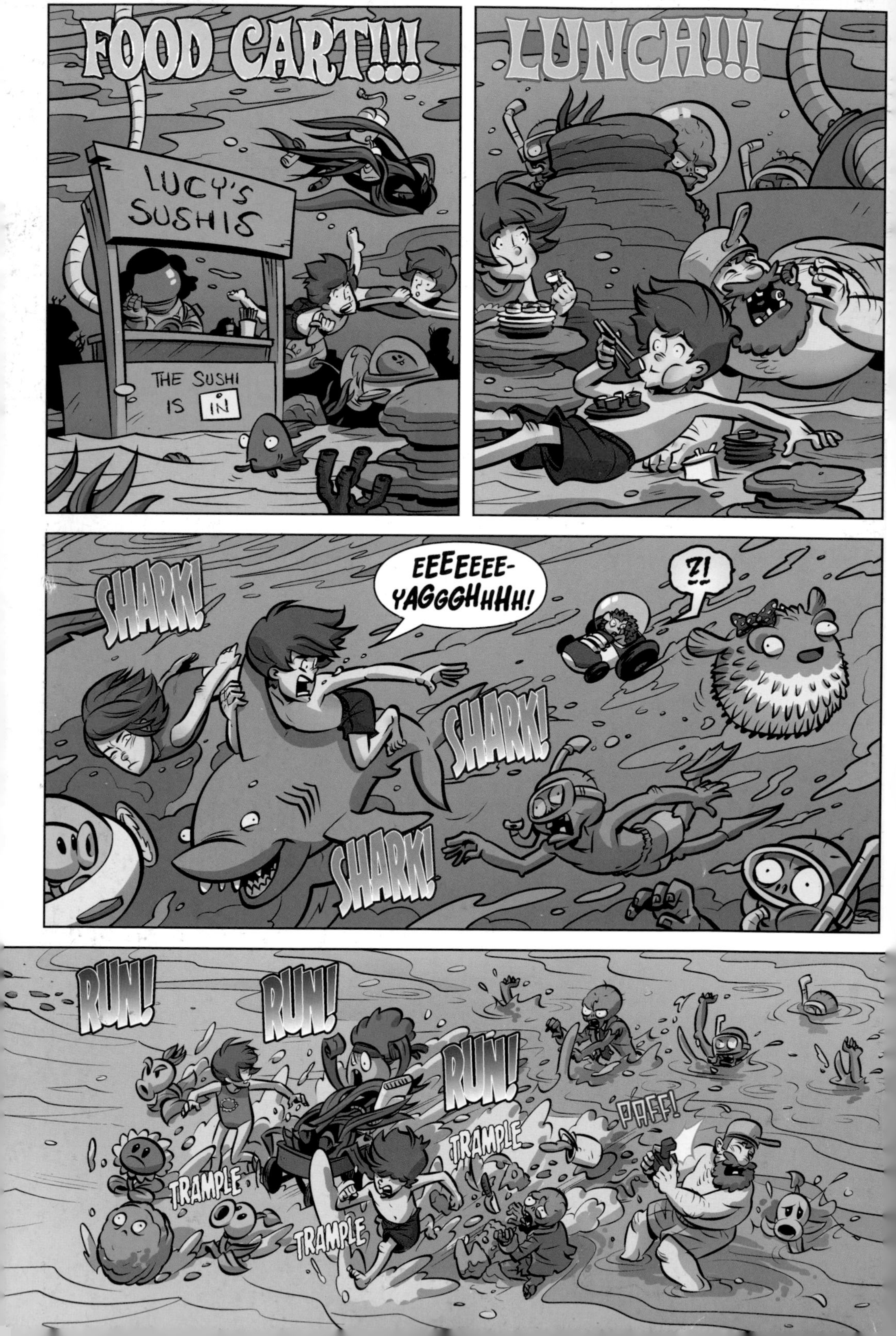
FOOD CART!!!
LUCY'S SUSHIS
THE SUSHI IS IN
LUNCH!!!
SHARK!
EEEEEEE-YAGGGHHHH!
?!
SHARK!
SHARK!
RUN!
RUN!
RUN!
PAFF!
TRAMPLE
TRAMPLE
TRAMPLE

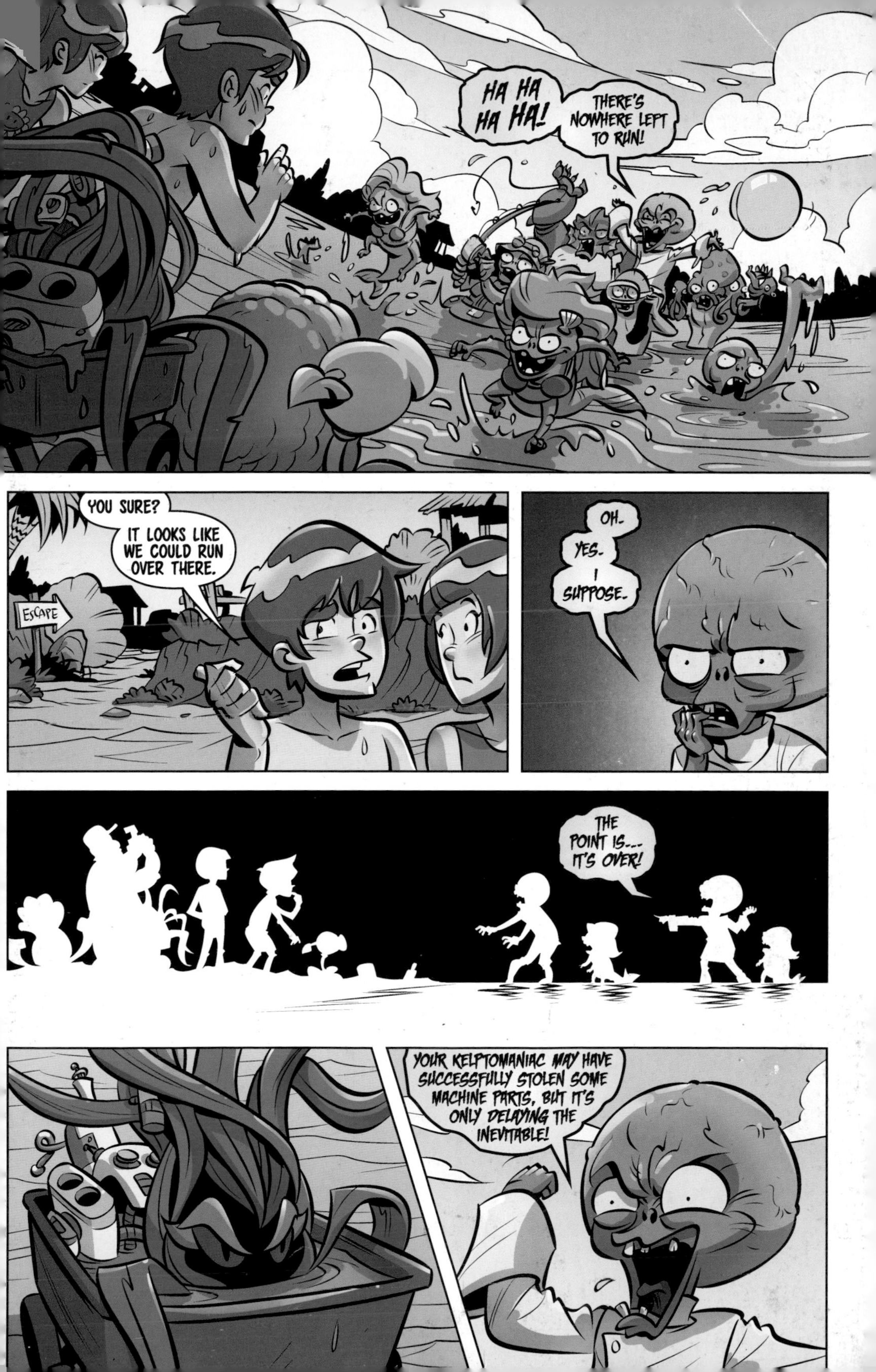
HA HA HA HA!
THERE'S NOWHERE LEFT TO RUN!
YOU SURE?
IT LOOKS LIKE WE COULD RUN OVER THERE.
ESCAPE
OH.
YES.
I SUPPOSE.
THE POINT IS... IT'S OVER!
YOUR KELPTOMANIAC MAY HAVE SUCCESSFULLY STOLEN SOME MACHINE PARTS, BUT IT'S ONLY DELAYING THE INEVITABLE!

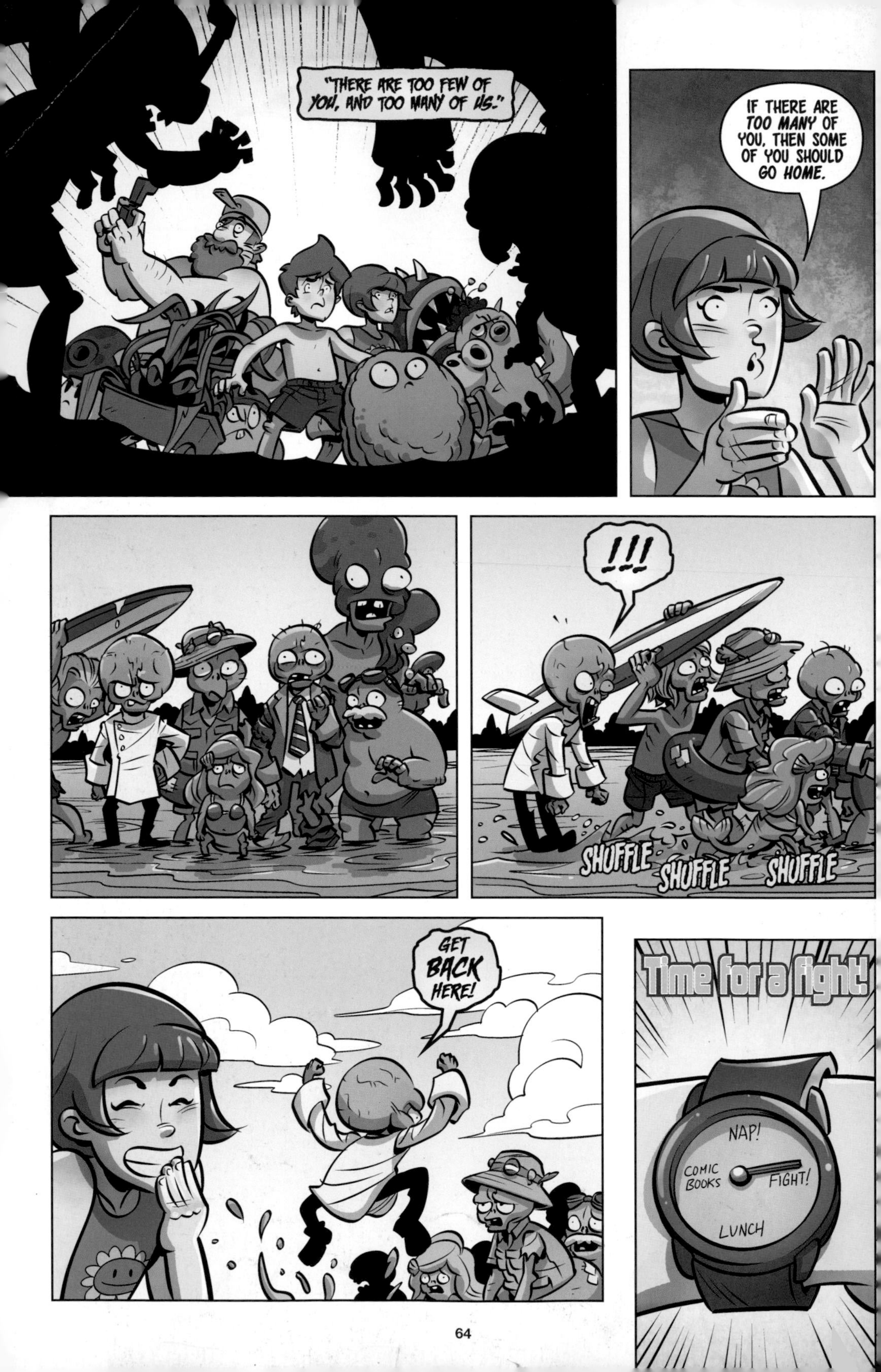
"THERE ARE TOO FEW OF YOU, AND TOO MANY OF US."
IF THERE ARE TOO MANY OF YOU, THEN SOME OF YOU SHOULD GO HOME.
!!!
SHUFFLE
SHUFFLE
SHUFFLE
GET BACK HERE!
Time for a fight!
NAP!
COMIC BOOKS
FIGHT!
LUNCH

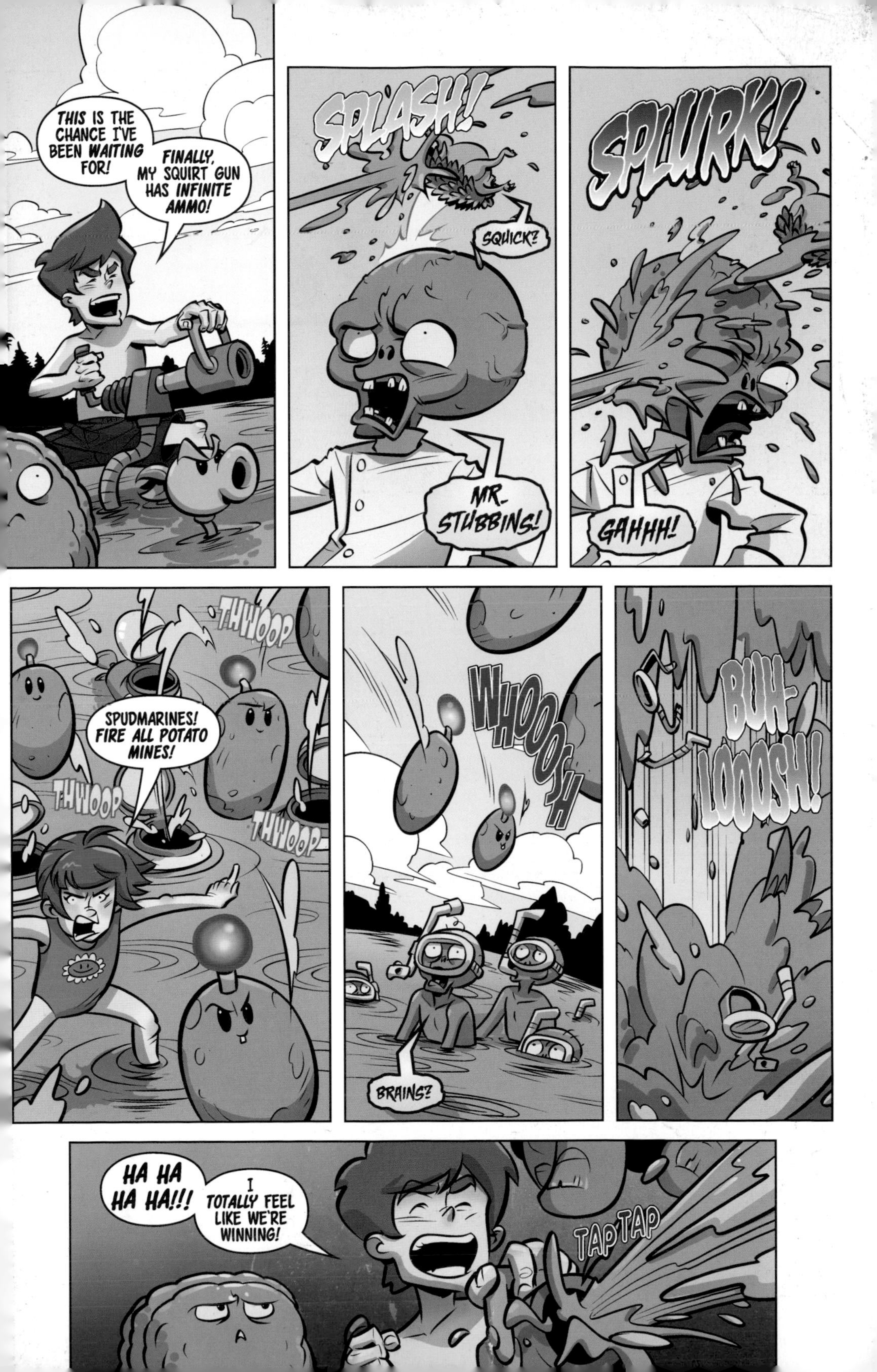

THIS IS THE CHANCE I'VE BEEN WAITING FOR!
FINALLY, MY SQUIRT GUN HAS INFINITE AMMO!
SPLASH!
SQUICK?
MR. STUBBINS!
SPLURK!
GAHHH!
THWOOP
SPUDMARINES! FIRE ALL POTATO MINES!
THWOOP
THWOOP
WHOOOOSH
BRAINS?
BUH-LOOOSH!
HA HA HA HA!!!
I TOTALLY FEEL LIKE WE'RE WINNING!
TAP TAP

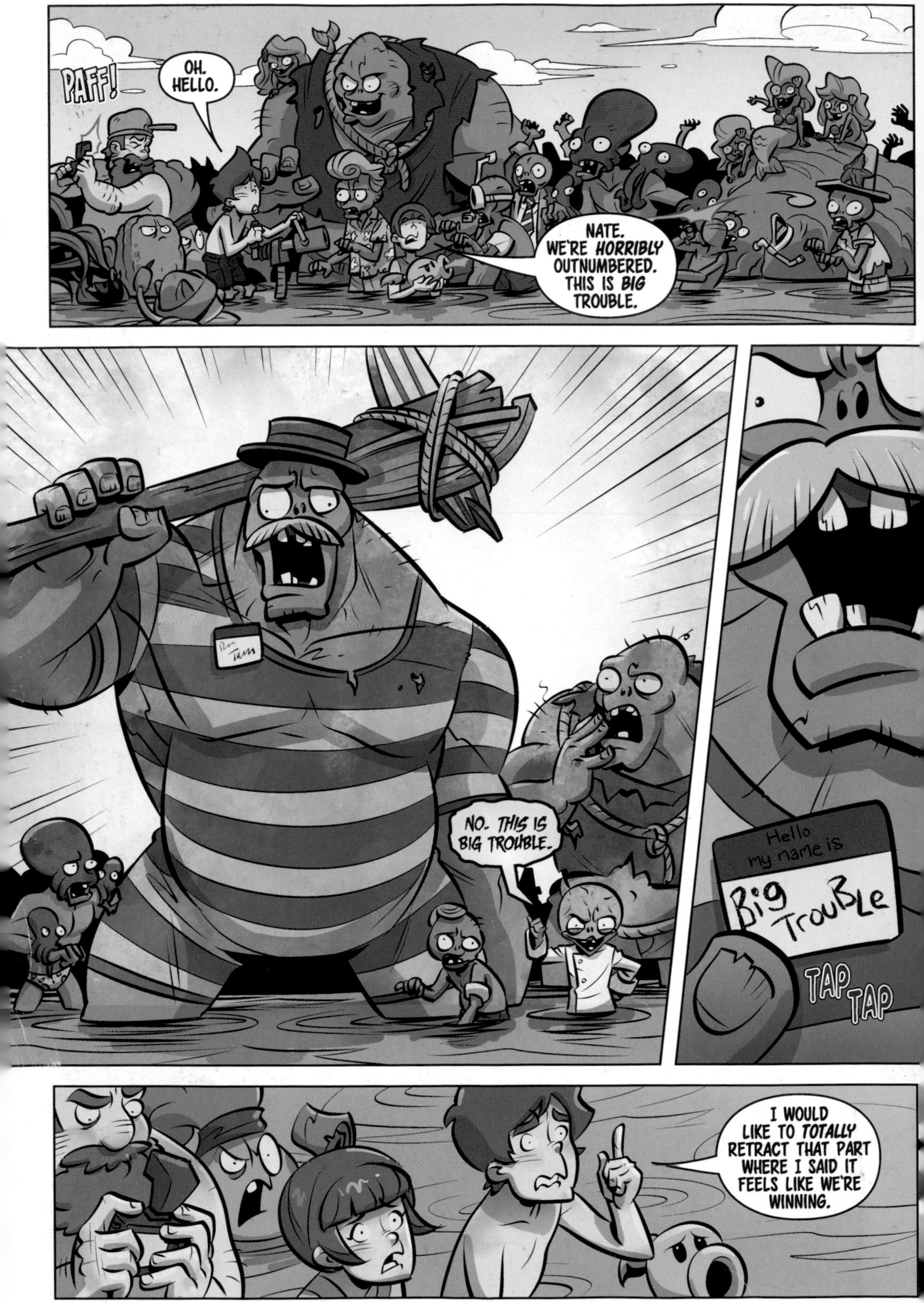
PAFF!
OH. HELLO.
NATE. WE'RE *HORRIBLY* OUTNUMBERED. THIS IS *BIG* TROUBLE.
NO. *THIS* IS BIG TROUBLE.
Hello my name is
Big TrouBLe
TAP TAP
I WOULD LIKE TO *TOTALLY* RETRACT THAT PART WHERE I SAID IT FEELS LIKE WE'RE WINNING.

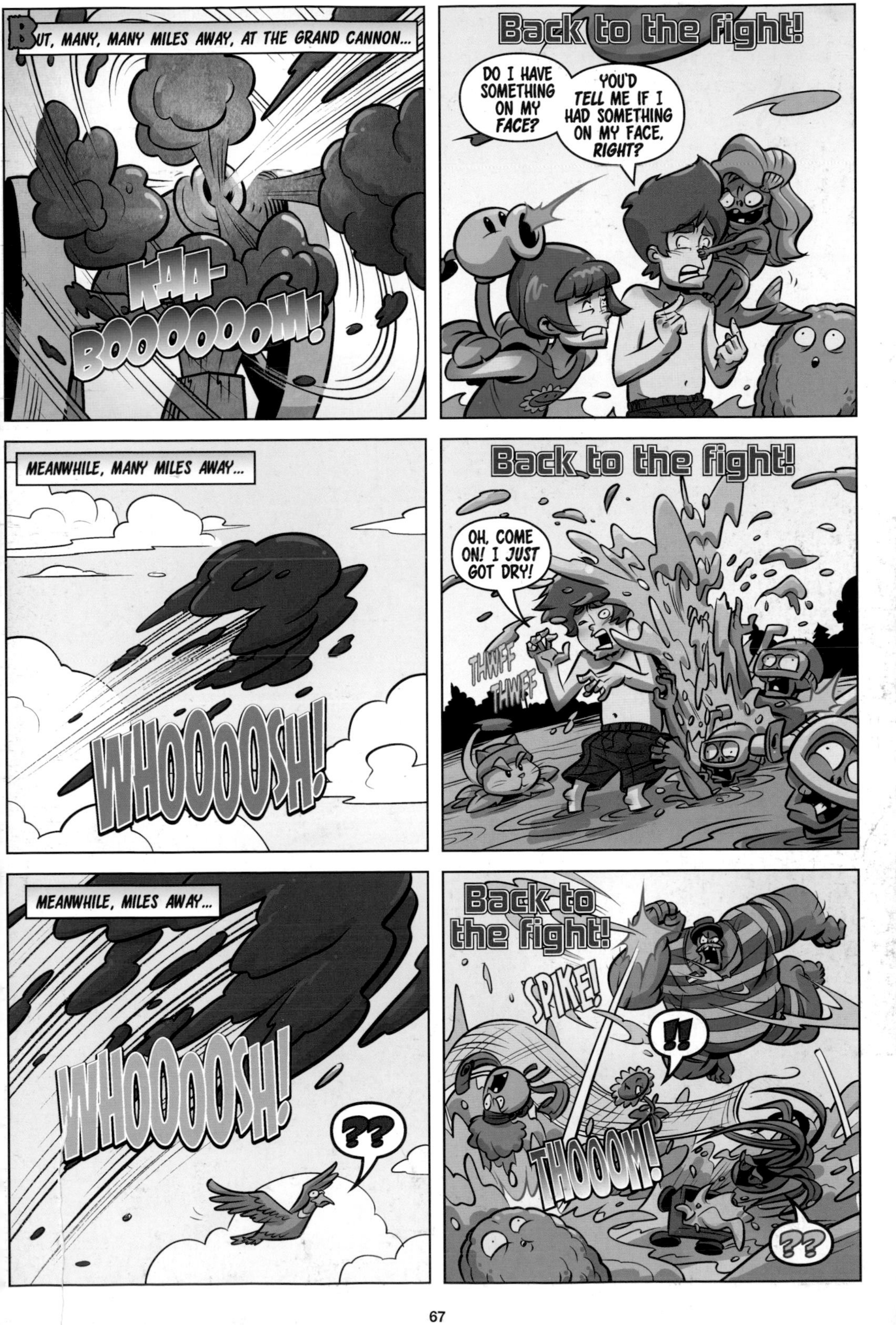
BUT, MANY, MANY MILES AWAY, AT THE GRAND CANNON...
KAA-BOOOOOOOM!
Back to the fight!
DO I HAVE SOMETHING ON MY FACE?
YOU'D TELL ME IF I HAD SOMETHING ON MY FACE, RIGHT?
MEANWHILE, MANY MILES AWAY...
WHOOOOSH!
Back to the fight!
OH, COME ON! I JUST GOT DRY!
THWFF THWFF
MEANWHILE, MILES AWAY...
WHOOOOSH!
??
Back to the fight!
SPIKE!
!!
THOOOM!
??

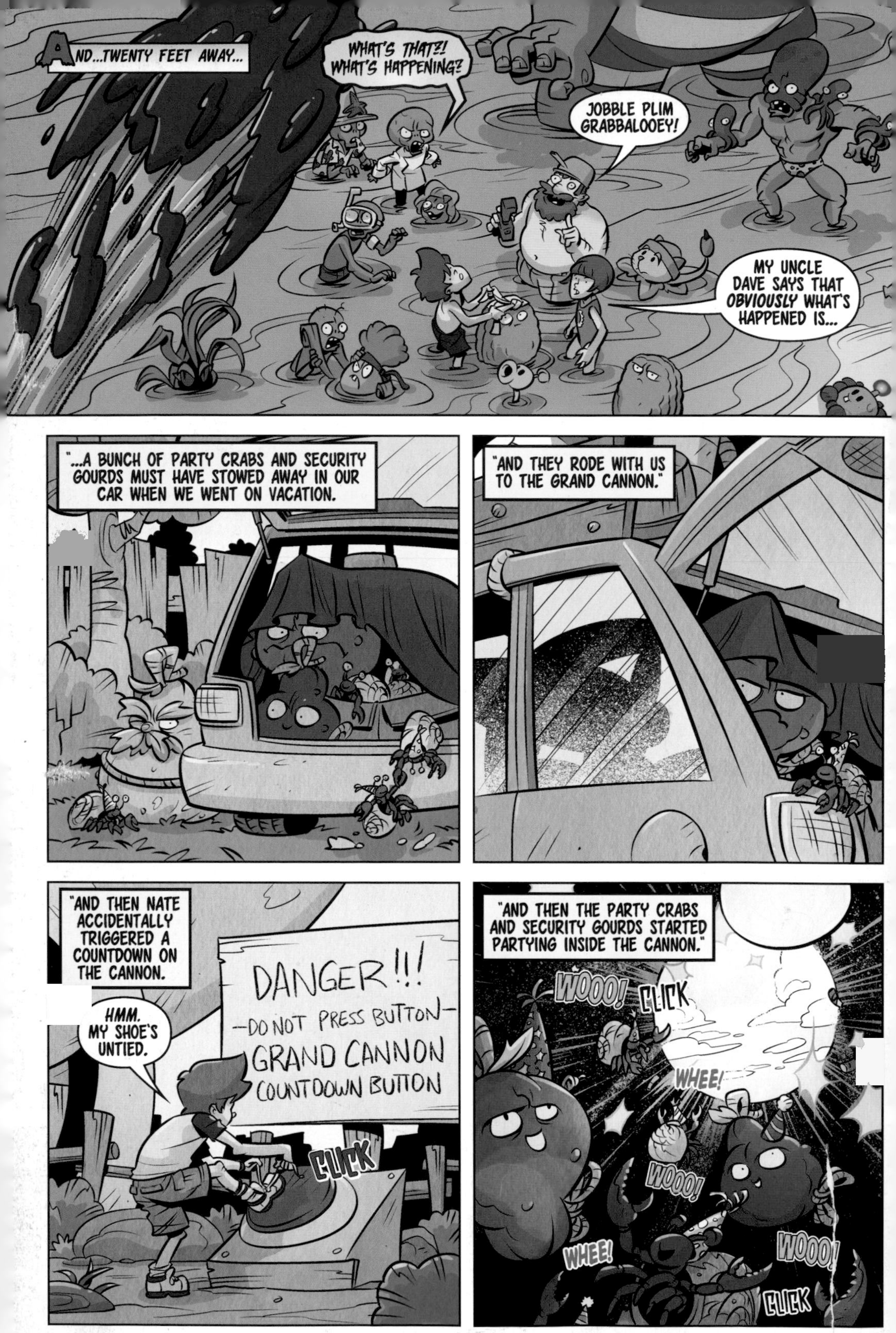
AND...TWENTY FEET AWAY...
WHAT'S THAT?! WHAT'S HAPPENING?
JOBBLE PLIM GRABBALOOEY!
MY UNCLE DAVE SAYS THAT OBVIOUSLY WHAT'S HAPPENED IS...
"...A BUNCH OF PARTY CRABS AND SECURITY GOURDS MUST HAVE STOWED AWAY IN OUR CAR WHEN WE WENT ON VACATION.
"AND THEY RODE WITH US TO THE GRAND CANNON."
"AND THEN NATE ACCIDENTALLY TRIGGERED A COUNTDOWN ON THE CANNON.
HMM. MY SHOE'S UNTIED.
DANGER!!!
—DO NOT PRESS BUTTON—
GRAND CANNON
COUNTDOWN BUTTON
CLICK
"AND THEN THE PARTY CRABS AND SECURITY GOURDS STARTED PARTYING INSIDE THE CANNON."
WOOO!
CLICK
WHEE!
WOOO!
WHEE!
WOOO!
CLICK

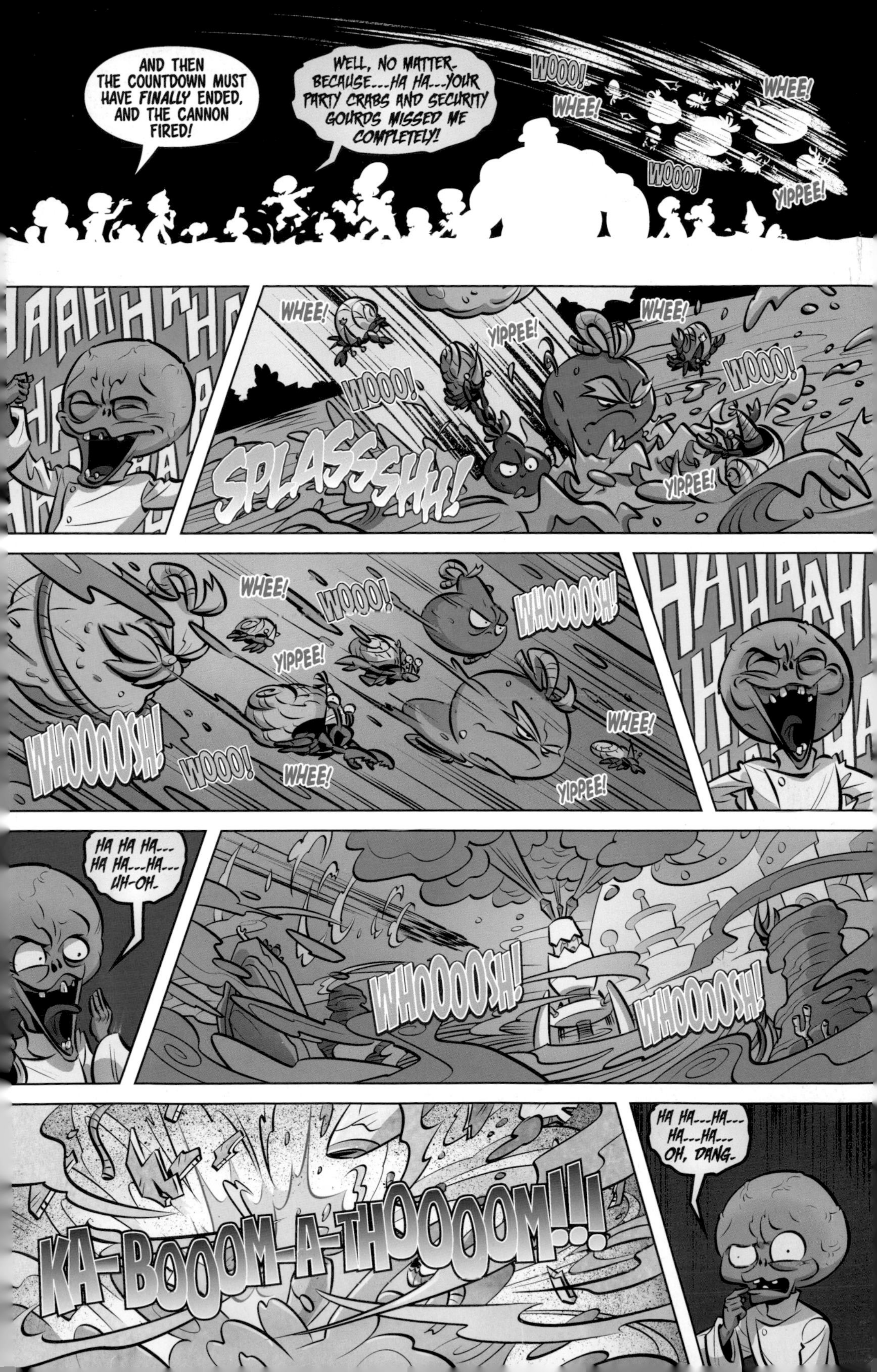
AND THEN THE COUNTDOWN MUST HAVE FINALLY ENDED, AND THE CANNON FIRED!
WELL, NO MATTER. BECAUSE... HA HA... YOUR PARTY CRABS AND SECURITY GOURDS MISSED ME COMPLETELY!
WOOO!
WHEE!
WHEE!
WOOO!
YIPPEE!
HAHAHAHA
WHEE!
WHEE!
YIPPEE!
WOOO!
WOOO!
SPLASSSHH!
YIPPEE!
WHEE!
WOOO!
WHOOOOSH!
YIPPEE!
WHOOOOSH!
WOOO!
WHEE!
WHEE!
YIPPEE!
HAHAHAHA
HA HA HA... HA HA... HA... UH-OH.
WHOOOOSH!
WHOOOOSH!
KA-BOOOM-A-THOOOOM!!!
HA HA... HA... HA... HA... OH, DANG.

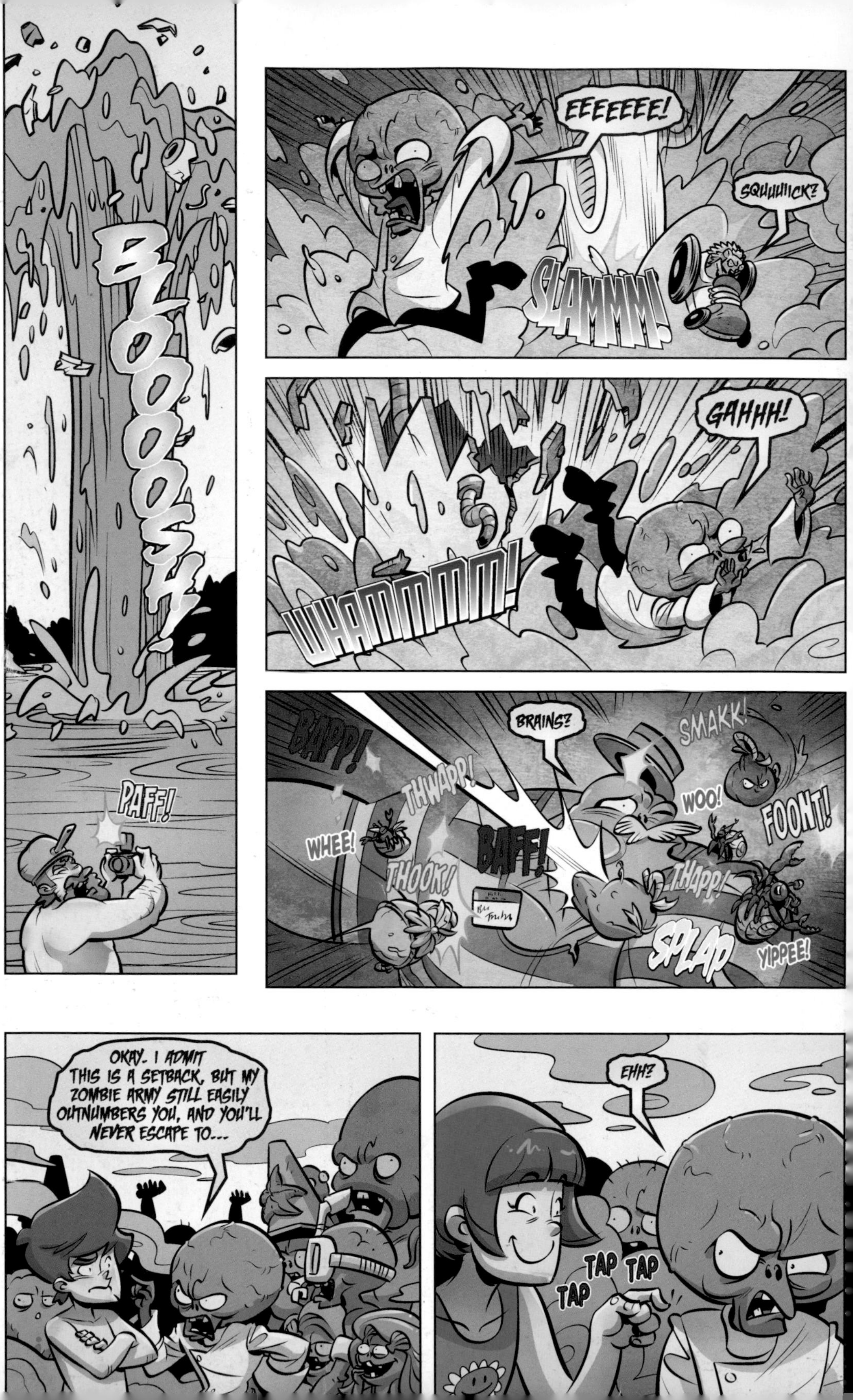
BLOOOOOSH!
PAFF!
EEEEEEE!
SQUUUIICK?
SLAMMM!
GAHHH!
WHAMMMM!
BAPP!
BRAINS?
SMAKK!
THWAPP!
WOO!
FOONT!
WHEE!
BAFF!
THOOK!
THAPP!
SPLAP
YIPPEE!
OKAY. I ADMIT THIS IS A SETBACK, BUT MY ZOMBIE ARMY STILL EASILY OUTNUMBERS YOU, AND YOU'LL NEVER ESCAPE TO...
EHH?
TAP TAP TAP

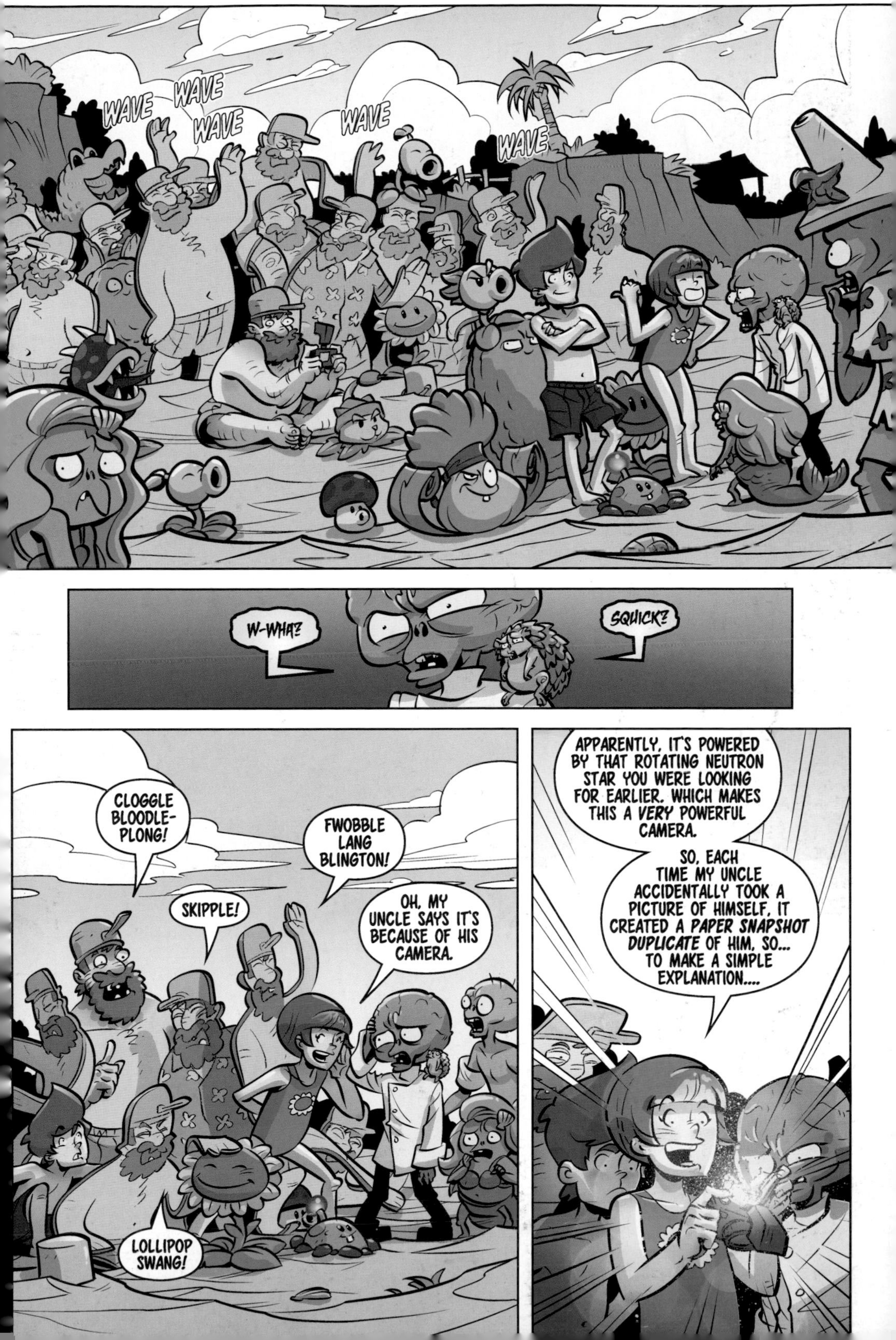
WAVE
WAVE
WAVE
WAVE
WAVE
W-WHA?
SQUICK?
CLOGGLE BLOODLE-PLONG!
SKIPPLE!
FWOBBLE LANG BLINGTON!
OH, MY UNCLE SAYS IT'S BECAUSE OF HIS CAMERA.
LOLLIPOP SWANG!
APPARENTLY, IT'S POWERED BY THAT ROTATING NEUTRON STAR YOU WERE LOOKING FOR EARLIER. WHICH MAKES THIS A *VERY* POWERFUL CAMERA.
SO, EACH TIME MY UNCLE ACCIDENTALLY TOOK A PICTURE OF HIMSELF, IT CREATED A *PAPER SNAPSHOT DUPLICATE* OF HIM, SO... TO MAKE A SIMPLE EXPLANATION....

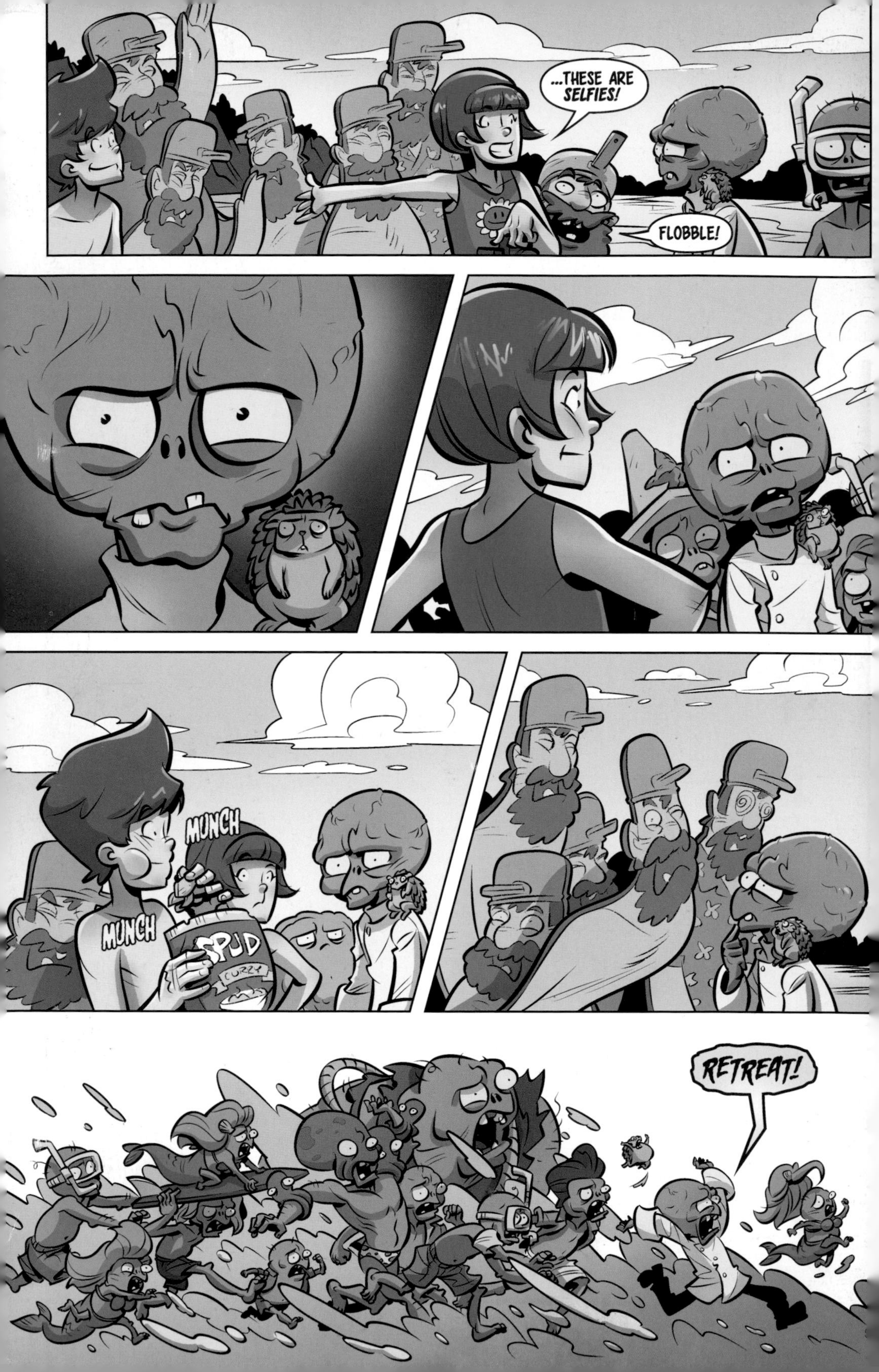
...THESE ARE SELFIES!
FLOBBLE!
MUNCH
MUNCH
SPUD
CURRY
RETREAT!

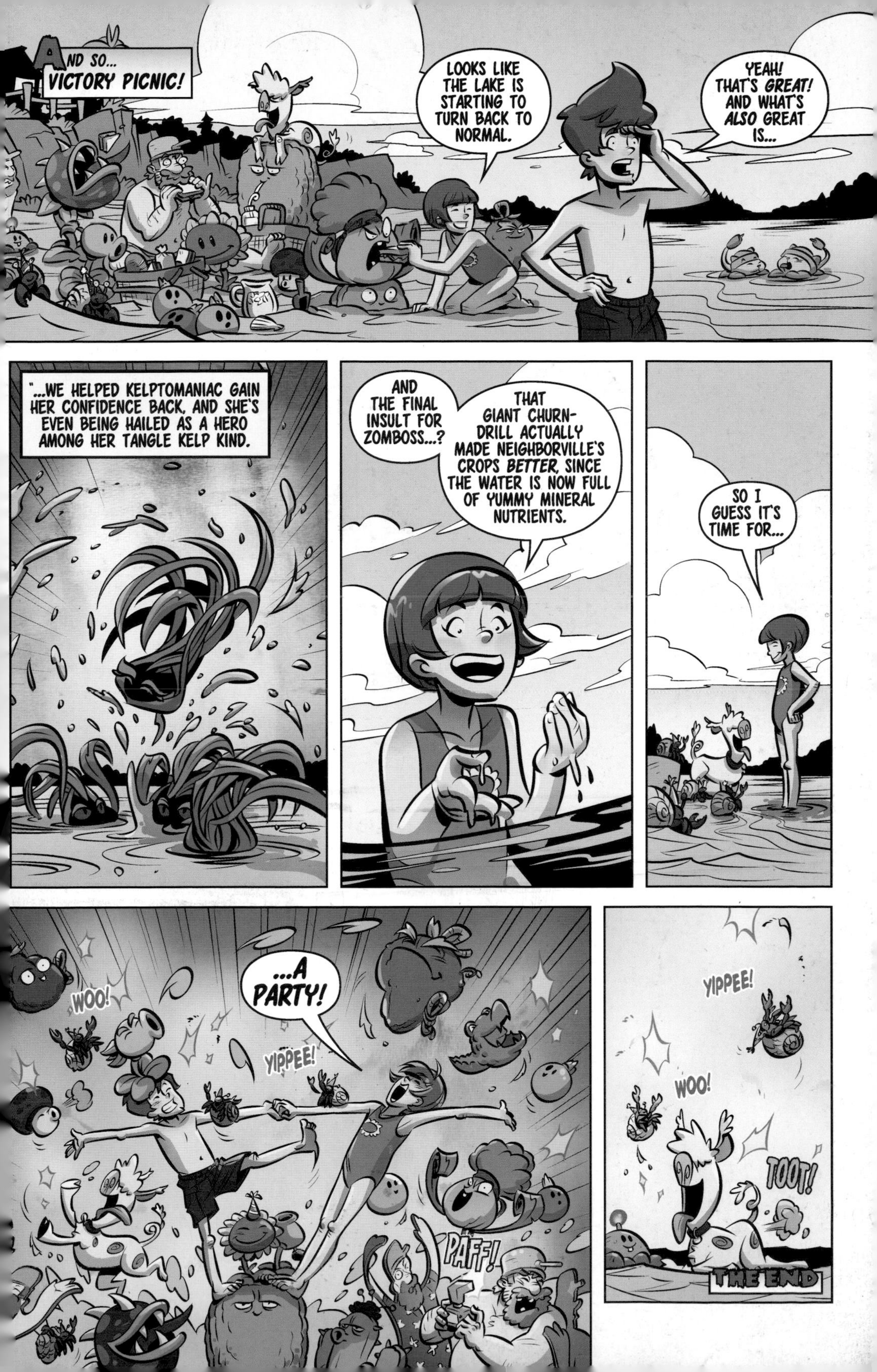
AND SO... VICTORY PICNIC!
LOOKS LIKE THE LAKE IS STARTING TO TURN BACK TO NORMAL.
YEAH! THAT'S GREAT! AND WHAT'S ALSO GREAT IS...
"...WE HELPED KELPTOMANIAC GAIN HER CONFIDENCE BACK, AND SHE'S EVEN BEING HAILED AS A HERO AMONG HER TANGLE KELP KIND.
AND THE FINAL INSULT FOR ZOMBOSS...?
THAT GIANT CHURN-DRILL ACTUALLY MADE NEIGHBORVILLE'S CROPS BETTER, SINCE THE WATER IS NOW FULL OF YUMMY MINERAL NUTRIENTS.
SO I GUESS IT'S TIME FOR...
...A PARTY!
WOO!
YIPPEE!
PAFF!
YIPPEE!
WOO!
TOOT!
THE END

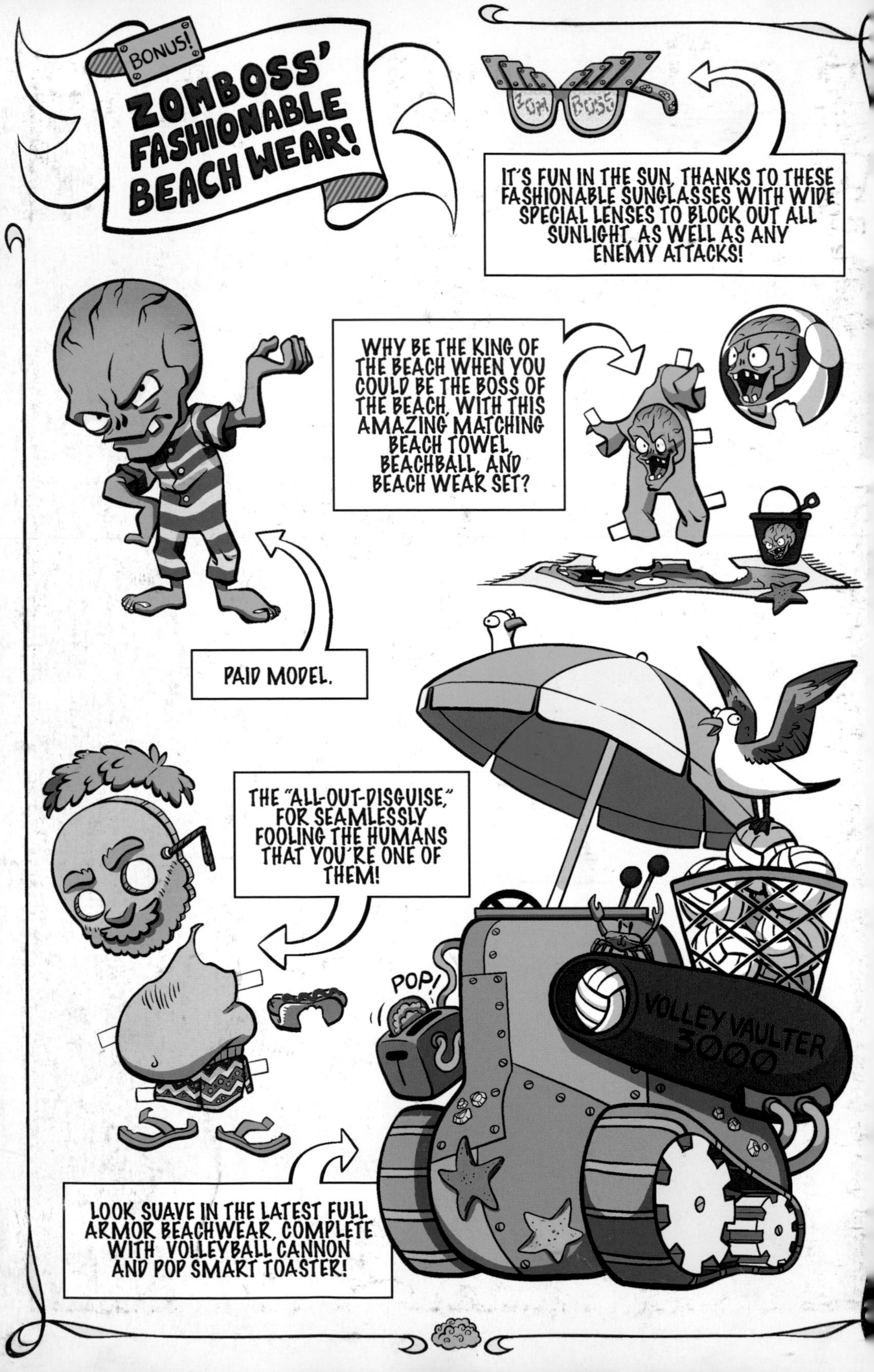

BONUS!
ZOMBOSS' FASHIONABLE BEACH WEAR!
IT'S FUN IN THE SUN, THANKS TO THESE FASHIONABLE SUNGLASSES WITH WIDE SPECIAL LENSES TO BLOCK OUT ALL SUNLIGHT, AS WELL AS ANY ENEMY ATTACKS!
ZOM BOSS
WHY BE THE KING OF THE BEACH WHEN YOU COULD BE THE BOSS OF THE BEACH, WITH THIS AMAZING MATCHING BEACH TOWEL, BEACHBALL, AND BEACH WEAR SET?
PAID MODEL.
THE "ALL-OUT-DISGUISE," FOR SEAMLESSLY FOOLING THE HUMANS THAT YOU'RE ONE OF THEM!
POP!
VOLLEY VAULTER 3000
LOOK SUAVE IN THE LATEST FULL ARMOR BEACHWEAR, COMPLETE WITH VOLLEYBALL CANNON AND POP SMART TOASTER!

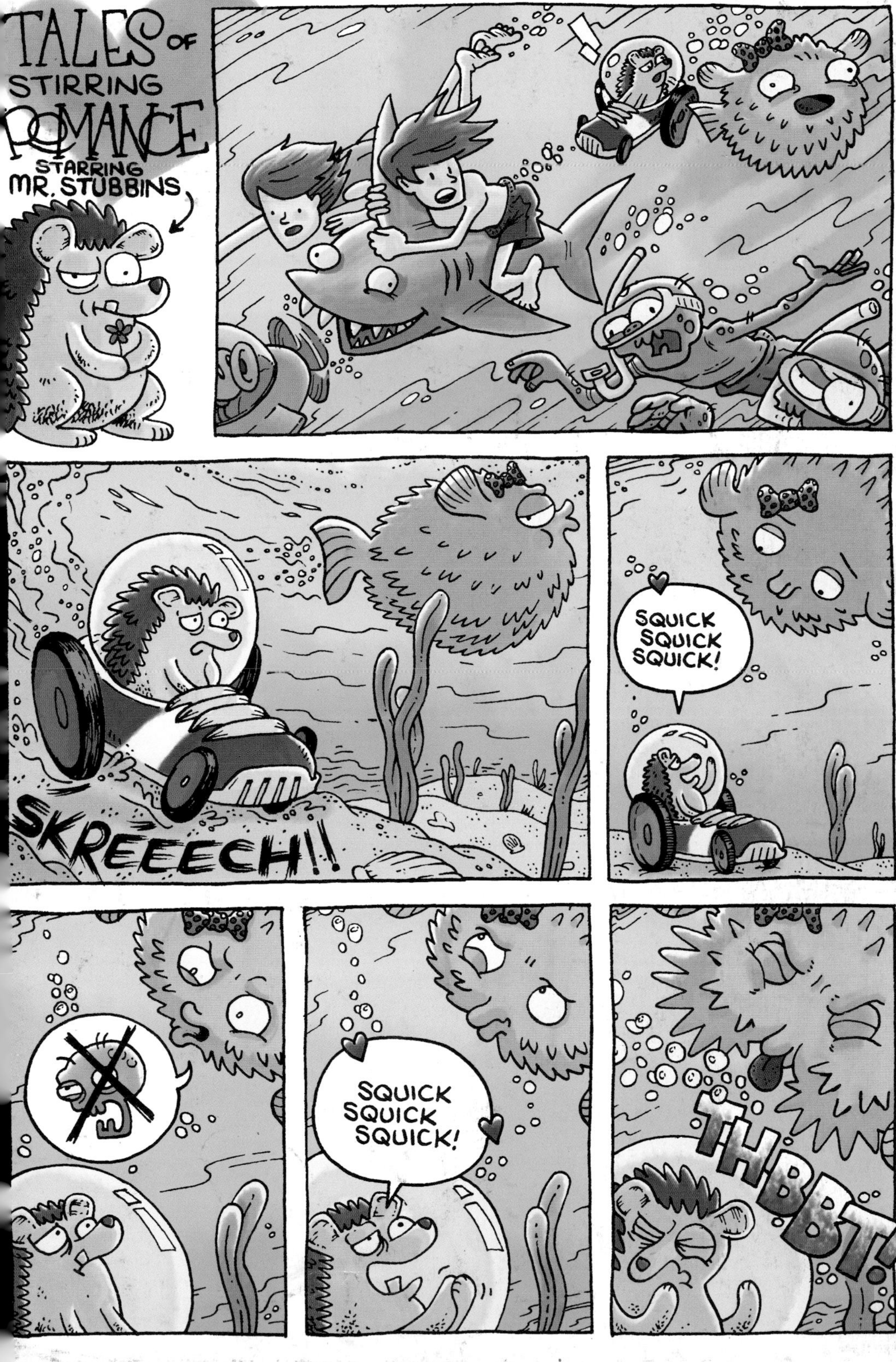
TALES OF STIRRING ROMANCE
STARRING MR. STUBBINS
SKREEECH!!
SQUICK SQUICK SQUICK!
SQUICK SQUICK SQUICK!
THBBT!

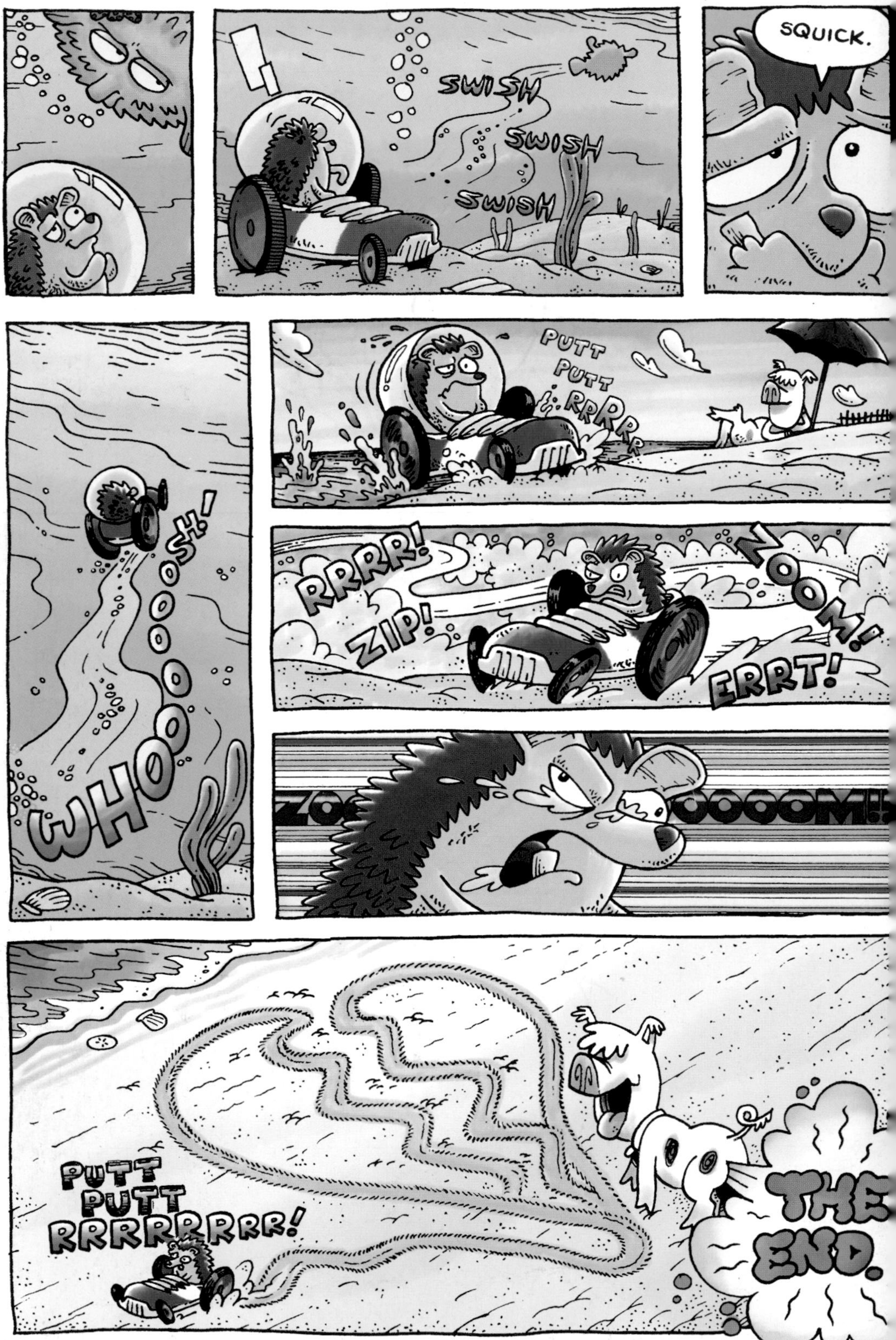
SWISH
SWISH
SWISH
SQUICK.
WHOOOOOOSH!
PUTT
PUTT
RRRRRR
RRRR!
ZIP!
ZOOM!
ERRT!
OOOOM!!
PUTT
PUTT
RRRRRRRRR!
THE
END.

PLANTS VS. ZOMBIES:
RUMBLE AT LAKE GUMBO
cover pencils by RON CHAN

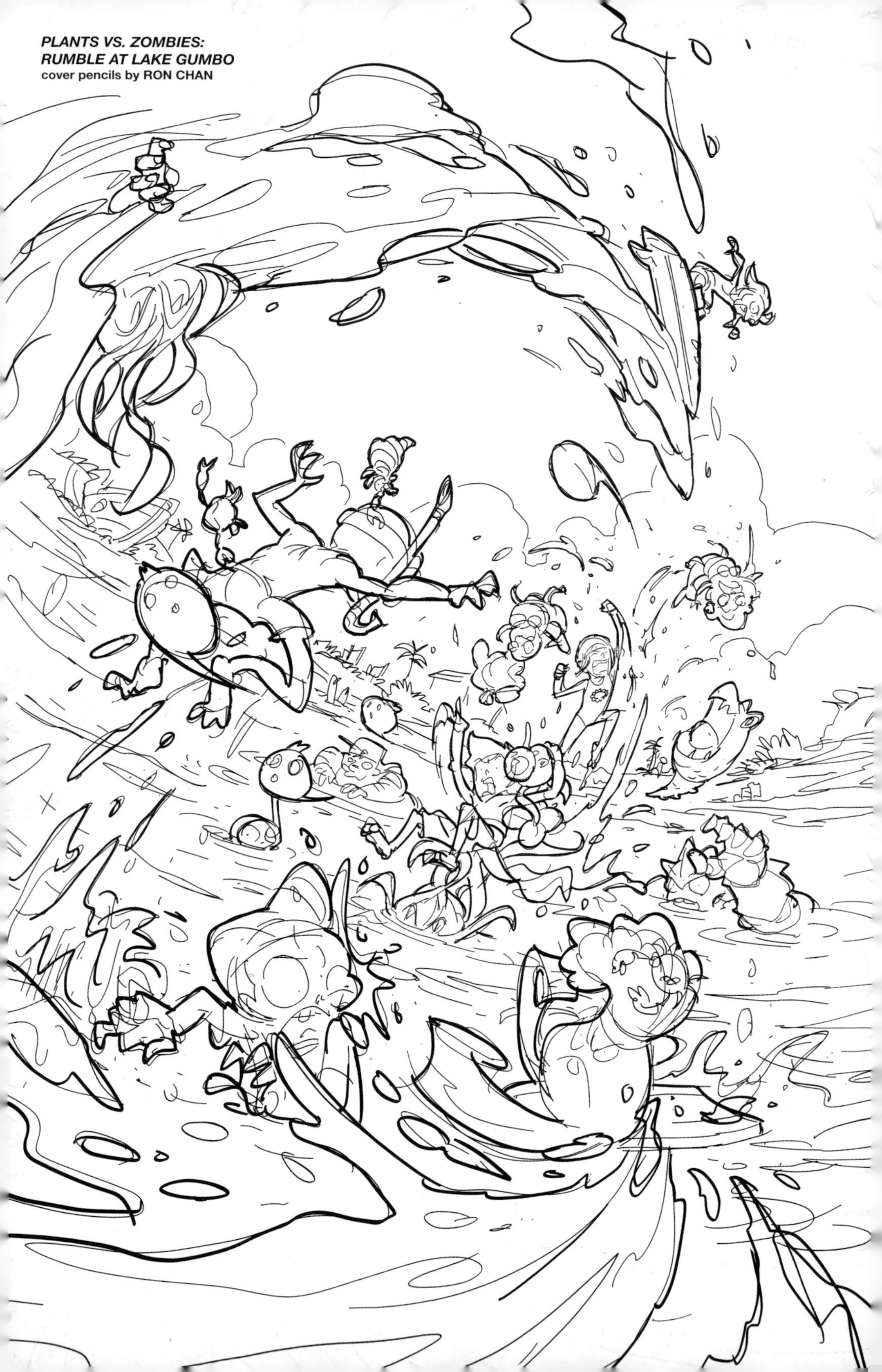

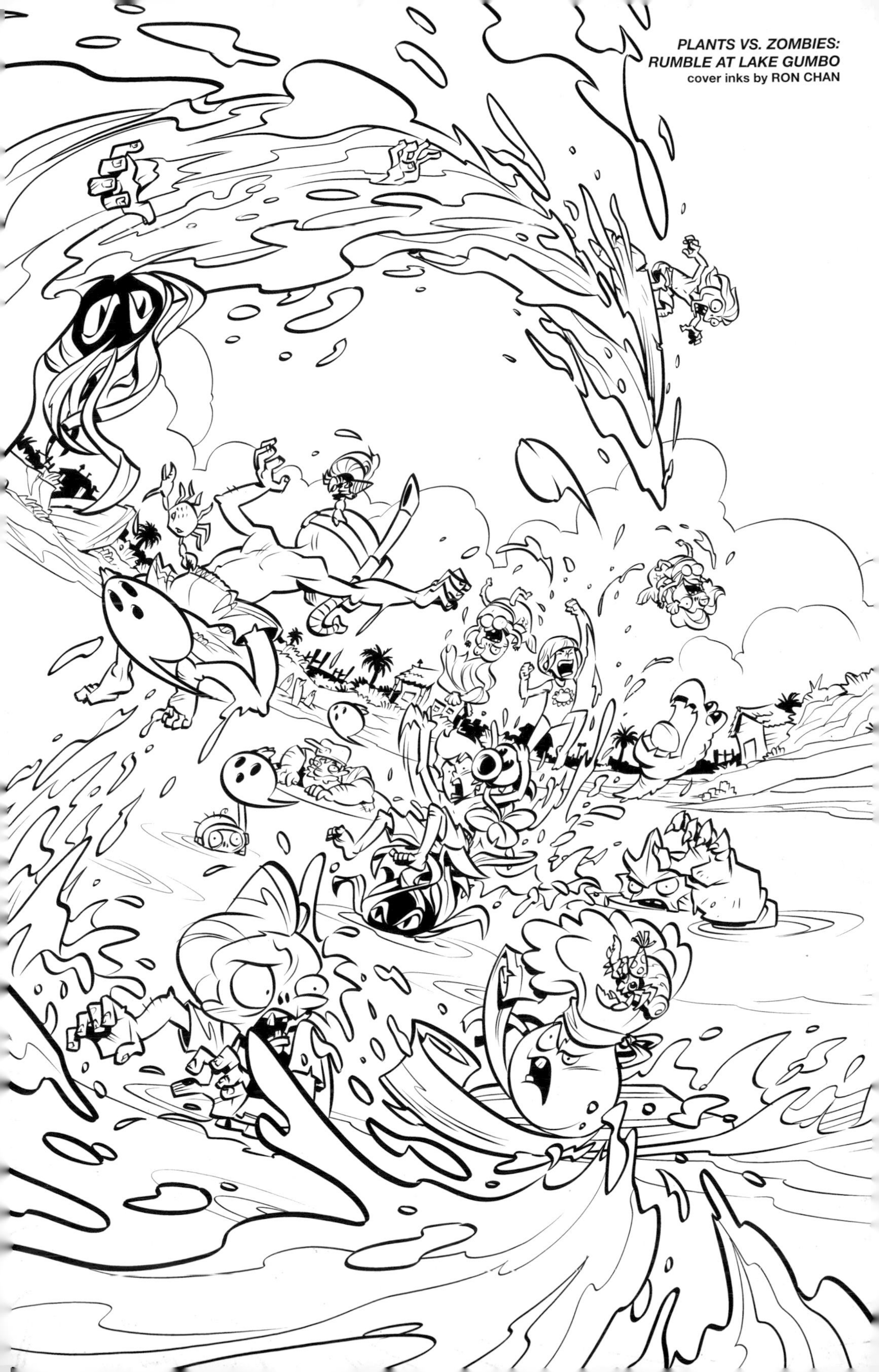

PLANTS VS. ZOMBIES: RUMBLE AT LAKE GUMBO
cover inks by RON CHAN

PENCIL ART FROM *RUMBLE AT LAKE GUMBO* STORY PAGES 32–35 BY ARTIST RON CHAN!

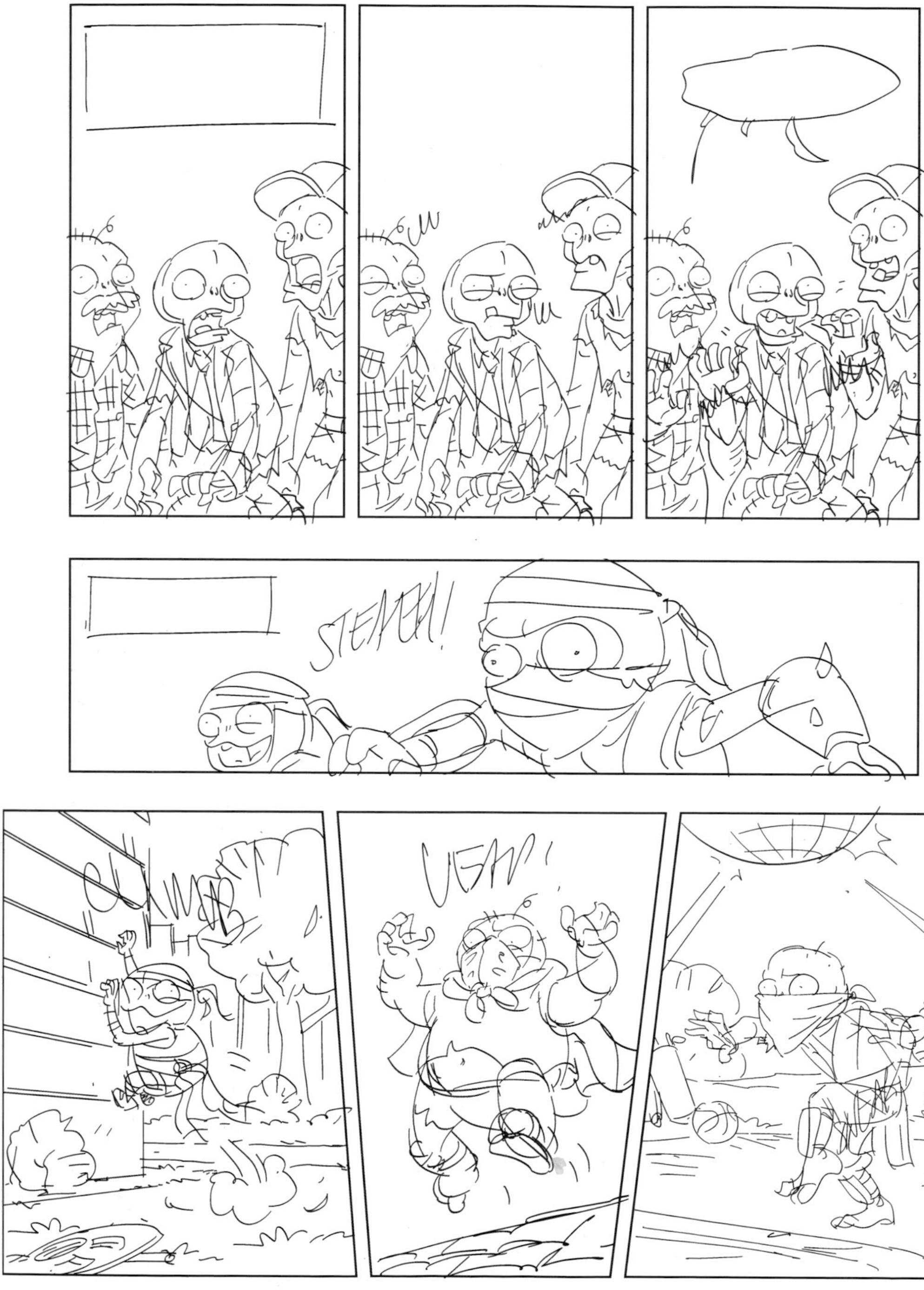
STENCH!

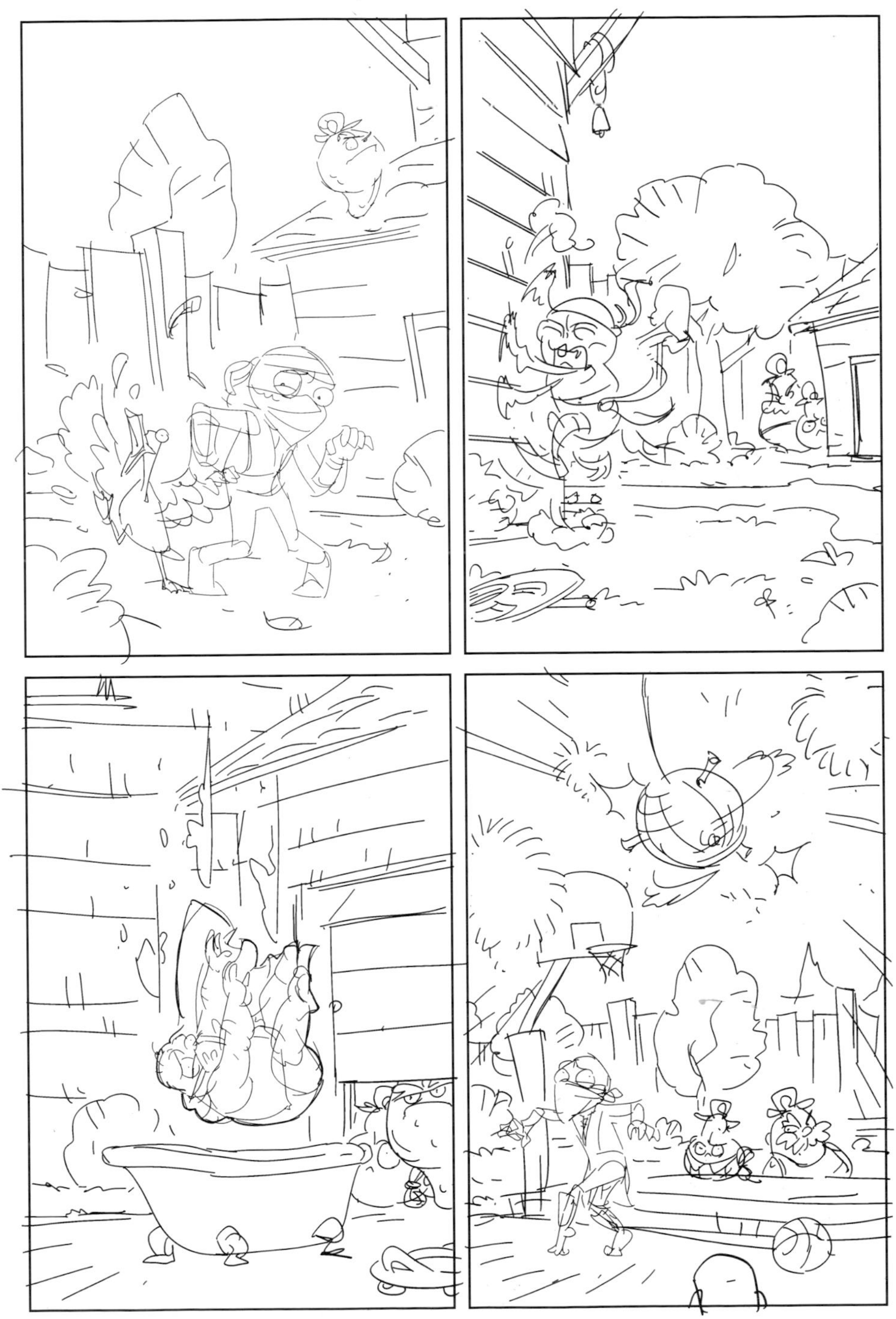

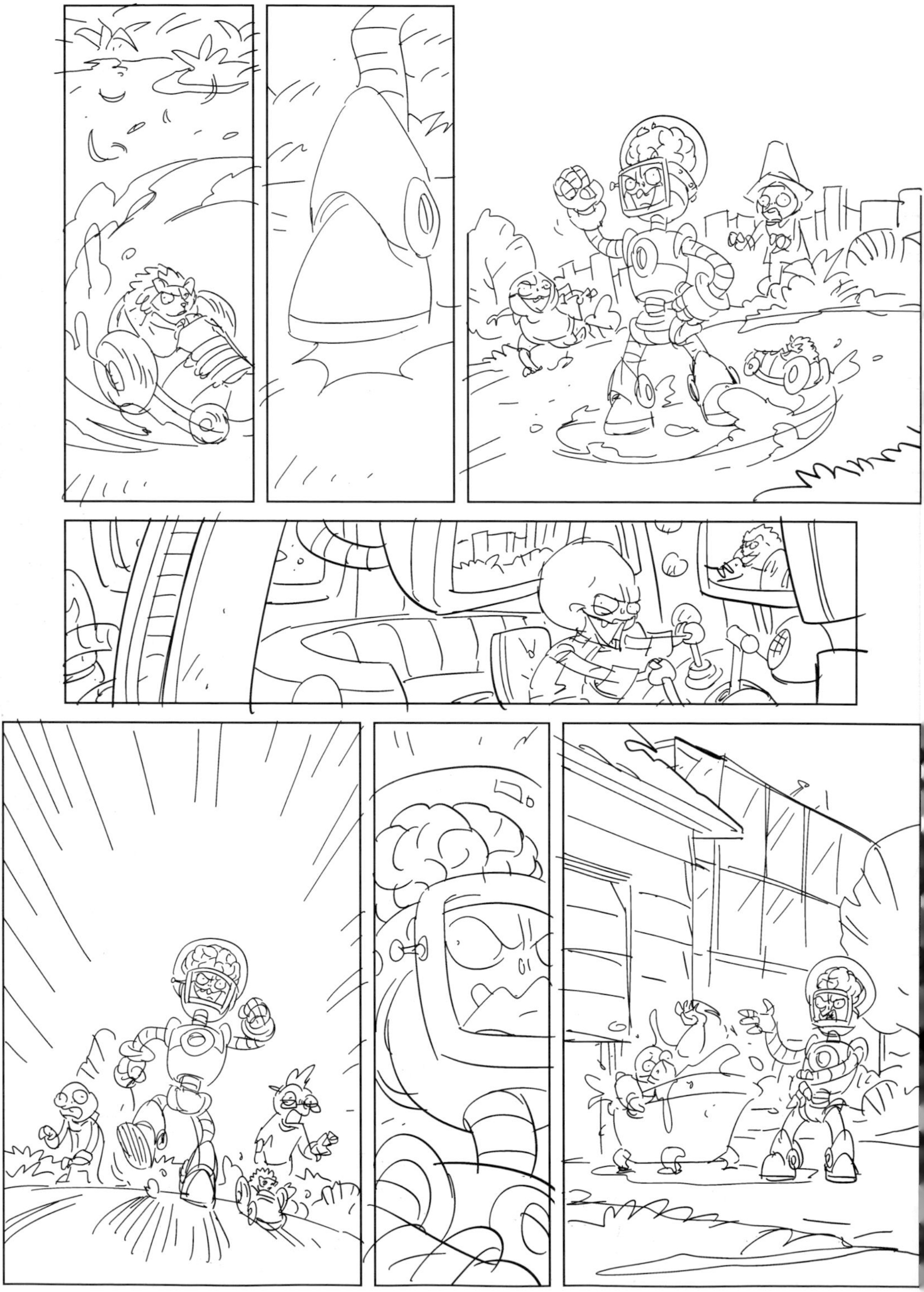

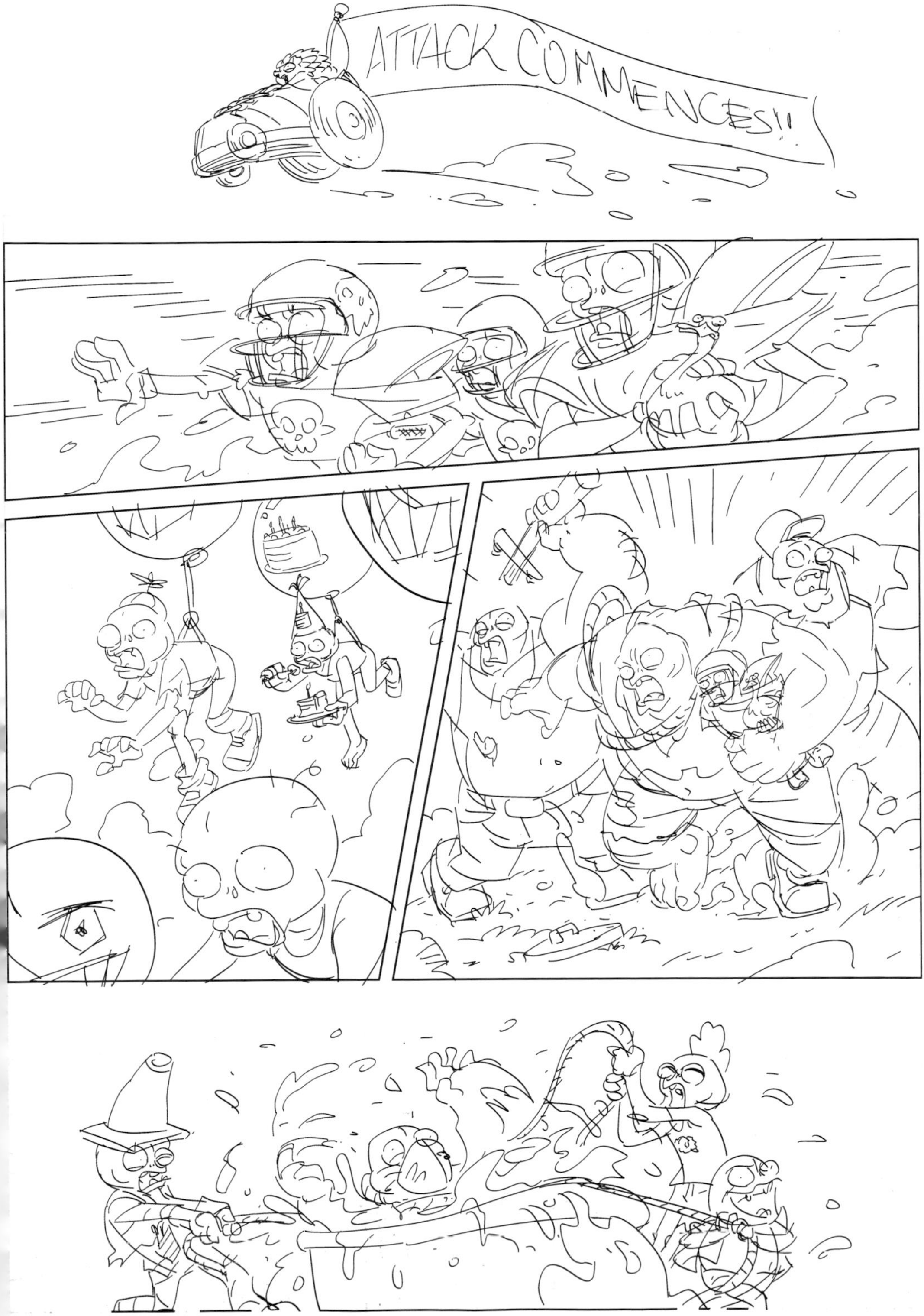
ATTACK COMMENCES!!

CREATOR BIOS

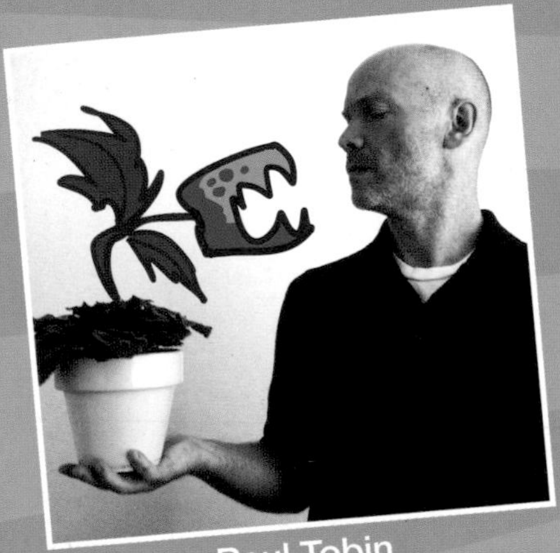

Paul Tobin

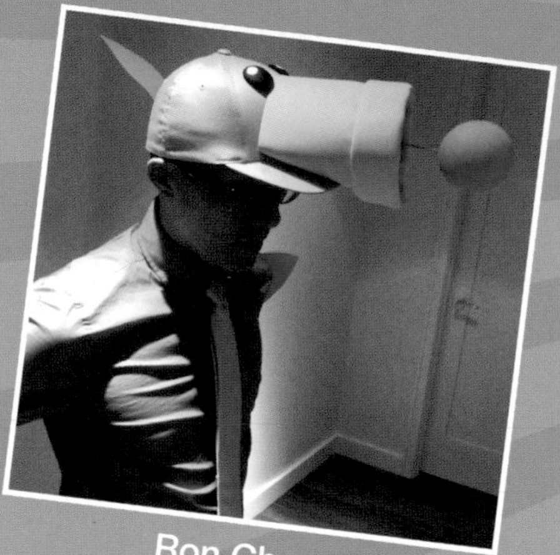

Ron Chan

PAUL TOBIN enjoys that his author photo makes him look insane, and he once accidentally cut his ear with a potato chip. He doesn't know how it happened, either. Life is so full of mystery. If you ask him about the Potato Chip Incident, he'll just make up a story. That's what he does. He's written hundreds of stories for Marvel, DC, Dark Horse, and many others, including such creator-owned titles as *Colder* and *Bandette*, as well as *Prepare to Die!*—his debut novel. His *Genius Factor* series of novels about a fifth-grade genius and his war against the Red Death Tea Society debuted in March 2016 with *How to Capture an Invisible Cat*, from Bloomsbury Publishing, and continued in early 2017 with *How to Outsmart a Billion Robot Bees*. Paul has won some Very Important Awards for his writing but so far none for his karaoke skills.

RON CHAN is a comic book and storyboard artist, video game fan, and occasional jujitsu practitioner. He was born and raised in Portland, Oregon, where he still lives and works as a member of the local artist collective Helioscope Studio. His comics work has been published by Dark Horse, Marvel, and Image Comics, and his storyboarding work includes boards for 3D animation, gaming, user-experience design, and advertising for clients such as Microsoft, Amazon Kindle, Nike, and Sega. He really likes drawing Bonk Choys. (He also enjoys eating actual bok choy in real life.)

Matt J. Rainwater

Steve Dutro

Residing in the cool, damp forests of Portland, Oregon, **MATT J. RAINWATER** is a freelance illustrator whose work has been featured in advertising, web design, and independent video games. On top of this, he also self-publishes several comic books, including *Trailer Park Warlock*, *Garage Raja*, and *The Feeling Is Multiplied*—all of which can be found at MattJRainwater.com. His favorite zombie-bashing strategy utilizes a line of Bonk Choys with a Wall-nut front guard and Threepeater covering fire.

STEVE DUTRO is an Eisner Award-nominated comic-book letterer from Redding, California, who can also drive a tractor. He graduated from the Kubert School and has been lettering comics since the days when foil-embossed covers were cool, working for Dark Horse (*The Fifth Beatle*, *I Am a Hero*, *Planet of the Apes*, *Star Wars*), Viz, Marvel, and DC. He has submitted a request to the Department of Homeland Security that in the event of a zombie apocalypse he be put in charge of all digital freeway signs so citizens can be alerted to avoid nearby brain-eatings and the like. He finds the *Plants vs. Zombies* game to be a real stress-fest, but highly recommends the *Plants vs. Zombies* table on *Pinball FX2* for game-room hipsters.

ALSO AVAILABLE FROM DARK HORSE!

THE HIT VIDEO GAME CONTINUES ITS COMIC BOOK INVASION!

PLANTS VS. ZOMBIES: LAWNMAGEDDON
Crazy Dave—the babbling-yet-brilliant inventor and top-notch neighborhood defender—helps young adventurer Nate fend off a zombie invasion that threatens to overrun the peaceful town of Neighborville in *Plants vs. Zombies: Lawnmageddon*! Their only hope is a brave army of chomping, squashing, and pea-shooting plants! A wacky adventure for zombie zappers young and old!
ISBN 978-1-61655-192-6 | $9.99

THE ART OF PLANTS VS. ZOMBIES
Part zombie memoir, part celebration of zombie triumphs, and part anti-plant screed, *The Art of Plants vs. Zombies* is a treasure trove of never-before-seen concept art, character sketches, and surprises from PopCap's popular Plants vs. Zombies games!
ISBN 978-1-61655-331-9 | $9.99

PLANTS VS. ZOMBIES: TIMEPOCALYPSE
Crazy Dave helps Patrice and Nate Timely fend off Zomboss' latest attack in *Plants vs. Zombies: Timepocalypse*! This new standalone tale will tickle your funny bones and thrill your brains through any timeline!
ISBN 978-1-61655-621-1 | $9.99

PLANTS VS. ZOMBIES: BULLY FOR YOU
Patrice and Nate are ready to investigate a strange college campus to keep the streets safe from zombies!
ISBN 978-1-61655-889-5 | $9.99

PLANTS VS. ZOMBIES: GARDEN WARFARE
Based on the hit video game, this comic tells the story leading up to the events in *Plants vs. Zombies: Garden Warfare 2*!
ISBN 978-1-61655-946-5 | $9.99

PLANTS VS. ZOMBIES: GROWN SWEET HOME
With newfound knowledge of humanity, Dr. Zomboss strikes at the heart of Neighborville . . . sparking a series of plant-versus-zombie brawls!
ISBN 978-1-61655-971-7 | $9.99

PLANTS VS. ZOMBIES: PETAL TO THE METAL
Crazy Dave takes on the tough *Don't Blink* video game—and challenges Dr. Zomboss to a race to determine the future of Neighborville!
ISBN 978-1-61655-999-1 | $9.99

PLANTS VS. ZOMBIES: BOOM BOOM MUSHROOM
The gang discover Zomboss' secret plan for swallowing the city of Neighborville whole! A rare mushroom must be found in order to save the humans aboveground!
ISBN 978-1-50670-037-3 | $9.99

PLANTS VS. ZOMBIES: BATTLE EXTRAVAGONZO
Zomboss is back, hoping to buy the same factory that Crazy Dave is eyeing! Will Crazy Dave and his intelligent plants beat Zomboss and his zombie army to the punch?
ISBN 978-1-50670-189-9 | $9.99

PLANTS VS. ZOMBIES: LAWN OF DOOM
With Zomboss filling everyone's yards with traps and special soldiers, will he and his zombie army turn Halloween into their scarier Lawn of Doom celebration?!
ISBN 978-1-50670-204-9 | $9.99

PLANTS VS. ZOMBIES: THE GREATEST SHOW UNEARTHED
Dr. Zomboss believes that all humans hold a secret desire to run away and join the circus, so he aims to use his "Big Z's Adequately Amazing Flytrap Circus" to lure Neighborville's citizens to their doom!
ISBN 978-1-50670-298-8 | $9.99

PLANTS VS. ZOMBIES: RUMBLE AT LAKE GUMBO
The battle for clean water begins! Nate, Patrice, and Crazy Dave spot trouble and grab all the Tangle Kelp and Party Crabs they can to quell another zombie attack!
ISBN 978-1-50670-497-5 | $9.99

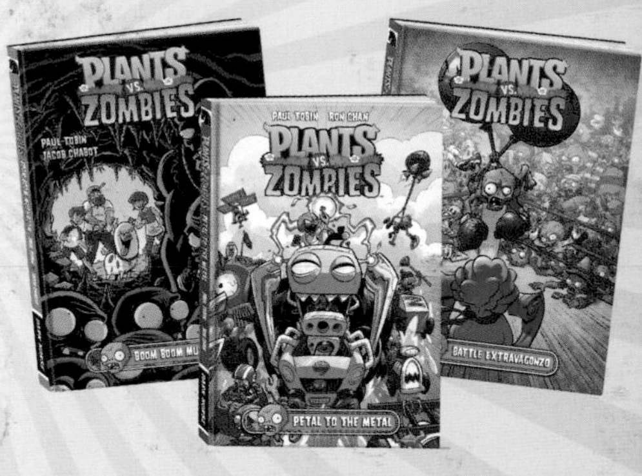
PLANTS vs ZOMBIES
PAUL TOBIN
JACOB CHABOT
BOOM BOOM MU
PAUL TOBIN RON CHAN
PLANTS vs ZOMBIES
PETAL TO THE METAL
PLANTS vs ZOMBIES
BATTLE EXTRAVAGONZO

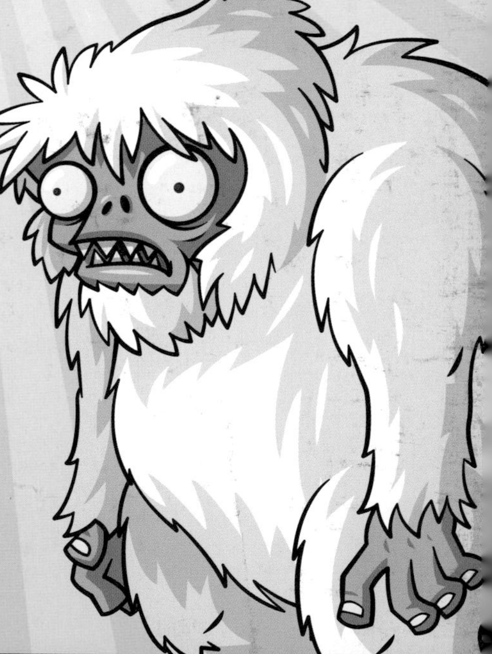

AVAILABLE AT YOUR LOCAL COMICS SHOP OR BOOKSTORE
To find a comics shop in your area, visit comicshoplocator.com.
For more information or to order direct visit **DarkHorse.com** or call 1-800-862-0052

DARK HORSE BOOKS
EA
PopCap

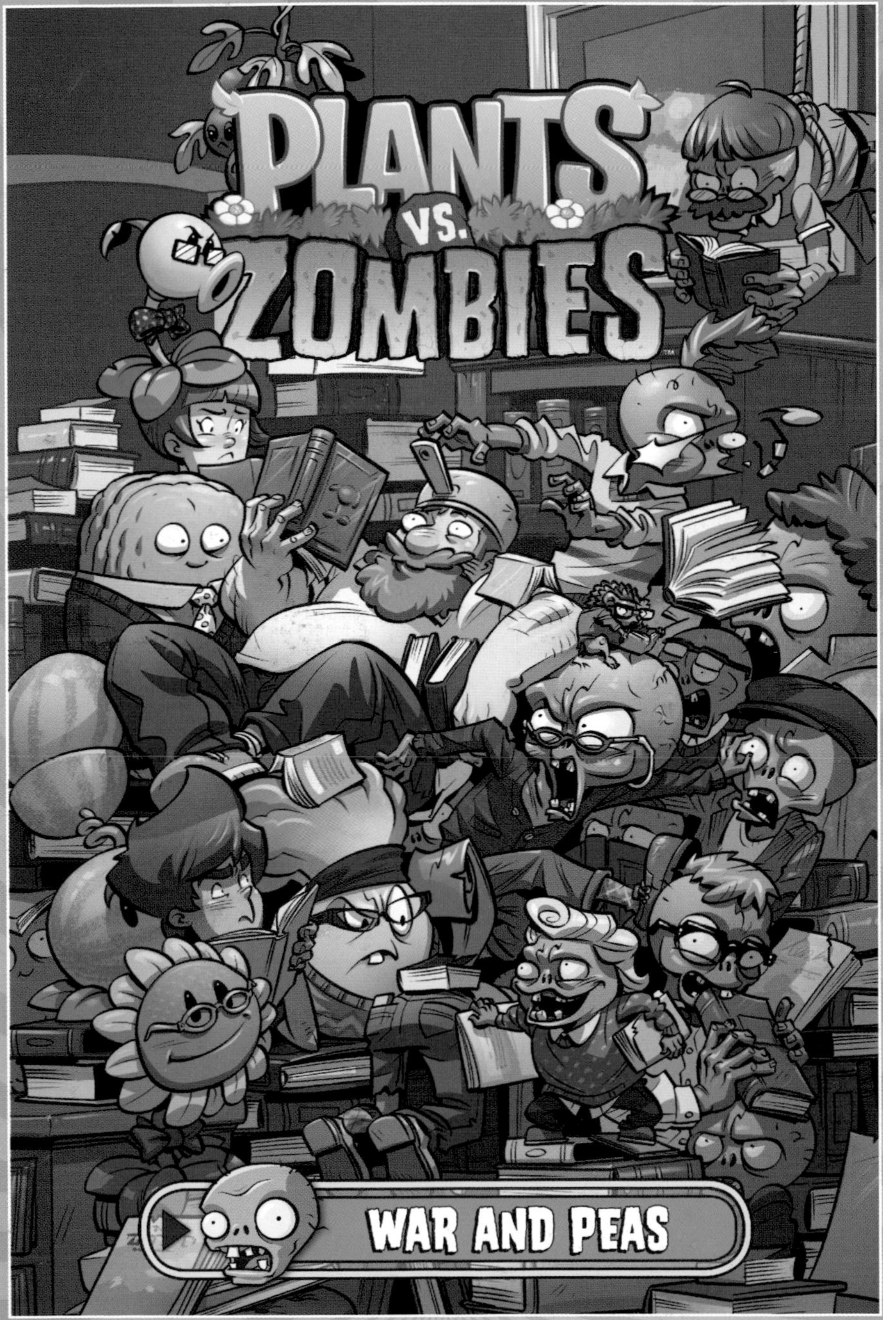
PLANTS VS. ZOMBIES
WAR AND PEAS

PLANTS VS. ZOMBIES: WAR AND PEAS—BOOKING IT IN OCTOBER 2018!

Let the bookish battle commence! When Dr. Zomboss and Crazy Dave find themselves members of the same book club, a literary war is inevitable! The position of leader of the book club opens up and the plants and zombies rivalry heats up as Zomboss and Crazy Dave compete for the top spot while Nate, Patrice, and their intrepid plants take on the zombies in a scholarly scuffle for the ages!

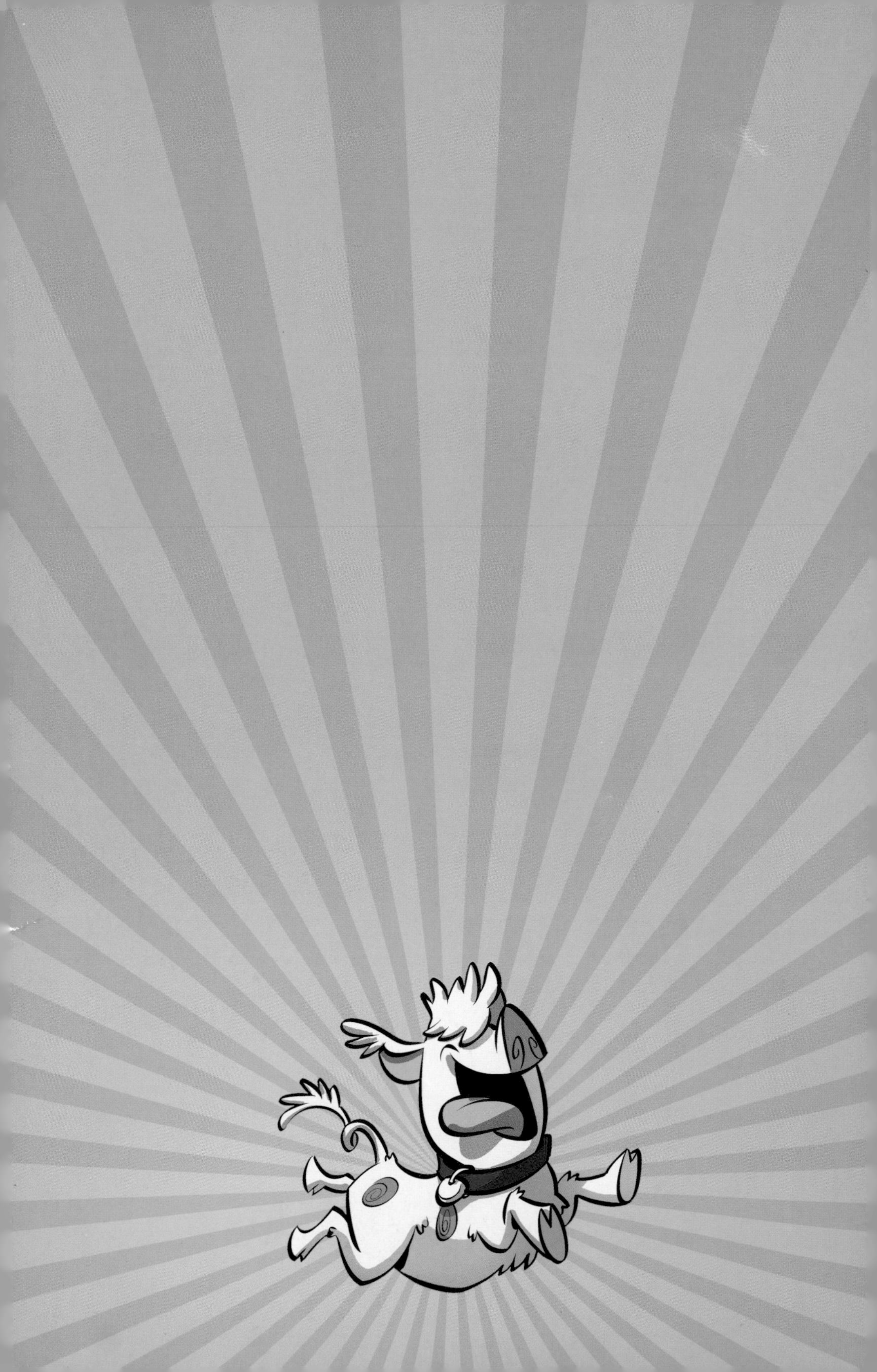

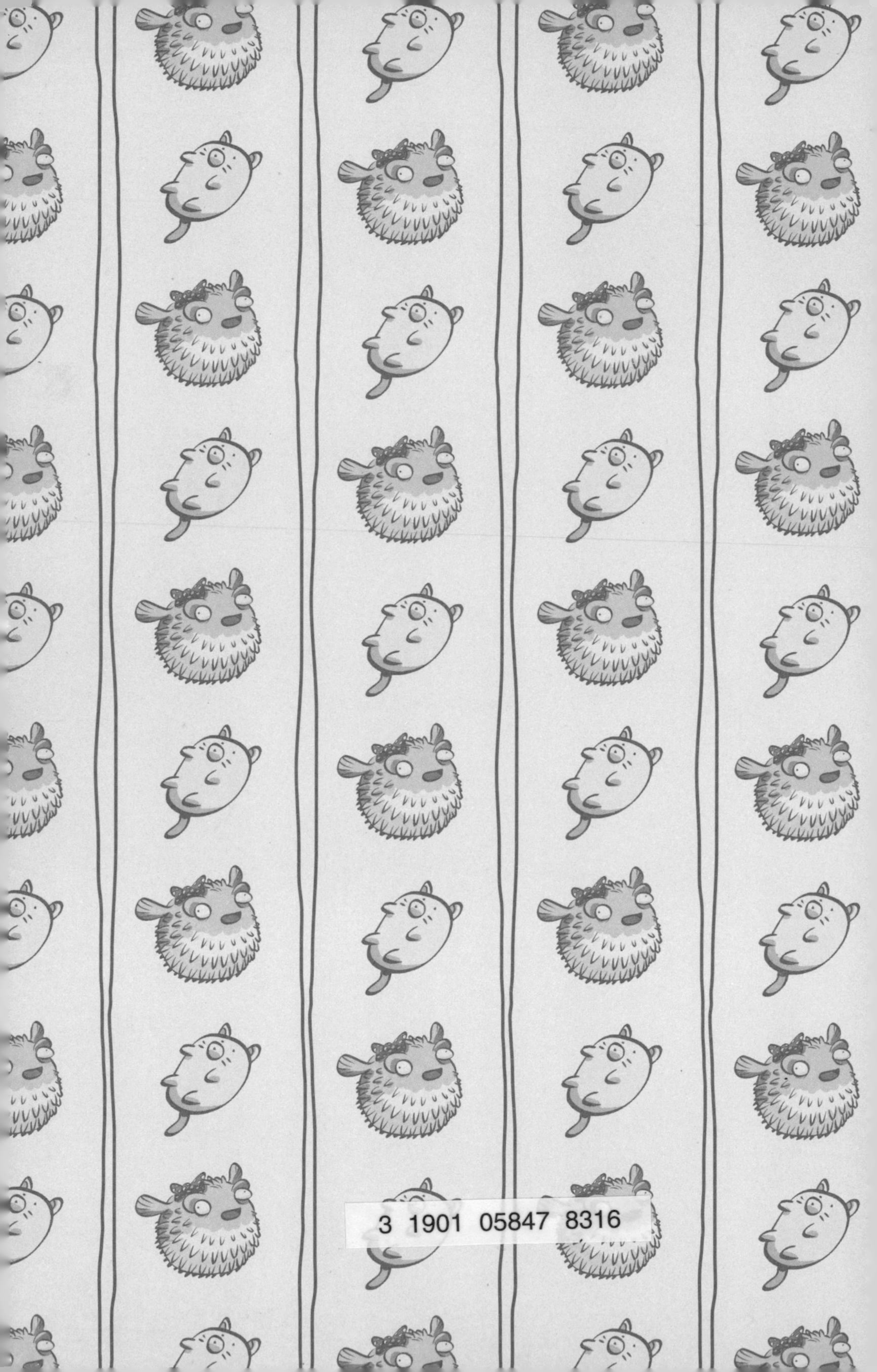